REASONABLE DOUBT

What Reviewers Say About Carsen Taite's Work

It Should be a Crime

"Taite also practices criminal law and she weaves her insider knowledge of the criminal justice system into the love story seamlessly and with excellent timing."—*Curve Magazine*

"This [*It Should be a Crime*] is just Taite's second novel…, but it's as if she has bookshelves full of bestsellers under her belt."
—*Gay List Daily*

Do Not Disturb

"Taite's tale of sexual tension is entertaining in itself, but a number of secondary characters…add substantial color to romantic inevitability"—Richard Labonte, *Book Marks*

Nothing but the Truth

"Author Taite is really a Dallas defense attorney herself, and it's obvious her viewpoint adds considerable realism to her story, making it especially riveting as a mystery. I give it four stars out of five."—Bob Lind, *Echo Magazine*

"As a criminal defense attorney in Dallas, Texas, Carsen Taite knows her way around the court house. …*Nothing But the Truth* is an enjoyable mystery with some hot romance thrown in."
—*Just About Write*

"Taite has written an excellent courtroom drama with two interesting women leading the cast of characters. Taite herself is a practicing defense attorney, and her courtroom scenes are clearly based on real knowledge. This should be another winner for Taite."
—*Lambda Literary*

The Best Defense
"Real Life defense attorney Carsen Taite polishes her fifth work of lesbian fiction, *The Best Defense*, with the realism she daily encounters in the office and in the courts. And that polish is something that makes *The Best Defense* shine as an excellent read."—*Out & About Newspaper*

Slingshot
"The mean streets of lesbian literature finally have the hard boiled bounty hunter they deserve. It's a slingshot of a ride, bad guys and hot women rolled into one page turning package. I'm looking forward to Luca Bennett's next adventure."—J. M. Redmann, author of the Micky Knight mystery series

Battle Axe
"This second book is satisfying, substantial, and slick. Plus, it has heart and love coupled with Luca's array of weapons and a bad-ass verbal repertoire…I cannot imagine anyone not having a great time riding shotgun through all of Luca's escapades. I recommend hopping on Luca's band wagon and having a blast."—*Rainbow Book Reviews*

"Taite breathes life into her characters with elemental finesse…A great read, told in the vein of a good old detective-type novel filled with criminal elements, thugs, and mobsters that will entertain and amuse."—*Lambda Literary*

Beyond Innocence
"Taite keeps you guessing with delicious delay until the very last minute…Taite's time in the courtroom lends *Beyond Innocence*, a terrific verisimilitude someone not in the profession couldn't impart. And damned if she doesn't make practicing law interesting."—*Out in Print*

"As you would expect, sparks and legal writs fly. What I liked about this book were the shades of grey (no, not the smutty Shades of Grey)—both in the relationship as well as the cases."—*C-spot Reviews*

Rush

"A simply beautiful interplay of police procedural magic, murder, FBI presence, misguided protective cover-ups, and a superheated love affair...a Gold Star from me and major encouragement for all readers to dive right in and consume this story with gusto!" —*Rainbow Book Reviews*

Switchblade

"I enjoyed the book and it was a fun read—mystery, action, humor, and a bit of romance. Who could ask for more? If you've read and enjoyed Taite's legal novels, you'll like this. If you've read and enjoyed the two other books in this series, this one will definitely satisfy your Luca fix and I highly recommend picking it up. Highly recommended."—*C Spot Reviews*

"Dallas's intrepid female bounty hunter, Luca Bennett, is back in another adventure. Fantastic! Between her many friends and lovers, her interesting family, her fly by the seat of her pants lifestyle, and a whole host of detractors there is rarely a dull moment."—*Rainbow Book Reviews*

Courtship

"The political drama is just top-notch. The emotional and sexual tensions are intertwined with great timing and flair. I truly adored this book from beginning to end. Fantabulous!"—*Rainbow Book Reviews*

"Carsen Taite throws the reader head on into the murky world of the political system where there are no rights or wrongs, just players attempting to broker the best deals regardless of who gets hurt in the process. The book is extremely well written and makes compelling reading. With twist and turns throughout, the reader doesn't know how the story will end."—*Lesbian Reading Room*

Lay Down the Law
"Recognized for the pithy realism of her characters and settings drawn from a Texas legal milieu, Taite (*Courtship*) pays homage to the prime-time soap opera *Dallas* in pairing a cartel-busting U.S. attorney, Peyton Davis, with a charity-minded oil heiress, Lily Gantry."—*Publishers Weekly*

"Suspenseful, intriguingly tense, and with a great developing love story, this book is delightfully solid on all fronts. This gets my A-1 recommendation!"—*Rainbow Book Reviews*

"This book is AMAZING!!! The setting, the scenery, the people, the plot, wow…."—*Prism Book Alliance*

Visit us at www.boldstrokesbooks.com

By the Author

Truelesbianlove.com

It Should be a Crime

Do Not Disturb

Nothing but the Truth

The Best Defense

Beyond Innocence

Rush

Courtship

Reasonable Doubt

The Luca Bennett Mystery Series:

Slingshot

Battle Axe

Switchblade

Lone Star Law Series:

Lay Down the Law

REASONABLE DOUBT

by
Carsen Taite

2015

REASONABLE DOUBT

© 2015 By Carsen Taite. All Rights Reserved.

ISBN 13: 978-1-62639-442-1

This Trade Paperback Original Is Published By
Bold Strokes Books, Inc.
P.O. Box 249
Valley Falls, NY 12185

First Edition: September 2015

Credits

Editor: Cindy Cresap
Production Design: Susan Ramundo
Cover Design By Sheri (graphicartist2020@hotmail.com)

Acknowledgments

Many headline grabbing true stories inspired this work of fiction: young people lured into joining terrorist training camps in faraway lands; bombings, both here and abroad, killing dozens and forever changing the lives of those who survived. This book is not based on a real act of terrorism, but as I finished the first draft of this story, the Boston Marathon bomber's case was in its final days and I, like many others, was moved to tears by the testimony of the victims and their families. Years of practice as a criminal defense lawyer mean that I always try to keep an open mind, to see both sides—the pain of the victim balanced against the intent of the accused, but blatant acts of terrorism can't be balanced. No matter what the motivation, the result is the same—senseless harm suffered by innocents. Yet, our justice system works precisely because we give everyone a chance to make their case, even when it's clear from the outset what the result will be. To everyone who sat in the courtroom and endured the ten weeks of trial, reliving the horror of that fateful Patriot's Day, you have my utmost respect. You are true patriots.

Thanks to everyone who helped me bring this book to life. Rad for giving my stories a place to thrive. Sandy Lowe for tending to every detail along the way. Cindy Cresap, my editor, for making me laugh out loud during edits even while you challenge me to be better with every book. A huge shout out to the entire Bold Strokes team, from PR to proofreading—thanks for everything you do!

Ashley Bartlett and VK Powell—the best first readers in the world! Your friendship means the world to me. Thanks for your honesty and your willingness to deal with my crazy schedule. Ruth Sternglantz, my bonus story editor—your willingness to talk through plot points, anywhere, anytime is a true gift of friendship.

Lainey, thanks for all the sacrifices you make, big and small, to allow me to pursue my dreams. I love you more every day.

To all my readers—thanks for making this journey so worthwhile. I cherish all the e-mails, notes, and words of encouragement. This story is for you.

Dedication

To Lainey, without a doubt.

CHAPTER ONE

Sarah Flores ducked as the bullet barreled past her head and into the wall behind her. She cast a quick look at the body on the bed. She could do more good chasing the suspect. She ran out into the hall and paused at the top of the stairs, listening for footfalls. Was he hiding on the landing or had he ducked into one of the other bedrooms on this floor? Seconds later, she heard a crash outside and dashed down the stairs and out the door. Her boss, Trip Sandler, met her on the front steps.

"I lost him." Sarah pointed up at the second story balcony. "He must've jumped," she said between gulps of air. "Come on."

Trip placed a hand on her arm. "Slow down. Mendez and Davis took off after him. We need to stay here and secure the scene."

He was right, but Sarah chafed at the order to stand down. It was against her instinct to stay behind, but she dutifully led her boss up the stairs and into the bedroom where she'd found the Atlanta Strangler's latest victim. The kill was too fresh to smell, but the woman on the bed was clearly dead.

Trip pulled on a pair of gloves as he circled the bed. "Is this the sixth or the seventh? I've lost count."

Sarah looked up from the body. "You know, when you start losing track, it might be time to call it a day."

"Why should I keep count when I've got you to do it for me?" He struck his forehead with a gloved hand. "Oh, wait, I only have you for the rest of the day. Who's going to keep track of all the dead bodies when you're gone?"

Sarah shook her head but didn't bother replying. Trip had been bellyaching about her upcoming transfer for weeks. He'd gone from cajoling at first, in an attempt to get her to stay, to his present mode of inserting guilt-tripping remarks into every conversation.

Didn't matter. He could do whatever he wanted. Tomorrow she'd be back in D.C. packing up her apartment, and the day after that, she would be on a plane to Dallas and a new job that didn't involve body counts. She'd spent her entire career as an agent in the FBI's Behavioral Analysis Unit investigating serial killers and witnessing the rituals of their carnage. She was ready for a routine of paper pushing, which was exactly what her new position in the fraud unit would entail.

She was almost done examining the body when another one of their team members walked into the bedroom. Peter Buckner, their resident nerd, looked the part. He was skinny, awkward, and sporting out of style glasses, but he could kick all of their asses when it came to calling up facts and figures on the fly or gaining access to computer databases that provided information crucial to keeping up their team's success rate. She could tell by his expression he didn't have good news, but she asked anyway, "Did they get him?"

"Nope. They barely even caught a glance before he vanished. We've got Atlanta PD on it and I've sent notifications to the airport, bus, and train stations, but we don't have much in the way of a description."

"I didn't get much of a look at him either. But he won't leave town," Sarah said as she finished making her notes. "He's escalating." She pointed at the body. "Look at these marks here. He did this while she was still alive. He's taking more risks, getting more juiced by the killing. No way will he take this show on the road when he's just hit his stride here, where he's most comfortable. Being chased today probably just amped up his adrenaline."

Trip leaned over her shoulder as she took pictures of the cuts, still clotted with blood, that formed a heart shape on the woman's chest. The cuts were deeper, more jagged than the ones on the previous victims. "She's right. Peter, get Baker from Atlanta PD on the phone. I want a meeting with their folks first thing in the morning. We need to give them an updated profile and talk new strategy."

Sarah looked up to see Trip staring at her. She'd worked with him long enough to know exactly what he was thinking. She shook her head. "No way."

"Come on," Trip said. "We'll get your flight rescheduled. Just a few more days."

"Right. It's always just a few more days. And what if another call comes in? A few more days after that?" She shook her head. "They're expecting me in Dallas."

"Right. All those paper pushers just sitting around with files full of bank statements for you to dig into."

Sarah laughed. The fraud unit at FBI Dallas would probably have a thing or two to say about Trip's characterization of their work, but the lack of excitement was exactly what she was looking for. The past six years as a special agent in the BAU had taken its toll on every aspect of her life: her sleep, her mental health, and definitely her social life. She had a hard time keeping up any kind of relationship when she had to fly out of town at a moment's notice, and most of what she saw on the job wasn't suitable for dinner conversation. Trip and some of the others had been doing the job a lot longer, but she'd watched everything about their personal lives fade until they were nothing without the work. She still had time to make a new life for herself, and the transfer to Dallas was what she needed to resist being defined by the evil she encountered on a daily basis.

"Just because there's no blood involved, doesn't mean the job isn't fulfilling," she said.

"Sure. I guess there's always the risk of a paper cut to make things interesting."

"Whatever." She shrugged off his teasing. He only did it because he was going to miss her. She was going to miss him too, along with the rest of the team. They'd been her family for the past six years, but it was time to find a new family. One bound together by something besides murder.

CHAPTER TWO

Ellery Durant idled her F150, certain this was the place she'd seen the treasure when she'd been riding as a passenger in April's tiny sports car the day before. Of course, now that she had space to haul away the find, it was nowhere in sight. She turned around at the end of the block and vowed this would be the final pass before one of the residents called the cops and reported her as a stalker.

She'd just about given up when she spotted the abandoned door on the street side of the sidewalk in front of a medium-sized bungalow. She pulled over and slipped on a pair of heavy leather work gloves before stepping out of the truck, quickly spotting the reason the object had been so difficult to locate. She lifted several busted piñatas and a sack of what appeared to be party debris, and set them to the side before removing the boards underneath them, careful not to scratch the wood. Once she'd worked the door free, she stepped back to admire her find. Years ago, this arched pine door had been brand-new, its lead glass panels bright and its auburn stain shine fresh and unmarred by the passage of time. Now, scratches and divots covered its surface, but Ellery could see only the opportunity to bring it back to life. She spread a blanket in the back of the pickup bed and carefully slid the door into place, securing it with a couple of bungee cords and some rope. She replaced everything in the pile exactly as she'd found it and drove home, eager to begin her work.

A light rain started to fall as she pulled into her driveway. She jumped out of the truck and rushed to get the door into her workshop before it could get too wet, thankful she'd found it before it had sat in the rain. Once inside, she spent a few minutes moving things around, trying to decide where to put her new project. When she'd converted the garage into her workshop, she worked hard to create an efficient space, but as each potential project piled up, she realized the organizational skills she'd relied on in her past didn't fit with her new creative career. At any given time, she had four to five projects going at once. As much as she enjoyed the feeling of accomplishment that came with finishing a new piece of furniture using the materials others had abandoned, she loved the freedom of bouncing from project to project more.

This old door would soon be new again, given a new purpose. A desk perhaps. Or maybe a wardrobe. The first step would be stripping away the beaten finish. The lead glass was a rare find and she might use it on another project altogether. It would make a beautiful wall cabinet.

Ellery looked at her current project, a custom order. The buyers wanted a large dining room table constructed from the old boards they'd saved when the unstable barn on their property had to be torn down. She'd finished the construction, and now it was time to sand the piece. She pulled a face mask from a drawer and fastened it in place. She loaded her sander with an eight grit belt and began to grind away the rough surface of the wood. The boards she'd chosen for the tabletop were each unique, and she loved bringing them new life. When the initial sanding was done, she reached for her orbital sander and applied a finer grit to add extra polish to the surface without taking anything away from the natural characteristics of the grain. She took her time, and when she was done sanding, she circled the table, smoothing her fingers across every inch of the surface until she was satisfied she'd done her best.

As she pulled off her mask, her stomach rumbled and she realized she was starving. She looked out the window and saw it was dark outside. Once again, she'd completely lost track of time. If not for the fact she was hungry, she might have stayed outside all night. Making a mental note to get a small refrigerator for the studio, she put away the sander and hung her canvas apron on a hook by her workbench.

When she opened the door to her workshop a thick wall of wet obscured her view of the house. The light rain from earlier had turned into a heavy downpour, and she was amazed she hadn't noticed the growing storm. By the time she reached the back porch, she was drenched in the cold wet of the early spring rain. She shrugged out of her coat and boots, left them on the porch, and walked into her chilly house.

She must've forgotten to turn the heat up this morning. A glance at the clock on the oven told her it was six thirty and she'd been in her workshop for several hours. Her cell phone lay next to the stove—another thing she'd completely forgotten. How quickly she'd gone from having it with her always to forgetting it even existed. She started to walk away, but habit drove her to give it a quick glance before she went to change clothes. There was one message and three missed calls. She scrolled through the numbers. One was from April, the woman she'd dated a couple of times over the past month, and the other two were from a number she didn't recognize. She clicked through to hear the message and April's smooth, bright voice came through the line. "Hey, it's April. Just checking in to see what you're up to. Looks like we're in for some stormy weather. They say it might even snow. Sounds to me like a wine and fireplace kind of night. If you're not busy, maybe we could get together. Give me a call if you're interested."

Ellery listened to the message again, this time hearing the subtle sexy undertones. She had to agree, it was definitely a fireplace kind of night, but beer would be more her thing, and part of her wished April realized that. She shook her head, knowing she wasn't being fair. Two dates wasn't enough time for April to glean that kind of intel. Besides, it didn't sound like what they'd have to drink was the first thing on April's mind.

With the phone still in her hand, she reached into the fridge and pulled out a locally brewed stout and twisted off the cap. The dark, creamy beer coated her mouth and warmed its way down her throat.

If she wanted April to get to know her better, she should invite her over and show her what she liked. She wasn't used to having time to do this dating thing. Up until a few months ago, she'd barely had time for a quick rendezvous with any of the number of eligible women who'd run across her path. Now that she had time to savor their company, she wasn't entirely sure how to go about it. Was it really as difficult as she was making it seem?

She drank half the strong brew while she rummaged through the kitchen, checking for supplies. Once she determined she had what she needed, she dialed April's number before she could change her mind.

April answered on the second ring. "I hoped you'd call."

"I just got your message. You're definitely right about the weather. It's a fireplace kind of night."

"Would you like to come over? I just opened a nice Malbec."

"Actually, I called to invite you over here," Ellery said. "What are your thoughts on homemade chili and a nice oatmeal stout?"

"Hmmm, well, beer's not my thing, but I love a good chili. I have the perfect wine to go with it. Can I bring anything else?"

Ellery paused, for a brief second wishing she could retract the invitation, before she mentally smacked herself. Wine, beer, what did it really matter? They didn't have to like all the same things to get along. April was pretty and accomplished and a decent conversationalist. At least she didn't ask a ton of questions about what Ellery did for a living and what she'd done before. It didn't matter what they drank or whether they liked the same things. They'd have chili and talk and maybe make out by the fire. A near perfect date. "I've got everything covered. Head on over whenever you're ready."

She hung up and spent the next hour putting together the chili recipe her great-grandfather had made famous. Like her work restoring and repurposing furniture, the simple steps of putting together ingredients to create a complex result was soothing, satisfying, sensual. When the doorbell rang, she'd reached her Zen place.

April thrust a bottle of red into her arms. "It's bold enough to stand up to a lot of spice. I assumed you'd make a spicy chili."

Ellery did her best not to cringe at the poorly delivered innuendo. She took April's coat and hung it in the closet. "Are you hungry?"

"Starved."

"Then follow me." Ellery led the way into the kitchen and motioned for April to have a seat while she gave the chili a final stir. Satisfied it was ready, she opened the bottle of wine and poured a single glass. When April raised her eyebrows in question, she raised her own bottle of stout in a toast. "Cheers to whatever suits you." She clinked the bottle against April's glass and took a deep drink.

"You do casual well," April said.

Ellery looked down at her worn jeans and rag wool sweater, a far cry from the sharply tailored suits she used to wear. April's attire wasn't much different from what she'd seen her in before. Her version of casual was high fashion—skinny black pants tucked into tall suede boots and a crimson sweater designed to hug every curve.

Ignoring the sexual undertone, Ellery handed April a bowl and pointed her in the direction of the large pot of chili. The family recipe was designed to feed a mob, and she'd made enough for a dozen dates, figuring she'd freeze whatever they didn't eat. As April dished chili into her bowl, Ellery pointed out a line of small serving dishes. "Cheese, sour cream, cilantro, jalapeños. Have some or all."

April held the bowl to her nose. "This smells divine. You never said you could cook. Your list of talents seems to be never-ending."

"Hardly. I've always liked to cook, but I haven't had time until recently."

April ate a spoonful and groaned. "Cooking is all you should do. Seriously, this is amazing."

"I'm glad you like it." Ellery smiled at April's unabashed enthusiasm. She hadn't really picked April as the chili type. Ellery had been selling her furniture from a pop-up shop when her friend and former colleague, Meg, stopped by with April in tow. They'd been checking out a fresh juice vendor a few booths down. April, looking like she'd stepped from the pages of a fashion magazine, seemed completely out of place at the outdoor market, but that night Meg called to say that April had asked for her number and she figured what the hell. They'd been on two dates, both of them the kind of dates she'd used to have—high end, high energy, and high profile. Sushi, steaks, champagne, and clubbing. Tonight was designed to see if April would fit into her new life where things were much more low-key. So far, she measured up.

They sat at a low table by the roaring fire and devoured the chili. April, a cardiologist with a thriving Dallas practice, was keyed up, and she dominated the conversation with stories about her hectic week. Ellery leaned back into the large cushions she'd propped up around the table, letting the heat of the fire and the flood of words flow around her. It wasn't that April's tales weren't interesting, but she feared if she listened too closely, she'd get swept back into the frantic style of life she used to lead as a high profile criminal defense attorney. Too much OPD, other people's drama, had consumed her every waking moment. For years, she thought she thrived on the constant frenetic energy of her busy practice, but over the course of the past year, the pace had culminated into a series of incidents that convinced her to make a break or lose her sanity.

Her former law partner, Meg, hadn't believed her when she said she was walking away, even went so far as to have a new firm logo designed with both of their names and ordered a boatload of new stationary. But Ellery had ignored Meg's attempts to get her to stay on, paid the cost of the new stationary, and taken the necessary steps to dissolve the partnership. So far, she hadn't regretted the move for a second.

"And that's when I told her no way would I sign off on that kind of procedure," April said.

Ellery looked up, oblivious to the subject of April's diatribe, but certain she was supposed to offer some affirmation. Luckily, the phone rang. April looked toward her cell phone, but Ellery pointed toward the kitchen.

"It's the house phone," Ellery said.

"Go on and get it. I can check in with my service."

Ellery picked up the extension and looked at the caller ID. She didn't recognize the number, but very few people had her home number so she answered the call. "Hello?"

"It's Meg. You throw your cell phone away with the rest of your life?"

Ellery laughed at the gruff sound of her former law partner's voice. "No, I'm just not tethered to it anymore. You should give it a try. Might stop you from having to pop antacids like they're candy."

"What, and give up all this glory? Not a chance."

"Suit yourself. I'm on a date, so make it quick."

"A date? At your house? Wow, you have changed. How will you get her to leave when you're ready for the date to end?"

Ellery glanced down the hall toward the living room. She hadn't actually thought that part through. Part of her new life was playing things by ear, but she wasn't about to discuss dating strategy with Meg while April was sitting in the next room. "Did you actually want something or do you just miss me?"

"Both. I need you to handle a tiny little thing for me in the morning."

Alarm bells went off and Ellery dug in. "If you need me to make you a piece of furniture, I'm in. Anything else, no way."

"I wouldn't ask, but it's Amir. I'm set for trial on another case in Denton, and he won't show up with anyone else. He trusts you."

"That's nice, but like everyone else, he'll have to learn to let go."

"It's not his fault you deserted all of us. It's for his son Naveed's case. Come on, just this once."

Ellery sighed. Amir Khan wasn't necessarily a difficult client, but he did expect personal attention to all of his business matters and his expectations could be trying. His son had picked up a case around the time that she'd first decided to quit the practice. Although he'd wanted her to represent him, she had introduced him to Meg and made it clear from the start that she would take over when she was gone. "What do you need me to do?"

"Nothing major. It's just an appearance. Hold his hand, see if the prosecutor has a rec, sign a pass slip, get a new court date, and you're on your way. An hour tops. I'll even pay you."

"Don't. I'd rather you owe me one."

"So, you'll do it?"

"This is it, Meg. Nothing else. Are you sure you want to blow the only work favor you're going to get from me on something this simple?"

"I promise I won't bug you again unless it's for lunch or drinks."

"Fine. I'll meet him at the courthouse, but I'll have to come by the office and get the file, so let him know it will be around ten before I make it down there."

Ellery hung up and instantly started sorting through details. All her suits were clean since she hadn't worn one in months, but she'd probably have to iron a shirt. Taking into account the fact she had to run by the office before going to court, she'd have to get up early. So much for having another beer.

"Everything okay?"

She looked up to see April standing in the doorway. "Just an unexpected change to my plans for tomorrow."

"Me too. Actually, mine has to do with tonight. I need to run by the hospital. I shouldn't be too long though if you're going to be up late."

"Sorry, looks like I have an early morning in store. Guess we should call it a night."

April's smile held a tinge of regret. "I had a good time. And don't worry, I completely understand about wacky schedules. This happens to me all the time."

Ellery managed a smile in return, but she wasn't feeling it. Interrupted dinners and late night phone calls used to happen to her all the time too, but she'd sworn off those things in exchange for a quiet life. She made a silent vow that she wouldn't let Meg talk her into any more favors. This would be the very last one. Former clients would stay former clients. The serenity of her new life was worth protecting.

CHAPTER THREE

So far, Sarah's first day at the Dallas FBI field office had been duller than dull. From the moment she arrived, the rest of the fraud unit eyed her as if she were an alien creature. She'd shown up in a suit, ready to make new friends, and engage in the kind of work that didn't involve gory crime scene photos and bullets whizzing past her head. Everyone else in the unit wore what was likely some version of business casual and, without exception, seemed unreasonably territorial about the incredibly boring work assigned to them. After a morning meeting with the field office director's secretary to get security issues squared away, the director, Robert Mason, introduced her around, and then showed her to a desk loaded with boxes full of paper and computer hard drives.

"You'll want to get started on these. Liz will be happy to fill you in." He waved to a woman seated in a cubicle across the way and left Sarah on her own. The expression on Liz's face told Sarah right away that the boss was exaggerating Liz's happiness about anything. She sighed. These people didn't know her, and it was probably going to be a lot harder to develop relationships with them since this assignment was more of a nine-to-five than an always on call job, but she was determined to make it work. She plastered a big smile on her face, walked over to Liz's desk, and stuck out her hand. "Sarah Flores, nice to meet you."

"Special Agent Elizabeth Dawson."

Dawson delivered the title with just a hint of tone and the firmness of her handshake was punishing. *Great, someone's got a bit of an insecurity issue.* Sarah kept smiling to hide the whir of personality processing going on in her head. Someday maybe she'd learn to shut down the constant need to analyze everyone around her, but it was more than a habit, it had been her life. "Mason says you're in charge of this project." She motioned to the stack of boxes on her desk. "What would you like me to do?"

"Mason's in charge, not me, but I suppose you can do what the rest of us are doing. The hard drives contain various bank records we obtained in conjunction with an investigation into several tax and investment fraud schemes. We're looking for unusual activity. There's an evidence log with the boxes you can use to organize your searches. You find something, you let us know, and we'll compare it to records the rest of the team is reviewing."

A dozen questions popped into Sarah's mind, but Liz's face was an impenetrable wall. Sarah decided to start digging into the records and, if the answers weren't readily apparent, when things got a little more comfortable with the rest of the team, she'd pose her questions then.

A couple of hours later, she had pages of notes, none of which amounted to much without some context. In between reviewing the records, she'd watched the group around her operate in an attempt to learn what she could about the existing dynamics. At least three other agents were working on this project with Liz, but no one stuck out as being on equal footing with her. Sarah saw them all converse and managed to catch snippets of what they had to say. Apparently, what they were working on had to do with the recent government crack-down on entities applying for non-profit status and the records review was supposed to root out those entities that didn't truly qualify for the tax privileges they'd received as a result of their status. Would have helped to know that from the start. She was going to have to figure out a way to uncover information on her own until the rest of the group started accepting her.

Around eleven, a low rumble from her stomach told her the coffee she'd had for breakfast was no longer doing its trick. She remembered the lunchroom that Mason had rushed her past earlier. Not likely any of these not-so-friendly types was going to ask her to lunch and she wasn't in the mood to stick around here anyway. She reached for her phone and dialed a familiar number. When the voice on the other end answered, she said, "Tell me you have time to meet me for lunch."

"Flores! Is that you? Are you here in town for real?"

Sarah warmed to the welcome in Danny's voice. "Got here last week. Tried to reach you, but your office said you were out of town."

"Rare vacation, but I'm back now. I can make lunch work if we can do it around here. Vacation means I'm kind of behind on work."

"Great. I'll come get you."

Sarah grabbed the keys to her car and checked out with the receptionist. She didn't bother saying anything to any of the other agents, figuring they probably wouldn't notice she was leaving and she didn't want to make them feel like they should've included her in their plans. Maybe it was time for her to expand her horizons and make friends outside of the job.

Danny Soto was a Dallas County prosecutor she'd met while working a serial killer case in the area last year and they'd become friends during the course of the investigation. Okay, so her friendship with Danny wasn't exactly expanding her horizons, but at least they didn't work in the same office. And Danny's wife, Ellen Davenport, was the executive director for a national sorority office—not the least bit involved in crime, so that was something. As she sped to the courthouse, she vowed she would find something to do this very weekend that didn't involve work of any kind.

Ellery looked in the rearview mirror before carefully backing her truck into the tiny space in the parking garage of the Dallas County Courthouse. Once the truck was parked, she took a second look in the mirror, unaccustomed to the reflection staring back at her. For the past six months, she'd spent most mornings roaming abandoned buildings, junkyards, and flea markets or working in her studio. Except for a few dates, none of her activities required combed hair or a business suit. Today, instead of her usual Levi's and T-shirts, she sported a light-weight black wool suit and a crisp pale blue shirt, both of which she'd had custom made while traveling in London a couple of years ago. Once upon a time she'd reveled in the feel of the expensive fabric and the well-tailored fit, but now the clothes were suffocating. Or maybe it was this place that was suffocating. Determined to get this errand over as quickly as possible, she grabbed her handmade leather briefcase and walked to the side entrance of the courthouse.

The line at security was surprisingly long considering her stop at Meg's office meant she'd shown up after the morning docket was usually well underway. She used the time in line to review the file. Amir Khan's son, Naveed, along with one of his cousins and two of their friends had been charged with burglary of a building. A security guard had spotted the young men leaving an office building in North Dallas in the early morning hours one weekend night, and called the police. Realizing they'd been spotted, the boys ran toward their car, but Naveed, who'd been waiting behind the wheel, took off before they got close. None of the boys had ratted Naveed out, but the witness gave the police his license plate information and he'd been picked up not far from the building and charged as a party to the crime. A window in the building had been broken, but it didn't appear anything had been taken and, according to Naveed, the whole thing had been a lark. Lark or not, the case had lagged on in the system, but charges had finally been filed last month and this was his first court appearance.

Amir had first come to her with this case right before she left the practice. He'd wanted to hire her to represent all of the boys, but she'd explained that it could be a conflict of interest. Unlike the other boys, Naveed had been accepted to an Ivy League school, and he had the most to lose with a criminal conviction on his record. She told Amir it would be better if Naveed had his own attorney and the chance to offer his cooperation to the district attorney in order to cut a deal that might result in the charges being dropped. The way she'd seen it, the boys' actions amounted to nothing more than misdemeanor criminal trespass, and Naveed's role was a minor one at that. She and Meg had been on the same page about the defense and she planned to reinforce the original plan to Naveed and his father this morning and then reset the case to give Meg more time to review the evidence and talk to the prosecutor about a resolution that would keep Naveed's record clear.

After what seemed like forever, Ellery finally reached the front of the line. She set her briefcase on the conveyor belt and walked through the metal detector. The security guard nodded as she waited for her bag to come out the other side and she nodded back. Briefcase in hand, she headed for the stairwell, knowing that no matter how long she'd been gone, two things were probably still true—neither the elevators nor the escalators were all functioning. The six flights were an easy climb and she emerged from the stairwell just a few feet from the court where Naveed's case was assigned.

He and his father were waiting on a bench outside the courtroom and they both stood as they saw her approach. A petite girl with ivory white skin and golden blond hair stood with them. Ellery shook Amir's hand and gestured for them to follow her down the hall. She stopped in an alcove near the elevators where the floor to ceiling windows offered the city's best view of downtown Dallas.

"Amir, Naveed, nice to see you both." Ellery waited a few beats, but neither of them offered up anything about the blonde who'd joined them, so she finally asked, "Who's this?"

Amir started to speak, but the girl beat him to it. "I'm Kayla, Akbar's girlfriend."

Ellery went on alert. Akbar was Naveed's cousin and, based on Meg's notes, the ringleader of their romp that night. She spoke directly to Amir. "I respect your desire to have family involved, but I must speak to Naveed in private. You understand, yes?" She punctuated her question with a nod to let him know she wasn't really asking, she was saying that was how it had to be. He nodded in return.

"Kayla, come with me. Miss Durant will speak to Naveed alone for a moment."

As they walked away, she heard Kayla whisper, "I don't understand why she doesn't trust you to hear what she has to say. Akbar's lawyer doesn't have secrets." Ellery felt a slow boil of anger and shook her head. No skinny little girl was going to tell her how to handle her cases.

"Miss Durant?"

She turned to look at Naveed who was gazing at her with a curious expression. Naveed, who was no longer her client. For a second, she'd forgotten this was a life she'd left behind. "I'm sorry." She looked back over at Kayla who was standing next to Amir, still bending his ear. "Just curious, why is she here?"

Naveed shrugged. "Akbar was here earlier with his attorney and she came with him. He left, but she stuck around. She's always around."

His comment prompted her to ask, "What about that night? Where was she then?"

"Akbar said no girls allowed that night. He said they had to prove themselves before they could tag along. No one brought their girlfriends."

She smiled. "Probably a good idea or your father would have to be hiring even more lawyers."

"I'm glad you're here."

"I'm only here for today. Meg's your lawyer."

"She doesn't like me."

"I doubt that."

"You talk to me. She only talks to my father. I have to spy to figure out what's going on. Akbar and the others are going to trial. She says that's what I should do."

"Really?" Ellery didn't try to hide her surprise. "When did she say that?"

"Last week. At least that's what she told father. Maybe I should. What do you think?"

Ellery paused before answering. Her knee-jerk reaction was to say that wasn't what they'd decided before, but for all she knew something had changed since she'd last worked on this case. It was possible Meg had gotten discovery from the prosecutor that led her to believe the state would have a problem proving their case. "I'd have to ask Meg. She's been working on the case, not me."

He repeated his earlier statement. "I don't understand why you can't represent me. She will only talk to my father, not to me."

Ellery had noticed Meg deferring to Amir the first time she'd introduced him and Naveed to her, but she figured Meg was just sucking up to one of the firm's more important clients. While she had focused on criminal law, Meg had more diverse interests, and she had expressed on more than one occasion her desire to get all of Amir's business. Apparently, in her quest to win the father, she'd lost the confidence of the son. "I'll talk to her. You're an adult. Just because your father is paying doesn't mean you aren't the one calling the shots. What do you want to do?"

"My father wants me to go to college."

"I didn't ask you what your father wanted."

"Sorry. I want to go to college. Eventually. First, I'd like to travel." He offered a rueful smile. "Far away from here."

"I hear you. I'll go talk to the prosecutor and reset your case to give you time to sit down with Meg and tell her what you just told me, review the evidence, and make your own decision. Okay?"

"I guess I don't have a choice."

"You could hire your own lawyer." Ellery knew Naveed's monthly allowance was probably more than most kids his age made in an entire summer of work.

Naveed shot a look at his father and Kayla. "That's okay. I'll work things out with the one I have."

Ellery followed his eyes and saw Kayla staring at him like a hawk observing its prey. She had no idea what the dynamic was between this young woman and Naveed, but she couldn't help a growing sense of unease at Kayla's presence.

She shrugged it off. Whatever Kayla's role was in their lives, it wasn't her problem. Time to do the favor she'd promised and get the hell out of here. She pushed through the double doors of the courtroom and then opened the door to her left to enter the DA workroom. She nodded to the prosecutor seated at the desk just inside the door and pointed at the door on the far side of the room which was pulled to. "Hi, James, is Danny in?"

"She's back there. Suffering from reentry. Enter at your own risk."

Ellery rapped on the door and a voice called out, "Come in."

She pushed through the door. Danny Soto, the chief prosecutor in this particular court, was seated behind a desk piled high with files. "Let me guess. You've been on vacation?"

"Yep and I'm beginning to wonder why I bothered," she said. "It's always worse when I get back. Thank God, this isn't a jury week. Whatcha got for me?"

"Hopefully, something easy. Naveed Khan. I'm here on his announcement setting."

"Ah, the Bank of America bandits."

"Bank of America?" Ellery looked at her notes. "I'm pretty sure it was just an office building."

"That Bank of America owns. Don't worry. They don't have a branch there anymore. If they did, I would have referred this out to the feds. So, we'll just call them the building bandits if it makes you feel better."

"The word bandit implies they actually took something. When my guy was picked up, he had no stolen property in his possession."

Danny waved her hand in the air. "I say bandit, you say getaway driver. Whatever. Do you need a rec?"

"I understand the other defendants are going to trial."

"I don't know about that. Maybe they set a date while I was out of town, but I don't think I even made an offer yet. Let me check the file." Danny yanked open a file cabinet drawer and thumbed through a row of folders until she found the one she was looking for. She pulled it out and flipped through the pages. "I've got Meg Patrick's name listed here as the attorney of record. Are you working this with her?"

"Not really. I'm officially no longer in practice, but I know this family, and Meg's in trial in Denton this morning so I told her I'd pass the case. I figured while I was here, I'd see what you're offering."

"No longer in practice, huh? Guess that's why I haven't seen you around for a while. What are you up to?"

"I make furniture." She felt herself bristle in response to Danny's raised eyebrows and she kept talking. "Out of stuff I find. Reclaimed materials. I have a shop online and I sell at various local shows."

Danny's expression held a mixture of surprise and awe. "That sounds cool. Bet you don't miss this grind."

She started to answer in the affirmative, but pulled up short. She hadn't missed it. Not until this morning anyway. Naveed's plea for help and his frustration about not getting the guidance he needed had tugged at her emotions and she sincerely wanted to help. This wasn't her case, but she was already invested in getting him the best possible result. "Not usually, no, but like I said, I've known this family for a while so it was no big deal to fill in." Time to turn this conversation away from her personal life and back to the reason she was here. "Do you have a rec?"

Danny glanced through the file one more time before setting it down. "Looks like your guy has no priors. If he'll testify against the others, I'll offer three years deferred."

Deferred meant Naveed would be on probation for three years and when the time was up, if he completed all the conditions of probation successfully, the case would be dismissed. Then he'd have to wait a few years to get his record sealed. While it might seem like a generous offer, it meant that the felony would linger on Naveed's record well into his college years and the time he'd start applying for jobs. Ignoring the voice in her head that whispered this was Meg's case and she shouldn't interfere, she said, "That's not going to fly. Worst-case scenario, this was a misdemeanor criminal trespass. Best case, you won't be able to prove my client had any knowledge of what those other kids were doing. Give him a conditional dismissal. He'll do whatever you ask—pick up trash on the side of the highway, pay a fine, anything. He's got a bright future ahead. No one was hurt and nothing was damaged. Don't let this one incident ruin a young kid's life."

Danny started to reply, but at that moment the door swung open and Ellery turned in her chair to see a tall, beautiful woman in a suit burst into the room. She expected Danny to tell the intruder she was busy, but within a second, the woman rushed Danny and pulled her into a hug.

"Who's your favorite federal agent?" she said.

"Get off me, crazy lady." Danny pointed at Ellery. "Can't you see I'm in a meeting?"

"Didn't sound like a meeting. It sounded like she was trying to shake you down. Have you gone soft?"

"Not hardly." They shared a laugh, and then, as if she'd just remembered Ellery was in the room, Danny introduced the stranger. "Sarah Flores, meet Ellery Durant."

"Nice to meet you." Ellery held out her hand and looked between the two. Like Danny, the stranger was Latina and they both wore suits, but the similarities stopped there. In contrast to Danny's boyish good looks, Sarah was decidedly feminine, from her perfect makeup to her stylish shoes, to the way the cut of her suit accentuated every luscious curve.

"Sorry for interrupting."

Sarah's eyes were locked on Ellery as she spoke. The scrutiny made her uncomfortable, but she couldn't put her finger on why. It was almost like Sarah could see her thoughts. She waited for Danny to ask Sarah to leave while they finished their business, but instead Danny said, "Hang for a minute. We're just finishing up." She switched her focus back to Ellery. "Okay, you were saying you want me to reduce the burglary to a criminal trespass and give your client a pass. Is that about it?"

"More or less." Ellery shifted in her chair. The dynamic had changed now that Sarah had entered the room, and she'd lost the momentum of her plea. "I can bring you his college acceptance letter if that helps you justify the reduction."

"Ted Bundy went to college," Sarah said. "Graduated with honors."

"Excuse me?" Ellery looked over at Sarah who raised her shoulders in a slight shrug.

"I'm just saying a college degree is not a good predictor of whether or not someone is going to obey the law."

She'd encountered these types of federal agents before. They drank the Kool-Aid and spent their careers believing anyone charged with a crime was a bad seed without any regard to extenuating circumstances. She had no patience for their black-and-white assessments of the world. "Take a poll of the population of any prison in the country. I'll bet you all the money in my wallet that at least eighty percent of the inmates never went to college."

"Well, besides the fact that I'm not about to wager money here at the courthouse when it's clearly illegal, I'll just say that's because the ones who went to college were too smart to get caught."

Ellery stood up, mentally adding cops like Sarah Flores to the list of things she didn't miss about practicing law. She looked at Danny. "Well, like I said, this is Meg's case. If you'll just sign the pass slip, I'll let her know to get in touch with you."

Danny scrawled her name on the paper to notify the court coordinator that they were still working out the case and handed it to Ellery with an apologetic look in her eyes. Ellery thanked her and pushed open the door as she stalked from the room without another word to Agent Flores. She paused before she walked back out in the hall to face Naveed and his father, disturbed at how angry she felt. It wasn't like her to let a cop get her so rattled, but Sarah's uninformed and unsolicited comments had gotten under her skin. And it certainly hadn't helped that Sarah was as attractive as she was annoying.

She took a deep breath. Maybe just being back at the courthouse was the issue. After all, she'd tried her very last case in this very courtroom. The memory washed cold down her spine and she pushed it away while she made a final decision about Naveed. She wasn't his lawyer and she had no business advising him. She'd give the file back to Meg, along with a brief summary of her conversation with Danny, and she'd be done with this case. No more favors. No more getting sucked back in. She wasn't a lawyer anymore and it was time to stop pretending she was.

Sarah watched the door close behind Ellery, still fixated by the exchange. When she'd first walked into the room, she'd been captivated by Ellery's good looks—short, stylish, dark brown hair, a strong jaw, and gray-blue eyes so deep you could drown in them. Happily. Her suit jacket hugged her lean torso, and Sarah had quickly determined she definitely wasn't carrying and therefore, probably wasn't a cop. Attorney, she'd concluded. She noticed the leather briefcase by her chair. Most likely defense counsel. Ellery's pose had been confident, like she belonged here, but the expression in her eyes signaled reluctance of some kind. She was entirely at ease bantering with Danny, but she didn't want to be here. What had she told Danny about why the case wasn't hers? Who was she doing the favor for? The details didn't matter, but Sarah couldn't shut down the questions, especially since everything about Ellery Durant, from her striking appearance to her feisty defense of her client was irresistible.

She managed to wait until they were at lunch to start grilling Danny. "What's the story with Ellery Durant?"

Danny glanced at her watch. "You've been in town how long? And you're already on the prowl? Why am I not surprised?"

"Fine for you to judge. You married people are all alike, forgetting how it used to be when you were single and lonely."

"You lonely? I find that hard to believe. I bet you have a different woman in every city."

"I might, but that doesn't change anything. In case you haven't noticed, I'm not traveling anymore."

"Ready to settle down?"

"Ready to start thinking about it." And she was, although this was the first time she'd said it out loud. While working in the BAU, she'd had built-in relationships with her fellow agents and she hadn't had the time or energy to give to anyone outside the close-knit group. She'd satisfied her need for intimacy with strangers in various cities, the location determined by her work. Her lifestyle had seemed easy at the time, but it had done nothing to prepare her for the long-term. Now that she had the opportunity to develop something more, she didn't have the first clue how to go about it. Maybe her attraction to Ellery was nothing more than the familiar call of hormones, but she could at least see if there was something more there. "Are you going to tell me about her or do I have to engage my super power detecting skills?"

"I don't know her well, not personally anyway. She didn't come up through the office. Her father was a big deal defense attorney in town and she started working in his practice right out of law school. She was good, born to be a trial litigator, but just as good at working out good deals for her clients. She wasn't one of those attorneys who thinks all law enforcement types are evil."

"Was? Did something happen?"

"I don't know, but she just told me she's not practicing anymore. Something about making furniture. You know, one of those deals where you find old stuff and what's the word? Repurpose it."

"That's odd."

"She seems happy."

"I guess. She seemed kind of annoyed."

"Well, you were a little annoying. And you're one to talk. Aren't you the one who left the prestigious BAU to thumb through papers in a fraud unit?"

"That's different," Sarah said, while hoping Danny didn't press her on the point. Unlike Ellery, she was still in the same line of work even if her new position wasn't nearly as dynamic as her work with the BAU. Pushing paper would allow her to stay in one place, have an actual home instead of an apartment that served as nothing more than a storage locker. Pushing paper wouldn't cause her to jerk awake from nightmares, ready to seize her gun from the nightstand. Maybe Danny was right. Who was she to judge Ellery for her decision to change occupations?

"Tell you what," Danny said. "Ellen's alumni group is hosting a candidate forum this Friday. The reception will be full of some of the most eligible women in Dallas. Ellen will be busy the whole time so you can be my pseudo date. If you're really settling down, you may as well start getting to know the locals. Pick me up at six."

Sarah laughed until she realized Danny was serious. She started to beg off, but her resolution to embrace her new life echoed in her mind. A night full of politics with Dallas's elite wouldn't have been her first choice, but what better way to plunge in and she'd at least have friends on hand if she started drowning.

CHAPTER FOUR

Sarah dug through her closet until she found the dress. The Dress. It was still wrapped in plastic from the last time she'd taken it to the cleaners. She tried to remember when that was, but couldn't quite place when she'd last worn it. Hopefully, it still fit. It had been way too long since she'd worn clothes that weren't designed to hide her government-issued Glock or shoes suitable for running down suspects, but tonight she was going all girl. She tugged the Louboutins she'd splurged on months ago, but hadn't had a chance to wear, off the top shelf of the closet. Danny's prediction about the number of eligible bachelorettes at this shindig had better be spot-on.

An hour later, she drove past the valet stand of the W Hotel and made a few laps around the block. The neighborhood around the hotel appeared to house a lot of new development, restaurants, retail, and a fancy apartment complex, all with private parking. It only took a few minutes for her to realize there was no street parking available, and when she looped by the American Airlines Center, she realized why. The arena was lit up and people were pouring into the building. The Mavericks were playing the Spurs, and no doubt the arena would soon be packed with fans cheering on their respective Texas teams. Resigned to leaving her car in the hands of strangers, she pulled into the hotel drive and surrendered her keys to the youngster who opened her door. He stared at her legs as she stepped out of the vehicle, and she tapped his shoulder to get him to meet her eyes. "Ticket?"

"Uh, sorry, miss." He handed her a stub. "Luggage?"

"No, I'm here for an event. I'll find my way." She strode away, certain his eyes were firmly fixed on her backside. Hopefully, this dress would have the same effect on the women at this event.

Moments later, she'd emerged from the elevator onto the top floor of the hotel. The entire space had been reserved for the reception. If breathtaking views made for generous donors, the politicians present could expect to go home with lots of new money. She walked to the floor to ceiling windows and stared out over the city, downtown to the left, the arena to the right. This was her home now, and she was ready to make the most of it. Maybe she'd check out the basketball schedule and catch the next home game. She'd rarely had time to take in planned events before since she never knew when her job would call her away. Now she could buy tickets well in advance and be certain nothing was going to disrupt her plans.

"Don't jump."

She turned at the sound of the familiar voice and smiled when she saw Danny and her wife, Ellen, walk toward her. "No worries. I was just taking in the sights."

Danny shook her hand and Ellen leaned in to kiss her lightly on the cheek. "I'm so glad you came," Ellen said. "Danny gets so bored at these things. Promise you'll keep her from falling asleep during the speeches?"

"Speeches?" Sarah glared at Danny who looked sheepish.

"Uh-oh. I may have neglected to tell her there would be speeches. I'm pretty sure I only mentioned gorgeous, rich, eligible women."

Ellen laughed. "Well, there'll be plenty of those. And the speeches will be short, I promise." She looked at her watch. "You've got an hour to find the woman of Sarah's dreams before anyone takes the stage. I'm sorry, you two, but I've got to do my thing. I'll catch up with you later. Sarah, it's great to see you." She'd barely delivered her last words before she disappeared into the crowd.

"Guess you're stuck with me," Danny said.

"You can be my wingman. I'm not leaving here without someone's phone number."

"Dressed like that you'll probably leave with a lot more than that."

"Settle down, tiger. Your wife's nearby."

Danny punched her in the shoulder. "As if."

Sarah smiled back at her, remembering how shamelessly she'd flirted with Danny the first time they'd met. Danny hadn't wanted to have anything to do with her, partly because they'd clashed professionally, but primarily because she'd already met Ellen Davenport and was completely captivated by her charms. She couldn't blame Danny. Ellen was beautiful and charming, and she could only hope to find a partner who was as well suited to her as Danny and Ellen were to each other.

"If only I could be as lucky as you. Let's start working this room. Where do you suggest we begin?"

"You stand here and look pretty and I'll get us some drinks, then we can make our way around the room. I know enough of these people to get you started on your quest to find the future Mrs. Flores."

Danny took off before Sarah could protest. She stood with her back to the windows and surveyed the room, glad she'd worn the dress, as this event was full of glitter. She spent the first few minutes playing a familiar game. The first couple she spotted could not have been more mismatched. She was short and dumpy, while he was tall and handsome. No noticeable age difference. Was she rich? Did she have a fantastic personality that outweighed their obvious differences in the looks department? Maybe he was her brother, pressed into service escorting his homely sister for a night on the town. Escort. Maybe he was being paid. Sarah shook her head. She knew she shouldn't be so shallow, but her generalizations were based on years of observing human behavior.

The next couple was more suitably matched. The taller of the two faced away from her, but Sarah could still tell her charcoal gray suit was a custom cut by the way it framed her slim hips and tight butt. In contrast to gray suit's close cropped brunette hair, the other woman's blond waves hung loose and free. Blondie wore a stunning maroon cocktail dress, and shoes that added four inches to her height, but still wouldn't bring her eye to eye with gray suit. Entranced, Sarah watched their interaction. The blonde kept glancing away as others passed by, occasionally stopping to pull someone else into their circle. Gray suit still stood with her back to Sarah, so she could only imagine her reaction to each interruption, but the stiff way her shoulders hunched each time Blondie looked away signaled she wasn't pleased. After a few moments, the blonde mouthed "I'll be right back," kissed gray suit on the cheek, and dashed off to a group of people gathering near the stage. Sarah watched Blondie until she disappeared into the crowd. When she looked back toward gray suit, she was gone.

Time for that drink. She looked around, but Danny was nowhere in sight. She must still be waiting at the bar. Deciding it was time to stop people watching and start assessing the dateability of the women in attendance, Sarah started walking through the crowd. Based on looks alone, the dating pool was stocked with potential, but she wasn't sure how to approach any of them. This wasn't like a bar where there was a better than average chance the woman next to you was up for a hookup. And she wasn't here for a hookup either. Sarah sighed. She was utterly inept when it came to anything other than simple pickup lines. She should just find Danny, have that drink, and spend the rest of the evening observing.

Decision made, she cut through the throngs of people until she finally found the bar. Danny was standing off to the side, drinks in hand, talking to none other than gray suit, and Sarah stopped in her tracks at the sight. From behind, gray suit was attractive, but the full frontal was breathtaking. Ellery Durant was as handsome as she remembered, from her warm eyes to the way her face crinkled into a smile at whatever Danny was saying. Excited about the prospect of a second chance to win her over, Sarah squared her shoulders and strode over to where Ellery and Danny were talking, convinced she was going to make a better impression this time around.

Ellery would rather be anywhere else. She glanced around the beautiful bar, at all the lavish food and well-dressed women, and felt no affinity with any of it despite the fact that just last year her firm would have probably been a headline sponsor of just such an event. Now, the only reason she was here was because April had goaded her into coming, promising that they would leave early and hole up somewhere decidedly unpublic for the rest of the evening.

She resisted looking at her watch, certain that every ten-minute interval was crawling by in half-time. Instead, she made a game out of watching the other women in the room interact with each other in a timeless social dance. April's sorority was throwing this shindig and, although she wasn't part of the committee putting on the candidate forum, April had insisted she had to be here to support her alumnae sisters. "It wouldn't look good if I missed. So many of them make referrals to the practice," she'd said.

Ellery got it. When you offered a service, you had to sell yourself first. It had been the same with her law practice. Lots of glad-handing, sucking up to people with money and power in hopes they'd send their business your way. Now, her work sold itself in the furniture she restored. People looked at the pieces she's transformed and they liked it or they didn't. They could afford it or they couldn't. Either way, whether she made money or not wasn't personal, it was pure economics. But still, this hadn't been at all what she'd expected when April had suggested they go out tonight.

She wasn't sure if she even cared. April was clearly still immersed in this world where money and appearance were paramount, but Ellery wasn't interested in being dragged back into her old life. She glanced across the room. April was surrounded by a circle of her sorority sisters and, judging from the raised drinks and loud laughter, they were having the time of their lives. She didn't begrudge them their fun, but she did want to kick herself for not staying home. Now that she was stuck here, she may as well get a drink and settle in since it didn't look as if April was going to be ready to leave anytime soon.

The bar was crowded, but luckily, she'd picked the fast line. When she finally reached the front, she ordered a beer and got a grateful smile from the bartender who'd been asked to pour all manner of complicated concoctions by the women who'd ordered before her. She declined a glass, left a generous tip, and started to walk back to her corner of the room when she heard a familiar voice call her name.

"Ellery?"

She turned and saw Danny Soto standing at the bar holding a beer bottle and a martini. She smiled and Danny walked toward her. "Hey, it's nice to see a friendly face."

"Tell me about it. I've been to a bunch of these things, but I'm not sure I'll ever feel like I fit in. I don't recall ever seeing you at one of these. Were you an Alpha Nu?"

"Nope. My dad would've had my hide if I did anything in college that distracted from studying. What are you doing here?"

"My wife, Ellen, is the executive director for the national office. I'm here in my capacity as supportive spouse. She's so busy, I probably won't see her until the end of the night."

Ellery pointed at the two drinks in Danny's hands. "I guess your role requires extra fortification."

Danny laughed. "Actually, one of these is for a friend. You remember Sarah Flores? She was in my office the other day when you came by."

Ellery started to reply, but she was interrupted by a voice from behind her.

"Are you going to stand there and talk about me or deliver my drink?"

Ellery turned and sucked in a breath. She'd never expected to see the aggravating woman she'd met earlier in the week at Danny's office again, but here she was, looking like she'd stepped out of the pages of a fashion magazine. This Sarah Flores looked nothing like any federal agent she'd ever met before. She finally realized she was staring and stuck out her hand. "Nice to see you again. Don't let me keep you from your drink delivery."

Sarah's smile flashed bright. "Nothing will accomplish that. And don't go." She took the drink Danny held out to her. "Stay and hang out with us. Please." She accented her words by tilting her drink as if to toast.

Ellery took longer than necessary to consider the simple request. Her first impression had been so clouded by Sarah's forceful cop attitude that she hadn't let the full depth of her stunning beauty seep in. This woman was every bit as captivating as she was aggravating, and Ellery was held in place by the magnetic pull of inexplicable attraction. She clicked her bottle against Sarah's glass. "I can stay for a bit. Are you here just to keep Danny company or to support one of the candidates?"

Sarah leaned close. "I don't know any of these people. I heard there would be an open bar and lots of beautiful women. I wasn't wrong, apparently."

"Cool it, Special Agent Hotshot," Danny said. "Ellery, I must apologize for my friend here. She's a bit of a cad."

"I am not. I just believe in taking life by the horns. Enjoying every moment. Even when I find myself at a stuffy event, I'm bound and determined to have a little fun. Besides, I was paying a compliment. Nothing wrong with that, is there?"

The candor Ellery had found annoying at the courthouse was refreshing in this venue full of people posing in order to garner votes. What harm could come from engaging in a little light banter? She raised her bottle. "Thanks for the compliment. Special Agent, huh? Is that a nickname or do you have a badge to back that up?"

"Oh, I have a badge, a gun, the whole thing. Would you like to see it?"

Danny cleared her throat. "Okay, that's my cue to find Ellen and see if she needs anything. You two have fun. Sarah, if you're going to leave without me, at least have the courtesy to send me a text."

As Danny walked away, Ellery took a long pull on her beer and tried to remember that she too was here with a date. Sarah's flirting was fun in the abstract, but she had no business flirting back when she planned to leave with April at the end of the evening. Time to strike a more serious tone. "Seriously, what agency are you with?"

Sarah looked around, like she was searching for an exit, and Ellery was instantly sorry she'd asked the question. She started to change the subject, but Sarah replied, "FBI. I just transferred from D.C."

"No wonder we've never crossed paths. What division?"

"Fraud. Nothing flashy."

"Do I detect a slight bit of regret?"

"No, it's just been a big adjustment for me. I mean the move. Different place, people. You know."

Ellery sensed there was more to this adjustment than Sarah was letting on, but she didn't push. "How do you know Danny?"

"Uh, I met her through work. You know, all paths lead to the same place kind of thing."

Again with the evasiveness. A local assistant district attorney and an FBI agent stationed in the nation's capital weren't likely to just run into each other at work. There was something about their connection that Sarah wasn't willing to share, which made Ellery instantly curious. *It's none of your business.* Before she could process her thoughts, Sarah changed the subject.

"So, Danny says you used to practice law, but now you're doing something else?"

"I restore and repurpose furniture."

"That's a bit of a change."

"Sometimes you need a change to make you feel alive. You know what I mean?"

Sarah didn't answer right away, but Ellery could tell by the light in her eyes, the idea resonated. Finding comfort in the warmth reflected back at her, she stared a bit too long into Sarah's eyes. She was still staring when she heard a voice over her shoulder and the feel of an arm around her waist.

"Ellery, dear, I've been looking everywhere for you," April's voice held a low, possessive growl. "Jana Kaplan would like to meet you. She's running for city council and she has some great ideas about small business development that I told her you would love to hear."

Ellery glanced at April and then back at Sarah who didn't appear to have broken her stare. She cast about for some way to keep the connection. "April Landing, meet Sarah Flores."

April reached out a hand. "A pleasure to meet you. Any chance you're related to Angel Flores, the city councilman?"

Ellery shook her head at April's inability to turn off the networking gene.

"Not that I know of," Sarah said, a hint of mischief in her eyes. "Is he one of the honest ones?"

"She's new in town," Ellery said, offering April a fake smile. Ellery knew April well enough to know she was conducting an internal calculation of how nice she had to be to the new girl based on how valuable she might be to her in the future. FBI agent might hold a lot of credibility for some people, but for April, a politician or business mogul was much more interesting. Time to steer April away before she could grill Sarah some more. "You said Jana was waiting."

"Yes, she's over by the bar. Come on and I'll introduce you."

April's smile was real now and Ellery supposed she should be glad. Smiling April was actually very beautiful and, if you could get past her constant need to be in the spotlight, she was a fun and interesting date. But she wasn't glad because walking off with April meant she was walking away from Sarah. She met Sarah's eyes and raised her shoulders in a gesture of defeat. Did she imagine she saw regret reflected back?

She started to tell April to go on and she'd be right there just so she could have one more moment of this magnetic connection, but at that moment, the floor shook and a loud boom echoed through the room. At first she chalked it up to one of the many small earthquakes that had been shaking the ground around Dallas in the previous months, but as people began to line the windows, pointing and shouting, she had a chilling sense of doom. Seconds later, a loud ring cut through the cries of the crowd, and she saw Sarah pull out her cell phone and glance at the screen. Sarah's entire demeanor morphed from flirting partygoer to duty bound cop. Her eyes took on a steely glint and her jaw was set.

Ignoring April's tug on her arm, Ellery asked Sarah, "Is everything okay?"

Sarah looked up, a far away expression in her eyes, as if she'd forgotten Ellery or anyone else was in the room. "I'm sorry. I have to go." She'd only taken a few steps before a voice cried out.

"Someone's bombed the arena!"

❖

Sarah watched as more of the crowd ran toward the windows in response to the shout about a bomb. She gripped her phone tighter as if she could squeeze the bad news out of it. She read the three-line text twice to make sure she wasn't hallucinating. *NTAS ALERT. Explosion at high value target. Report in immediately.*

Holy shit. The very first National Terrorism Advisory System alert and it was in her backyard. No need to look out the window to know what happened. She started toward the doors, but Ellery's voice cut through the dark cloud of her thoughts. She started to answer, but she was interrupted by more shouts.

"Was it a bomb?" "Look, it's burning like crazy!" "It's on Channel 4, right now." She couldn't tell who was doing the shouting, certainly more than one person. With no televisions in the room, everyone started whipping out their cell phones and calling out whatever facts poured in from Twitter, Breaking News, and Facebook. She grabbed Ellery's arm and pulled her close. "Find an exit and wait there. Stay inside. Find a TV if you can—it's your best bet for getting news, cell service might get sketchy real quick."

"What's going on?"

Sarah shook her head. "I don't know, but it's bad. Do whatever you can to keep folks calm." She looked down at her hand that was still on Ellery's arm. Ellery who was here with a date. For all she knew, this might be the first day of the end of the world. Deciding she didn't give a damn about Ellery's date, she leaned in close, so close her lips grazed Ellery's ear, and whispered, "Sometimes you do need a change to make you feel more alive. Let's hope we all get a chance to find out what makes us happy."

She didn't wait for a reaction before she took off. She made it as far as the door of the bar when she heard a voice calling her name. Danny. She waved for Danny to follow her, pausing only when they were out of the room.

"What is it?" Danny asked.

"Don't know, but I just received an NTAS alert with a report right fucking now text."

"So where do you report?"

"Good question. I'm a hellavu lot closer to the arena than I am to the field office. I'm headed there now and I'll figure out the rest on the way."

"I'm going with you."

"Slow down, pal. You should stay put. Your wife's in there and someone needs to make sure everyone stays calm."

"TV says there's a lot of casualties."

"It's probably too soon for them to know that. Besides, I wasn't aware prosecutors were on the list of first responders. Seriously, Danny, staying here and keeping people calm is as important as anything else you could do."

"You feds, always hogging the glory."

"Yep, that's us." Sarah knew Danny was kidding, but she also knew Danny realized the potential severity of the situation. "I'll do better if I know my friends are safe. Go find your wife. Okay?"

Danny nodded. "Promise me you'll check in when you can."

"Deal." Sarah didn't risk another look at her face before hauling ass out of the room, cursing the shoes she'd coveted in the store. She didn't bother with the elevators, instead locating the nearest stairwell, removing her heels, and jumping the steps three at a time as she practically slid down the banister. When she reached the ground floor, she spotted a group of security guards near the door, working hard to keep guests from flooding out into the street. She looked at her phone and, as she had suspected, she no longer had any signal. She strode up the nearest guard and flashed her badge. "Special Agent Sarah Flores, FBI. You have a radio?"

The guy glanced at his buddies and then reluctantly handed it over. As she ran through the frequencies, he asked, "What can you tell us?"

What she wouldn't give to have an answer to that question, but rather than admit she was just as clueless as every civilian clamoring at the doors, she merely shook her head. Finally, she found the local police band and listened for a moment before chiming in with her name and location as she started walking toward the site of the explosion, ignoring the protests of the security guard who wanted his equipment back. It could be the end of the world for all he knew, but he was squealing like a baby over a walkie-talkie.

As she got closer to the arena, the smoke and dust hung in the air, making it difficult to assess the location and extent of damage. She heard shouting and she could see the distant red and blue lights of emergency vehicles approaching. She pushed through until she saw a group of Dallas police officers standing by the fountains in front of the arena in a semblance of organization. They'd strung yellow tape between two traffic cones in a makeshift perimeter. She jogged over, but the officer standing closest to her stepped closer as if trying to keep her at a distance.

"Ma'am, we need you to stand back while we assess the damage."

"Special Agent Flores, FBI." She reached into her purse and pulled out her badge. "I'm here to help. Where's ground zero?"

He handed back her badge without even really examining it. "We think it only affected a small portion of the building, but there are a lot of casualties." He pointed to the west end. "Looks like most of the wounded are over there, but there are a lot we haven't been able to get to and we won't be able to get close until the rubble is cleared away."

She imagined he and his fellow officers were completely out of their league with a catastrophe of this proportion. Who wouldn't be? She glanced around, wondering if anyone else from her agency had arrived on scene yet. Most of the people she saw looked like civilians who'd poured out of the arena, dressed in the colors of their favorite team and looking like their world had been upended. But wait a minute. She scanned the crowd again, certain she'd seen a familiar face. She strode toward a group clustered on the walk that ran around the arena. Sure enough, there was Liz from the office huddled with a different group of cops. Liz looked up as she approached, not even trying to mask her surprise. "What are you doing here?"

"Guess I could ask the same thing," Sarah said. "I was at a reception at the W when I got the page."

"I live over there." Liz pointed at the apartment building across the street. "I heard a loud noise and windows starting shaking. At first I thought it was another one of the earthquakes that's been happening lately, but then I looked outside."

Liz's voice faltered and her words trailed off, the image of supremely confident agent fading in the face of tragedy. At least it proved she was human. "Have they established a command post? Have you reported in?"

Liz shook her head. "The local departments have protocols in place, but I doubt they've been having drills. It's going to be a little while before we can get things under control."

Sarah flashed back to 9/11 when she was a fairly new agent with the bureau, stationed in D.C. Any protocol they'd thought they had had been obliterated by the surge of confusion of being attacked on multiple fronts. In the capital and in New York, people had pitched in, protocol be damned. She pointed to the west end of the arena. "Well, I'm headed that way to see what I can do. You with me?"

Liz nodded, seemingly grateful to have someone else take the lead. As they made their way through the crowd to the site of the explosion, Sarah took a moment to look back at the W. The windows of the bar where she'd been less than an hour ago overlooked this scene and she wondered if Ellery was still there. As if on cue, she heard a familiar voice call her name and she saw Ellery headed her way. She told Liz she'd meet her in a moment and stepped aside to wait for Ellery to catch up to her. When she did, Sarah touched her arm. "Are you okay?" she asked.

"I'm fine. How about you? It's kind of crazy out here."

"Definitely. You shouldn't be here. We don't know enough about the situation." She lowered her voice to a whisper. "For all we know there could be others."

"I couldn't just sit up there and do nothing. I asked the cops at the front entrance if I could help, but frankly I think they're so paralyzed at the thought something like this could happen, that they didn't know what to tell me. And then I saw you. You look like you've got a plan. I know basic first aid and CPR. Put me to work."

"My plan is to stay alive and help as many people as I can." Sarah should catch up with Liz, but she couldn't help but take a moment to drink in the sight of Ellery. The suit jacket was gone and her sleeves were rolled up past her elbows. The muscles she'd only seen hints of before were now readily apparent. Ellery was strong and she was here. She'd be foolish not to take advantage of her help even if this dashing woman's presence threatened to distract her. For a second she considered asking about April Landing, but the thought was fleeting. Ellery was here alone, and she'd sought her out to help. She'd be foolish to question it. She reached out a hand. "Stick close."

She didn't wait for Ellery to reply before she dove back into the crowd, Ellery's strong hand firmly gripping hers as she led the way. When they finally made it to the west entrance, Sarah pulled up short. Seeing the damage from a distance was no substitute for standing right in front of it. The glass windows of the hotel had shielded them from the acrid smell of burning rubble and flesh and the piercing cries of the wounded. Relatively speaking, the actual damage to the building was smaller than the cloud of dust and debris had led her to believe, but there was absolutely no doubt it had been deadly for more than just a few.

She looked back to see Ellery's face harden at the sight of the devastation before releasing her grip. With a simple nod, Ellery strode away toward a group of fireman and started working with them to clear chunks of cement debris from a section of the bomb site.

"Sarah, where did you go?"

Sarah turned to find Liz standing behind her. "Sorry. I'm here now."

"Great. Come over here. These guys could use some help."

Sarah took just a moment to glance back at Ellery. She was lifting a piece of concrete as if it was a feather. Her expensive suit and her handsome face were smeared with soot and her eyes blazed with a fierce determination that won Sarah's admiration. As she started to walk away, she realized she had more in common with Ellery than probably either of them realized.

CHAPTER FIVE

Two weeks later

Ellery tacked the final piece of leather into place and stood back to assess her work. She'd given the well-worn brown leather she'd recycled from old theater seats a sleek new life as a midcentury channel back chair, and she was pleased with the clean lines and the simplicity of the piece. She gazed around her studio at the massive amount of work she had accomplished in the last two weeks. This new collection was different from her previous work. These pieces were lighter, more utilitarian, modern and bright. She'd taken a lot of her inspiration from the theater seats. She'd bought them for practically nothing at a flea market months ago, but it wasn't until after the night of the bombing that she'd been inspired to incorporate them into her work. As she carefully salvaged the leather from each chair, she'd offered a prayer for the victims of the bombing whose lives had forever changed.

She had stayed at the site of the explosion for hours, helping clear debris and assist the first responders in any way she could. At some point during the night, April found her there and tried to get her to leave or at least promise to come over when she left, but she stayed until dawn and then she'd gone straight home. In the shadow of their mortality, she could no longer pretend she and April still had anything in common, even if doing so would have never given companionship in those dark hours.

When she had finally arrived home she had at least a dozen messages from her parents. She'd called and spoken briefly with her father, but his dizzying round of questions made her wish she hadn't. He'd wanted to talk about every last detail. Was it a bomb? What kind? Foreign or domestic? How long before they had suspects in custody, and more importantly, who would represent them?

Ellery had listened to his questions, but she hadn't engaged, finally managing to convince him that she was okay and too exhausted and too busy to dwell on the details. What she'd seen that night had been too horrific to process, even with him. All she could do, like the rest of the nation, was spend the next twenty-four hours glued to the television, watching the major networks wield various theories about who had been behind the fatal blast. Pundits talked and politicians postured, but hours passed with no new information beyond an increased tally of injured and dead.

She found her solace in work and she'd barely left her studio, even sleeping some nights there on the couch. Karen, the owner of the showroom in the Design District that sold many of her creations, had finally shown up on her doorstep when she couldn't get in touch with her. Ellery assuaged her concern by showing her the new collection she'd started and then shoved her out the door so she could keep working. Other than a wave at her neighbor, Leo, when she met the kid who delivered groceries to her door, she hadn't spoken to another soul since. Now, two weeks out, she was beginning to feel restless.

Four more pieces. Karen had scheduled an event showcasing up-and-coming designers, and when she'd seen this new work, she'd insisted that Ellery participate. The additional pieces would round out the collection and Ellery had plenty of ideas. She didn't know whether she should be happy or sad that a national tragedy had spurred her creativity to new heights.

She shrugged. It wasn't fair, but then nothing really was. You lived your life, did your best, and hoped for the best in return, but everyone present that night had learned nothing was certain. The most important thing was to have no regrets, which was one of the reasons for abruptly breaking things off with April. The moments before the explosion she'd shared with Sarah Flores made it clear she was done dating women like April, but apparently, it had taken a monumental tragedy to get her to act on her impulse.

Sarah Flores. Special Agent Sarah Flores. She'd lost track of Sarah in the crowd that night. Had she saved lives? Had she been hurt doing so? In what distinct ways had the bomb changed her life? If she'd had her number, she liked to think she would call her to ask these questions, but the truth was solitude seemed to be her best friend right now. Still, a lingering desire to know more about Sarah edged closer into her consciousness with every passing day.

She probably hasn't become a hermit. Ellery laughed at her self-chiding inner voice. Going off-grid was so against her nature that it had taken days to get used to it, but now that she had would she be the same person when she emerged? Maybe tomorrow she would start her reentry into the real world with a phone call. She could let Karen know she was close to being done, set a time for her to come by and see the rest of her work. Maybe she would call her parents and check in or join Leo on his front porch for an afternoon beer. Maybe.

Sarah walked through the office, nodding to the support staff. She'd brought donuts that morning which meant she was everyone's hero. Things sure had changed over the past couple of weeks, and she knew it wasn't just the donuts.

"Hey, Flores, got something you should take a look at."

She looked over to see Liz sitting at her desk with a couple of the other agents hunched over her shoulder. Since the night of the bombing, when they'd worked side by side, Liz, and by extension, the rest of the group, no longer treated her like an interloper. She smiled at them, happy to be part of a team again. "Be right there." She handed the donuts to Beverly, the secretary they shared. "Save me one apple fritter, okay?"

Bev smiled. "You got it."

She strode over to Liz's desk and the rest of the group made space for her. "What's up?"

"We got in a bunch of records for nonprofits with foreign ties. I just started looking at them this morning, but look at this one." She pointed to the screen.

Sarah followed her finger and saw the name Welcome Home International, WHI. According to their website, they had formed in 2011 and were headquartered in Dallas. Established for the purpose of aiding refugees who entered the US from the Middle East to assist with basic needs and education. Sounded innocuous enough, except for the Muslim stigma. "Okay, I'll bite. Something funny going on with their financing?"

"Maybe. I've just started looking, but they don't appear to have much in the way of assets. They operate out of a local mosque. One of their board members is Amir Khan, who just happens to be a relative of Sadeem Jafari, who happens to be on a CIA watch list. I'm wondering if we should pass this along to them or Homeland Security."

Sarah took a moment to consider. Everyone in law enforcement was frustrated by the fact that two weeks out they weren't even close to making an arrest in the bombing case. No one had claimed responsibility, and if the CIA or Homeland Security had any viable leads, they weren't talking. She had more invested in catching the assholes who'd bombed the arena than most. The images of the dead and broken bodies she'd helped pull from the wreckage were forever etched in her mind, but she also knew the minute they handed over this information to another agency, they'd be shut out. No matter what anyone said about the improvement of interdisciplinary relations since 9/11, relationships between the agencies had slipped back into a natural state of competition. She shook her head. "Let's dig a little deeper into the financials and then talk to Mason before making that call. Deal?"

"I was hoping you'd say that. I'll start digging through the bank records." She motioned to the stack of boxes on the other side of her desk.

"Great. Mind if I take a box?"

"You got it."

Sarah hefted one of the bankers' boxes and hauled it over to her desk. She opened it, randomly selected a bulging file, and started poring over the bank account entries. She still loathed this part of the job, but she'd gotten used to the monotony. The day of the explosion was, sadly, the most excitement she'd had in a long time. She should feel bad about that, but she attributed part of the excitement of that day to seeing Ellery at the reception.

Tall, handsome Ellery. Who was apparently attached. Sarah had asked Danny about the woman who'd shown up to claim Ellery moments before the explosion occurred, but all Danny had been able to tell her was that Dr. April Landing was a cardiac surgeon, one of the more successful alums of the Alpha Nus. Well, la di da. She hadn't liked the way April had claimed Ellery, mostly because she'd wanted to do some claiming of her own.

She shook off the distracting thoughts. They'd been working overtime since the explosion, part of an interagency effort to track down the people responsible. Because no one had claimed credit it seemed more likely the bombing had been a homegrown incident rather than a foreign terrorist plot, but every lead had to be pursued, no matter how unlikely. Part of her wanted to be out in the field, interviewing witnesses, assessing possible suspects, not sheets of paper. She was used to getting her information in the flesh, not reading between the lines on a bank ledger. Daily, she had to remind herself she'd chosen this path for a reason—so she could have a life outside the job. But she was working as hard as ever, just as affected by the tragedy of it all, but without the same level of satisfaction she used to have from tracking a real life suspect rather than running down fuzzy accounting. To top it all off, she was never going to meet an Ellery if she spent every waking moment behind this desk.

Her cell phone rang and jerked her out of her pity party. She recognized the 202 area code and answered on the second ring. "Flores."

"So, they didn't get you in the blast."

Sarah smiled at the sound of Trip's voice. "Took you long enough to call and find out."

"Oh, I already knew you were okay." His signature deep booming laughter echoed through the line. "I know everything and don't you forget it."

"Then why do I sense you called me for a favor?"

"I may know everything, but I can't do everything. A couple of names came across my radar and I wanted to pass them along to someone I trust before I share them elsewhere."

A surge of electricity flew down Sarah's spine, and she hunched over the phone and glanced around her desk as if someone might be listening in. "Maybe I should call you back on another line."

"No need. Be sure to check your mail when you get home. I sent you all that stuff you left behind in your desk."

"Okay." Sarah knew he was talking code and all she wanted to do was get off the phone and head home. "Anything else?"

"We miss you, kid. You know if you ever want to come back here, you'll always have a spot."

A tug, a small one, pulled at her, but she kept her response casual. "Thanks, pal. Tell everyone I said hello."

Sarah spent the next few minutes paging through the files on her desk, but she could have been looking at gibberish for all it mattered. Her mind was back on the cagey conversation with Trip and she was consumed with curiosity about whatever he was sending her way. *Focus, Flores, focus.* She stood and took a lap around the offices, ostensibly to get a donut, but she walked until her head was clear. When she sat back down at her desk, she reopened the bank files for Welcome Home International and started combing through the entries in earnest. Before long she started noticing a disturbing pattern and she began scribbling notes on a legal pad.

"Hey, Flores, you want to join us for lunch?"

Sarah looked up to see Liz and Sam, one of the other agents, standing by her desk. She glanced at the time on her computer, surprised to see it was almost one o'clock. She pointed at the files on her desk. "I think I'm going to stick with this."

"Really?" Liz asked. "My stack was a big bunch of nothing. Come on, we're going to Pappasito's."

"Thanks, but I may need to head out a little early today. I've got some stuff coming into the apartment—the last of my move from D.C."

The tiny lie slid off her tongue with ease and the group trooped out without her. Sarah waited until she was sure they'd left before gathering up the files on her desk and making her way over to Beverly's desk. "Hey, Bev, call me crazy, but I prefer to look through documents on the computer." She hefted the stack of files. "Any chance I can scan these?"

"You could." Bev paused and smiled. "Or you could look at the set that's already scanned."

Sarah let loose a big smile. "You're a lifesaver."

"They're on the network drive." She wrote a note and handed it over. "Here's the location."

Sarah took the note. "Thanks a million. Hey, any reason Liz has all the boxes on her desk?"

"What can I say? She likes paper."

"That makes one of us." Sarah started to walk away, but then paused. "Oh, yeah, I meant to tell you that I need to head out early this afternoon, but you can reach me on my cell if you need anything."

"No problem. I'm sure if anyone needs anything it can wait until tomorrow."

The comment made Sarah think of the call from Trip and how this new job was the polar opposite of her last one where she'd been on call twenty-four seven and nothing could wait until the next day. She'd thought she'd grown to hate the constant interference in her life, but now she wondered if the boredom in her new position was just the other extreme. She thought about the entries she'd flagged in the bank records and considered whether she was making too much out of them, just for the sake of having some level of excitement in her life. It was clear she wasn't getting excitement in any other way. The only time she'd been out since she'd come to town was the night of the reception at the W when her chances with a hot woman had been thwarted by the woman's date and some terrorists. Not a great track record for her new lease on life and not much appeared to be changing since she was transferring all the bank records for WHI onto a flash drive to review at home. Right now, the only thing she had to look forward to was a potential lead in a case that would probably be snatched from her if it turned out to be viable.

Trip's offer echoed in her head. Maybe she should go back to her old unit. The nightmares and viciousness she confronted on a daily basis might be a fair trade off for feeling like she was really accomplishing something.

She spent the rest of the drive home mulling over her life choices, decidedly unsettled by the time she reached her apartment. She'd leased a place in Uptown, close to Danny and Ellen and close to the gayborhood. She'd been to the local bars a couple of times since she'd been back in town, but they were the same as bars everywhere—full of women looking for something for the night, but not necessarily any longer than that. If she wanted more, she was going to have to find it elsewhere, but the thought of getting involved in something other than her job was a foreign concept and required a level of commitment she wasn't sure she possessed. She flashed back to the evening of the reception. Politics. The only thing about that event that had been palatable was the promise of lots of eligible, desirable women, but the one she'd settled on had been taken.

Get over it, Flores. Ellery Durant isn't the only woman in this city and you shouldn't have expected your love life in a new city to just fall into place. Once the furor from the bombing abated, there would be lots more events and many opportunities to meet someone. *Just because you've decided to settle down doesn't mean women are going to line up for the opportunity to be Mrs. Sarah Flores.*

She laughed at the realization that the singular focus she applied in her work didn't necessarily translate to her personal life. Trip had always been on her ass about her impatient nature, telling her she couldn't force things to happen. He was right, of course, but knowing it didn't necessarily make it easier to wait it out.

She thought of Trip again as she checked her mail. Just as he had said, there was a plain brown envelope in her box. She was dying to know what was inside, but waited until she was in her apartment and the door was locked before sitting down at her dining room table and peeling back the seal.

She shook out a single piece of paper with a few lines of typewritten names: Sadeem Jafari, Hashid Kamal, Abdul Kamal.

She recognized the first name. Liz had mentioned him in relation to Amir Khan and said Jafari was on a CIA watch list. No surprise that Trip had also heard the name. She turned the paper over, but the rest of the page was blank. She flipped it back over and repeated the names to herself as she opened her laptop and started a Google search. Hashid and Abdul Kamal, aka Michael and Brian Barstow, were brothers, in their early twenties, and they were both listed on a Homeland Security terrorist watch list, which she verified by signing in to the agency's official database. Neither of them had a criminal conviction, but they'd been flagged as supporters of ISIS as a result of postings they'd made to several blog sites.

Sadeem, on the other hand, was a bit of a mystery. He wasn't in the FBI database and Google searches showed only a successful local business leader whose philanthropic interests were well known throughout the DFW Muslim community. She could understand why Hashid's and Abdul's names had come across Trip's radar, but Sadeem was a mystery. She searched for another half hour, but nothing she found led her to believe Sadeem was either connected to the other two men in any way or that he had any big secrets of his own to hide. If he was really on a CIA watch list, they were keeping the reason a secret from their sister agency.

She circled back through her searches and started looking at the names of the charities he supported. His primary interest appeared to be the Global Enterprise Alliance, which didn't ring a bell. She switched to the LexisNexis database and started digging. GEA was a US based Muslim charity whose stated primary purpose was assisting refugees from Middle Eastern Arab countries adjusting to life in the United States. As she read the mission statement, the words sparked a memory. She'd read a similar statement, earlier that day in fact.

Sarah dug the flash drive with the WHI records out of her bag and plugged it into her computer. She'd expected to find a copy of the WHI charter and IRS application for 501(c)(3) non-profit status along with the bank records, but neither of those documents was included in the file. Chalking it up to a careless scan job by one of the clerks at the office, she took to the Internet. One quick search netted what she was looking for. There it was, right there on the WHI website, virtually the same statement about purpose as that listed on the GEA site, but she checked her excitement. It could mean anything. Two charities with the same purpose wasn't unusual, but what if there was another connection? She started another search, but her cell phone rang, interrupting her thoughts. She didn't recognize the number, but she answered anyway, thinking it might be Trip. "Flores."

"Hey, it's your good pal, Soto."

"Hey, Danny. What are you up to?"

"Probably the same as you. Working. I know you think you guys are having all the fun, but our office has been pretty busy since the bombing."

"I imagine. Anything I should know about?"

"I could ask you the same thing, but I doubt you'd tell me anything."

"Not fair."

"I know. The boss has me on another task force. He can't stand to be shut out of the biggest crime event to hit Dallas ever, so we have to act like we're working on the bombing while handling all our other cases. I haven't been home for dinner in two weeks and the wife's about to shoot me."

"I kinda doubt that, but I know how you feel. The fraud unit definitely isn't taking the lead on any of this, but we're spending all our time working leads that go nowhere."

"But you have some free time, right?"

"Is that a trick question?"

"No tricks, only treats. A friend of ours has a gallery opening Friday night and I promised a certain someone I would invite you."

"Let me guess. Lots of eligible, worthy bachelorettes?"

"So she says."

"I'm not much into the art scene. I mean, I know what I like, but making conversation with a bunch of connoisseurs isn't really my thing."

"No worries. It's not that kind of art. It's a big warehouse in the Design District and the exhibits are all practical art pieces, furniture, pottery, that kind of thing. If you sit in chairs or eat off plates, you'll have plenty to say. In fact, you've met one of the artists. You remember Ellery Durant, she's the attorney who—"

"Who's involved with a top flight cardiac surgeon? You think continuing to throw me together with unavailable women is the way to welcome me to your fine city?" Despite her protest, Sarah warmed to the idea of seeing Ellery again.

"It's your city now and who said Ellery was unavailable? I saw April Landing canoodling with some other woman just last week."

"Please tell me you did not just say canoodling." Sarah hoped her teasing tone hid her excitement at the prospect that Ellery Durant was back on the market.

"Are you going to come with us or not?"

Sarah forced calm into her voice. "Sure, why not? Am I supposed to show up with you or solo?"

"Well, that was easier than I thought it would be," Danny said with a hint of mischief in her tone. "Come over here and we'll ride together. It'll be fun."

"Can't wait." And she meant it.

Distracted from her work, Sarah realized she was starving. Her fridge was bare. Even after this much time away from her old job, she still wasn't used to a regular schedule that allowed her to keep her fridge stocked without having to worry about last-minute out of town trips causing everything to spoil. She sorted through her stand-by stack of delivery menus and settled on Thai. While she waited for the order to arrive, she poured a glass of red wine and returned to her laptop. By the time her food arrived, she was armed with enough facts to start connecting some of the dots. GEA was a sister organization of WHI. While their stated purpose was nearly identical, WHI had been formed several years before GEA. Neither organization shared board members, but Amir Khan and Sadeem Jafari were cousins. Sarah spent another hour searching for connections between these two men and their organizations to the other names Trip had given her, but she came up with nothing.

Tired of trying to cipher out some meaning to what she had found, she took her searches in a completely different direction while she ate. It didn't take long to find out more about Ellery Durant. She'd been a hotshot criminal defense lawyer for over a decade, having worked on several high profile trials with her father, Gordon Durant, while she was still in law school. She'd graduated at the top of her class and probably had a host of offers from prominent big law firms in Dallas, but she'd gone into practice with her father and, though she'd dabbled in various areas of the law, she'd excelled at criminal defense, winning a big victory in a murder case shortly before she retired from practice. A courtroom artist's rendering of Ellery during a particularly heated federal trial showed her confident and commanding, almost fierce, in the courtroom. Sarah had testified in many trials, but based on the accounts she read, she shuddered to think about being on the other end of an Ellery Durant cross-examination.

Social sites shared a glimpse into Ellery's love life, featuring photos from various events, but she rarely appeared with the same date. Sarah typed in April's name and was pleased to see that she too showed up to many functions with a different woman on her arm, leading her to believe it was unlikely she and Ellery were anything more than casual. That would explain why April had moved on because who would walk away from a hunk like Ellery? One picture of them together showed what a strikingly hot couple they made. Maybe Ellery had only been seeing April for sex. The very idea was painful and she shelved it. Better she get back to work, which, while boring, wasn't as dangerous as wanting something she couldn't have.

CHAPTER SIX

"This is your best work yet."

Karen Tron walked around Ellery's studio, stopping to touch, stroke, and coo over all the new pieces she'd created. Finally, she asked, "It'll do for the show?" She held her breath waiting for the answer. Her previous work had been popular with Karen's customers, but the Designer's Showcase was a carefully curated event that could spur unlimited success.

"Are you kidding? These pieces will *make* the show. I'm going to have to open a bigger space. And you'll need plenty more because these pieces are going to sell out and we'll have a long wait list."

"I've been a bit focused." She'd spent the last few weeks, sawing, hammering, sanding, and varnishing, every action designed to wipe away the memories of the evil that she'd witnessed the night of the explosion. If the product of her catharsis was a sold out show, that was her best revenge.

"I can have it all, right?"

Karen's enthusiasm was contagious, and Ellery met her grin with one of her own. Smiling felt good. It felt real and new. Maybe she was ready for reentry. The gallery show opening was a week away, so she better be since she wasn't well known enough to pull off the eccentric and slightly reclusive artist bit. "It's all yours."

Karen spent the next hour making detailed notes and photographing all the furniture she planned to display at the show. A week's time wasn't much to put together the exhibit, but she'd shrugged off the trouble, saying it had been worth the wait. Ellery hoped so. For once, the work had felt more like an accomplishment than an escape. Although the materials she worked with were often more complex than they seemed at first, that was where the similarities to her old life ended. The work was soothing instead of stressful and, at the end of the day she had something to show for it beyond a fat bank account. She could point to each piece and claim pride of craftsmanship.

When Karen left, Ellery went into the house and looked around. It was time to come out of her shell and get back to living, and she'd start by making a real dinner instead of subsisting on protein bars and Coke. She opened the cupboards and the fridge and made a list of what she needed and then grabbed her keys and headed to the door. The ring of the house phone stopped her. Very few people called her on the landline and most of them were telemarketers. On impulse she walked over and checked the caller ID. Dad. She picked up the phone. "Checking up on me?"

"Always."

"I'm fine. You'll be glad to know I'm even considering venturing out of the house."

"That's a relief. I won't keep you. I just wanted to know if you're free Friday."

"Hey, we can talk now. My foray to the outside world can wait."

"Well, actually, I'm going to be in town and I could see you. Sorry about the short notice."

"I'd love to see you and it's kind of a perfect time since I just finished up a big project. What brings you down here?"

"Oh, you know…I'll explain when I get there."

His voice got lower and his tone was cautious, like he didn't want to be overheard. Ellery went on alert. "Is Mom coming with you?"

"She can't get away. You know how it is."

"Well, actually I don't. Not anymore. My new life doesn't come with many deadlines. Although I have been working on a bunch of new pieces for a gallery opening Friday night. You can be my escort and I can get you all the wine and cheese you could possibly want."

"You never know. Maybe that'll work. We'll talk when I get there."

"Need me to pick you up at the airport?"

"That would be great. I'll text you when I land. Love you, Ellery."

"Love you too, Dad. See you Friday."

She clicked off the line and stared at the phone as she replayed the odd call in her head. There were clues there, but she couldn't puzzle them into anything that made sense. His visit was pretty sudden and he didn't want to talk about it over the phone. She contemplated calling her mother, but if they were having issues, she didn't want to stir things up. She shrugged off her questions. Friday was only a few days away and she would have all her answers then. A few minutes later, her phone rang again. Shaking her head at the crazy level of activity after weeks in isolation, she answered even though she didn't recognize the number. "Hello?"

"Ellery?"

"Yep." The caller was a woman and her silky smooth voice echoed a memory, but Ellery couldn't place it. "Who's this?"

"It's Sarah Flores. You may not remember me, but I met you—"

"The night of the bombing. And before that at the courthouse." Of course she remembered Sarah. She'd been the highlight of that fateful evening. "I wondered what happened to you that night. You're okay, right?"

"Uh, yeah. I mean as okay as anyone could be who got an up close look at what evil could do. I guess you made it home okay?"

"Not a night I want to ever relive, but I feel lucky to be alive."

"That makes two of us. That's part of why I'm calling."

"I don't follow."

"I was talking to Danny and she mentioned you have a show this weekend. She also mentioned you might not be seeing Dr. Landing any longer."

"We were never anything but casual. She was more a vestige of my old life than anything else." Ellery mentally kicked herself for providing the extra information. Sarah didn't need to know her life story. Not yet, anyway. "Is there a particular reason my dating habits are important to the FBI?"

Sarah laughed and Ellery thought she detected a slightly nervous edge. "Well, your status is only important to this particular agent. I'll be at the show this weekend, but I figure you'll be really busy then. Any chance you're free for coffee today?"

Between Karen's visit and the strange call from her father, Ellery's work was already off-track, but she really wanted to see Sarah and she'd do it even if it meant she went without groceries and got hopelessly behind getting extra pieces ready for the show. She did her best to sound casual. "One of the perks of being my own boss means I can take a coffee break whenever I want. You have a place in mind?"

"I haven't had a chance to explore all the good coffee shops in town. How about you name the place?"

"Wild Detectives in Oak Cliff. Two o'clock. See you then."

A few minutes after Ellery hung up the phone, she realized she was not only going to leave the house for the first time in days, but she was an hour away from seeing Sarah Flores again and the prospect excited her more than she was willing to admit.

Sarah grabbed her keys and walked over to Liz's desk. Liz was still poring through the box of Welcome Home International's bank records. "You find anything else interesting?"

"Not yet," Liz said. "It looks like the wire transfers you found didn't start until last year, and most of these files date back before then. The box I gave you contained the most recent records."

"The difference is Amir. That fits with when he started directing the overall organization. Before that, he was involved, but not in charge. We should get his personal bank records."

"What's that going to prove? I don't think he was embezzling, and surely he wouldn't be stupid enough to funnel the money to a terrorist group through his personal accounts?"

"You're probably right," Sarah conceded. "But I'd like to eliminate all possibilities before we take this to anyone else."

"Not big on interagency cooperation?"

"I might be if I'd seen it ever work before." Sarah actually had seen it pulled off very effectively before, but Trip had avoided channels for a reason, and she'd taken enough of a risk talking to Liz about any aspect of what she'd found. In deference to Trip's trust in her, she'd held back the names he'd shared and limited what she told Liz to the information about the strange wire transfers out of WHI's account that all seemed to go into a black hole via the Cayman Islands. Not unusual for a foreign business enterprise to take steps to cut tax liability, but for a charity which wasn't subject to the same tax regulations, the banking maneuvers stood out like a sore thumb. The only reason she could think of to route the money in this manner was to hide the ultimate beneficiary and, if the funds were really being used for charitable purposes, there was no good reason to do so.

"I have a couple of friends at HSI," Liz said. "Maybe I can talk to them and see what they think."

It was a perfectly reasonable idea, but the idea of involving Homeland Security Investigations at this point sounded alarm bells in Sarah's head, and she cast about for a way to stall her. "Do me a favor. Give me a little more time to comb through what I have left. If you're going to talk to them, then let's at least have reviewed everything first so we don't waste their time."

"Sounds like a plan. You headed out?"

"Just need to run an errand." The lie was easy since no matter how well she was getting along with everyone at the office, she wasn't sure she'd ever be ready to share her personal life with them. What a contrast to when she was with BAU when their conversations all sounded like a session in the locker room. But that was different, because the dates she bragged about with her team were more like conquests she'd bagged rather than relationships she was building. She didn't have a clue if Ellery would turn out to be relationship material, but if she ever wanted to have a relationship, she'd have to start thinking that way.

Thirty minutes later, she walked into Wild Detectives and found Ellery already seated at a table, dressed in jeans and a sky blue sweatshirt that highlighted the color of her eyes. Unlike the night at the reception, today she was wearing dark rimmed glasses for a bookish look that only added to her appeal. Better yet, she was reading a book. An actual book, not an electronic version on her tablet or phone. Ellery hadn't noticed her yet, so she took a moment to scan the table. Keys, a pencil, and nothing else except the book in Ellery's hands. Strong looking hands, well-kept, but worn. Were they soft on the inside?

Further speculation ceased when Ellery looked up from the book and caught her staring. A wide grin spread across her face and her attractive quotient skyrocketed. Sarah returned the smile and walked over to her table. "Sorry I'm late. I don't quite have a handle on Dallas traffic yet."

"No worries. I would have picked someplace closer to your office, but it's kind of barren out there."

"So, you already know where I work? Have you been stalking me?"

There was that grin again. "I swear I've kept my distance, but you're at the FBI field office, right? I've been there a time or two."

"In your previous life?"

"Yep." Ellery's eyes shifted to something or nothing in the distance and she skirted quickly to a different topic. "So, what's your poison? They make an incredible cappuccino, but I always get the local brew."

"I'll have whatever you're having." She'd defer to the coffee conversation now, but she was determined to bring the conversation back around to Ellery's past. She was more curious than ever now that she detected Ellery wanted to avoid the subject. She leaned back in her chair and crossed her legs, taking in the scene while Ellery went to the counter to get their drinks. Nice place. Not a chain, but it was definitely trendy with a cross between a beatnik and hipster vibe, but it wasn't crowded. It wasn't just a coffee shop either. There was a full bar, but it didn't seem like the kind of place that attracted drunks even though there were a few folks sipping flights of whiskey while they thumbed through the books and magazines for sale.

Ellery seemed to know the man behind the counter. She smiled when she talked to him, and her stance was confident, but open.

She used her hands while she ordered, and although Sarah couldn't hear what she was saying, she could tell by the time it took and the gestures she used that their exchange had extras, beyond a simple "two cups of coffee please." Maybe he was asking about her. Did Ellery meet other women here, at her favorite coffee shop?

Ellery looked back at the table and caught Sarah staring again. She didn't mind the stares, especially since she caught more than a hint of admiration in Sarah's approving gaze, but there was something underneath that she couldn't put her finger on, something that made her squirm. It was like Sarah could see into her, like she was cataloging her every feature. Maybe to see if she measured up?

She waved off Wade's offer to help and picked up their drinks and headed back to the table. As she slid the cups onto the table, she bent close to Sarah's ear and whispered, "Like what you see?"

Sarah's brown eyes met hers. "I do."

Ellery felt the tug of a grin again and she gave in to it. "You're kind of fearless. I like that in a person."

"Duly noted. Although I should tell you it's kind of an agency requirement."

"Is that so? You have a lot to be afraid of in the fraud division?"

"You'd be surprised."

The memory of Sarah rushing off to help the night of the bombing surfaced and Ellery instantly regretted her flippant remark. "Actually, I wouldn't. I remember the last time we saw each other. You were the first one out the door of the reception, like you were used to running toward danger. Am I right?"

"I just followed my instincts. I've been close to the action during other terrorist attacks."

"You said you moved here from D.C. Were you there during 9/11?"

"Yes."

Sarah's one word answer spoke volumes. "And you don't much like to talk about it," Ellery said.

"Do you analyze all your dates?"

"Do you? Don't think I didn't notice your keen observation skills while I was ordering coffee?"

"Looks like we're even then. Although my skills aren't all that keen if you caught me in the act."

"True," Ellery said. "But I've had a lot of practice observing people. It used to be one of my primary skill sets."

"And now?"

"And now, I just use my finely honed skills on people I want to observe."

"Like your dates?" Sarah asked.

"Like you."

"Tell me what you see."

Ellery leaned back in her chair, taking a moment to put her thoughts together. "I'll start from the outside. You dress nicer than most agents around here, especially if you just came from the office where the dress code is kind of business casual, whatever that really means. So you either care more about your appearance or you have some other source of money than your government salary, or both." She paused and looked down at Sarah's Prada loafers. "You value comfort, but not at the expense of looking good. Your new co-workers probably didn't care for you much at first, but maybe by now they've warmed up to your charms."

"Charms, huh?"

"Oh yeah. You've got charm in spades."

"I guess you've worked your way to the inside now."

Ellery took a sip of coffee and watched Sarah. To her credit, she didn't squirm under the careful dissection. She seemed almost amused at the examination. "Your confidence is attractive."

"Some people find it kind of off-putting."

"Some people don't know a good thing when they see it."

"Why did you stop practicing law?"

Ellery barely kept from spitting out her drink at the abrupt curveball. Instead she swallowed, slowly and carefully as she worked her facial features into what she hoped was a neutral expression. "Guess you were tired of being under the microscope."

"You can put me under the lens all day. I enjoy you watching me, but I'm also curious about you and why you've made the choices you have."

Ellery held up her cup. "How do you like this choice so far?"

"The coffee's topnotch and so is your ability to deflect."

Wow. Ellery had to give Sarah credit. She didn't pull any punches. "You have a very interesting way of flirting with someone."

"Flirting is for amateurs. I'd like to get to know you better and I'd like for you to get to know me. Both of those things require honesty. I call it like I see it."

Ellery hid for a moment behind the cup of coffee as she contemplated the gauntlet that Sarah had just thrown down. She was definitely interested in getting to know Sarah, but Sarah's confidence signaled she was after more than a casual assignation. "As long as we're being honest, you seemed a bit more rakish when I last saw you. I definitely got a playgirl vibe that night."

"And you're disappointed now?"

"No, not disappointed. Surprised maybe."

"I'll admit my go-to instinct is playgirl, but I'm working on that. Someday I'd like to settle down, fall in love, raise a family."

Ellery heard a trace of wistfulness in Sarah's voice and she asked, "Is there a particular reason you haven't done any of those things yet?"

"I let the job get in the way."

Ellery started to tease that most of the fraud unit investigators she'd run across worked pretty regular hours and how could it be so hard to settle down if that's what Sarah really wanted, but she sensed there was more to it than that. More that Sarah wasn't willing to share. Since she had things of her own she wasn't interested in sharing, she decided to change the subject. "Tell me about your family. Where did you grow up?"

"The question is where didn't I grow up. My dad's an admiral in the navy. My mom was the dutiful spouse until she found something more interesting to occupy her attention while stationed in Turkey. She stayed there when Dad's orders brought him back to D.C. Eventually, he remarried someone who had a better idea of what she was getting into."

"Are you close with either of them?"

"Not really. I try to see them a couple of times a year, but it's hard to find the time."

Ellery filed these facts away with the others she'd gathered. She'd sort through them all later, but for now her impression of Sarah was a jumble of contradictions. Before she could process the high points, Sarah interrupted her thoughts.

"Now it's your turn. Family?"

"Mom and Dad are still married. She's a law professor at Northwestern and he's supposedly retired from practice, although I think he gets her clinic students riled up now and then about some interesting, newsworthy case."

"Raised by two lawyers. You have my deepest sympathies."

"Hey, I thought you liked lawyers. Isn't Danny Soto a good friend of yours?"

"I like her despite the fact she's a lawyer." Sarah laughed. "I'm kidding. Mostly. So, back to you. You were raised to follow in your parents' footsteps."

"Something like that. Mom and Dad practiced together when I was young, but Mom got tired of the push and pull and quit private practice to teach. I started working at the firm when I was still an undergrad. I followed Dad around and learned the ins and outs of the business until I finally graduated from law school and joined him in the practice."

"So, at some point your dad moves to Chicago with your mom and you up and quit."

"Something like that." Ellery took a sip of coffee as she contemplated how much she felt like sharing. She hadn't told anyone about the catalyst that had spurred her to quit, but the slow buildup before she'd left her practice had been a long time coming. Her new career didn't involve late night phone calls from indignant clients, power-hungry prosecutors, and eccentric judges. Now it was just her, making broken relics into something new. "Like anything, it had run its course."

"I hear you." Sarah met her eyes, but her expression indicated her mind was far away.

"How about we call a truce on delving into each other's past and plan a little future activity?"

"And what's wrong with the present?"

"I guess I just figured you might have to get back to the office. Or do you federal employees often take whole afternoons off?"

As if on cue, Sarah's cell phone rang. She picked it up and glanced at the screen. "Sorry, I have to take this. I'll be right back."

Ellery watched her walk across the room, out of earshot, marveling at how different this date had been compared to the several she'd shared with April. April had always been willing to fill their time with conversation if it revolved around her, and Ellery had been fine with that since it meant she didn't have to talk about her feelings or the real reasons she'd left her practice. She'd thought she'd been fine with it, but now that Sarah, full of questions, had appeared on the scene, she found she didn't entirely hate the attention, even as it made her squirm. Something about Sarah's laser focus made her feel like the most important person in the room. For someone who'd left a high profile practice thinking she would like to try to just blend in, the feeling was at once disconcerting and exhilarating.

"Sorry about that," Sarah said as she strode back to their table. "I need to get back to the office. Guess that answers your question about us federal employees. You can rest in comfort knowing that your tax dollars are hard at work."

"Too bad. I was hoping to steal you away for the rest of the afternoon. Maybe show you my studio."

"Raincheck?"

"Definitely. I'm going to be a bit swamped before the show Friday, but I'll see you there, right?"

"You can count on it."

Ellery watched as Sarah walked out of the shop and lowered herself into a shiny midnight blue Corvette. Her initial surprise at the expensive make was quickly replaced by the realization it was the perfect choice. Sarah Flores was as sleek as her ride.

Sarah sped back to the office wondering what was so urgent and secret that Mason couldn't tell her about it over the phone. She'd hoped to spend the afternoon with Ellery, but she'd have to be satisfied with the conversation they'd shared which had been surprisingly revealing. Raised by lawyers, Ellery had probably fallen into the profession rather than it being a dream of her own, which explained why she'd grown tired of it.

But she'd been good. Better than good. Based on the Internet searches Sarah had done the night before, Ellery consistently ranked in the top of her field according to both her peers and former clients. She'd taken over her father's practice which had included a variety of types of work, but what she really excelled at was criminal defense and she'd won many high profile cases that others had thought were doomed to conviction.

Sarah knew to be that good, you had to have passion. What had killed the passion for Ellery? She'd watched carefully as Ellery discussed her parents, the practice, and her new profession. The light in her eyes had brightened as she moved from subject to subject, and it was clear her passion had transferred to her new work, but Sarah detected lingering regrets about her former line of work. Did she miss it? Did she miss the attention?

Sarah pulled into the parking lot of the field office and shut off the engine. Now that she was back at the office, she needed to focus. She wasn't sure why she cared so much about Ellery's past. If she was still a big shot criminal defense attorney, their careers would curtail their chance of any kind of meaningful relationship. She should be glad things had turned out the way they did.

Mason and Liz were at her desk when she walked in. She chose to ignore their furtive looks. "Are you two prowling my desk for donuts?"

"Do you have any boxes of the WHI files other than the ones that were on your desk?"

Sarah forced herself to remain calm while she considered the question. Something was up. Mason's usually easygoing tone was short and brusque, and Liz looked like she was about to throw up. There was something in those records that tied WHI to the group who'd carried out the bombing, and someone besides the assembled group realized it. The case was about to slip out of her grasp. She should be glad. *You wanted to get away from the real crime, and terror couldn't be more real, right?*

But the bombing had been personal, if only because she'd been blocks away when it happened. She and her friends could have died. Ellery could have died. Lots of people had. She'd helped pull them from the wreckage with her own two hands.

Let it go. As she thought the words, she realized they weren't going to give her a choice. In a few seconds, she'd answer and the remaining files in her file cabinet would be hauled off to be examined by someone she hoped was qualified enough to decipher them. *Let it go.*

She reached down and unlocked the cabinet next to her desk and pulled out a box. "Here are the files I was looking at earlier. No more boxes."

Mason took the files and left without another word. Sarah confronted Liz. "What the hell was that all about?"

"He pulled me into his office after he finished up a conference call. Pressured me for an update. I couldn't tell him we had absolutely nothing, so I mentioned the wire transfers. I made sure he knew we didn't have anything concrete. Thirty minutes later, he came out and told me to box everything up, that 'our resources were being redirected.'"

Sarah nodded, schooling her expression into one of nonchalance instead of the supreme satisfaction she felt about the split-second decision she'd made when she'd handed over the box. She believed Liz, but she didn't know her well enough to trust her with the information that, while she'd told the truth about not having any more boxes of files, she still had a copy of every last one of them on her laptop at home.

CHAPTER SEVEN

Ellery glanced at her cell phone and saw Meg's number displayed on the screen. Again. It was her third call in the last fifteen minutes. She looked at the clock on her dashboard. Her father's plane had already landed and he'd be walking out of the airport any second, leaving her no time to pull into the cell phone lot and take the call. She wondered which of their old clients was insisting on meeting with her now. Probably Amir again since Naveed's new court date was coming up soon. At some point she was going to have to refuse to be pulled back in, and she made a mental note to meet with Meg next week to let her know she was just going to have to be more firm with their former clients.

On her second circle around through the parking structure at Love Field, Ellery spotted her dad walking toward a shiny red Porsche Cabriolet. She angled her truck into a space directly behind the expensive sports car and rolled down the window. "Dad, over here!"

He looked up at the sound of her voice, his furrowed brow showing his confusion. She called out again and he finally redirected and made his way over to the passenger door. She put the truck in park and hopped out to meet him. "It's good to see you," she said.

He stuck out his hand. "Good to see you too." He glanced back at the Porsche, a touch of wistful in his eyes. "I guess you've got new wheels."

She placed his one suitcase into the rear seat and motioned for him to climb into the truck. She waited until she was behind the wheel, pulling away from the curb before responding. "I sold the

Porsche. It wasn't real practical for my new line of work. Plus, the money came in handy. Don't you like my new ride?"

He glanced around the interior. She could tell he was fishing for something nice to say. She didn't care what he thought. She was proud of this truck. It might not be as luxurious as her fully loaded sports car, and it certainly wasn't as fast, but it was practical. It wasn't like she could load some curbside find onto the hood of her Porsche.

He finally offered his appraisal. "It's very roomy."

She laughed and he joined in. Even after all the years they'd lived and worked together, she continued to be astonished at how different she was from either of her parents. Neither one of them had even pretended to understand how she could walk away from a lucrative practice to start a business making furniture. She imagined they'd had many conversations about the waste of her law degree and years of networking they'd put into the firm. At first, she'd cared enough to try to make them understand, but she'd quickly realized despite the DNA they shared, she would never define success the same way they did. While that was okay, she held some small hope that when her father saw her studio and tonight's show, he'd finally get her.

"Are you hungry?" she asked. It was just after nine and they were near one of her favorite breakfast spots.

"Breakfast would be great."

She took a right turn onto Mockingbird and drove toward Market Diner while they talked about easy, inane subjects like the weather. They were almost at the restaurant when her phone rang again. Damn. She'd meant to turn it off after she picked up her dad. She looked at the screen. Meg again. She'd already left three messages. Ellery's thumb hovered over the ignore button. She could hit ignore and then shut the phone off. Meg would leave more messages and she could deal with them later. Or, she could pick up now and make it clear she was not to be disturbed for any legal work. Probably not a bad conversation for her father to witness. She answered the call. "Hi, Meg. Miss me?"

"Where are you?"

Ellery pushed past the anxious tone in Meg's voice, refusing to be bullied back into the practice. "I'm in the car with my dad. He's in town for a visit. Not a good time for you to light up my phone with a million messages about cases you want me to work. In fact, it's never going to be a good time for—"

Meg cut her off. "Didn't you listen to any of my messages? All hell's breaking loose. You need to get down here right now and straighten this out. I just had a huge potential client walk out and I'll probably lose a bunch more by the time they're done."

"Slow down. You're not making any sense. Who's they? What's going on?" Ellery pulled into the parking lot for the restaurant and parked the truck.

"Homeland Security agents are here with a search warrant for all the files you've worked on, paper, digital—everything. I don't have the affidavit yet, but based on the questions they're asking, they may already be at your house. It's on the news. Now, how about you tell me what's going on?"

Ellery froze. The phone was still in her hand and Meg was still barking into it, but anxiety kept her from making out any words beyond "search warrant," "Homeland Security," and "on the news." She looked at her dad and he took the phone from her hand and put it on speaker.

"Meg, it's Gordon Durant. Are the agents still there?"

"Yes. There are ten of them. Complete overkill. They want all files Ellery worked on for the last six years, computer records, everything."

"And they have a warrant, not just a subpoena?"

"Yes."

"I need to know which judge issued the warrant. Find out right now, and call me back at this number. Have they talked to any of your employees?"

"They tried, but all of them are well trained. I don't want to leave them alone, but I'm due at the courthouse for a hearing this morning. I'm going to have to contact the court and get a reset."

"You do that, but get that judge's name first and call me back. Okay?"

"Okay. Thanks, Gordon. I'm glad you're here."

Ellery watched him hang up the phone, too stunned to process the conversation they'd just had. All she could think about was the possibility that federal agents might be at her house, going through her things for some unfathomable reason. "I need to get home."

He ignored her comment and reached for the radio, punching it on and tuning it to the local news. The story was breaking news.

"Sources say federal agents are currently searching both the home and offices of a prominent criminal defense attorney, Ellery Durant. We don't have official confirmation, but a source close to the investigation tells us they are following a lead developed as part of the investigation into the bombing of the arena. We have a reporter on scene and we'll be back with updates as they develop on this very important story."

He pressed the other buttons on the radio and found similar stories on other channels. "Doesn't sound like the press knows anything concrete yet."

His words brought her back to the present. "What's that supposed to mean?" She didn't try to hide the growl in her voice.

"Nothing. It's just a good thing they aren't reporting specifics. Gives us time to get ahead of the game. Does the firm still have Lena Hamilton on retainer?"

Ellery shook her head. Her life was being turned upside down and all the great Gordon Durant could think of was how to spin the story. Lena Hamilton was a power player in the public relations field and she commanded high dollar fees to bolster the reputation of their clients when necessary. The very idea she'd need the same kind of treatment was mind-blowing, and she wasn't prepared to even consider the idea. "We're going home and we're going to get to the bottom of this." She started the truck and reached for the gearshift, but her father placed his hand on hers.

"Honey, I've only got your best interests in mind. We don't have to call Lena, but you're not going home. If that news report is right, agents are already there and the press is probably lined up out front waiting for a shot of your first reaction to the raid. Let's get you set up somewhere, and I'll go to your house and make sure they're playing by the rules."

He was right. As much as she wanted to see for herself what was up, absolutely no good could come from her showing up and confronting the agents searching her home. Public protestations of innocence would hardly help when she didn't have a clue what she was accused of doing. Right now, she needed to be somewhere she could take a breath and think. Someplace quiet and out of sight. "Okay, I'll get a room at the Melrose. Do you have your laptop with you?"

"It's in my suitcase. Take the whole thing. It'll make you look less conspicuous. Once I have a handle on what's going on, I'll meet you there."

A few minutes later, Ellery pulled into the parking lot at the Melrose hotel. She hopped out of the truck and grabbed her dad's suitcase while he walked around the truck to climb into the driver's seat. She lingered for a moment while he adjusted the seat and mirrors, but he seemed more intent on getting where he was going than discussing the matter any further. "Call me as soon as you know something," she said.

"Count on it." He pointed at the hotel. "Get a room and stay put. I'll be in touch." Seconds later, he was gone.

Ellery watched until the truck was out of sight, then she climbed the steps to the hotel. There wasn't a wait at the reception desk and she approached the man behind the counter and waited for him to get off the phone.

"Welcome to the Melrose," he said. "Do you have a reservation?"

She shook her head. "I don't, but I'm hoping you have something available."

"You have good timing. We were all booked up for tonight, but I just got off the phone with a cancellation. It's for the Presidential Suite, though. Will that work for you? If not, I can make a couple of recommendations for nearby accommodations."

A few years ago, she would've thought nothing of dropping the extra cash on an extravagant suite. She'd changed since then, and the luxury and the expense felt out of sync with the rest of the choices she'd made, but right now she needed to feel safe and that meant not trolling around the city looking for a hotel room. "I'll take it."

The bellman seemed mystified at her one small suitcase, but he dutifully showed her around the suite. Ellery had been to many community events at this historic hotel, but she'd only stayed overnight a few times and, even then she'd usually booked a regular suite. The Presidential suite had three rooms, including a dining room with a table designed to accommodate eight guests. *Maybe I'll invite the media and hold my own press conference. Too bad, I don't have a clue what I'd say since I don't have any idea what brought this fresh hell down on my head.*

Time to remedy that. She opened her dad's suitcase and pulled out his laptop. She used the hotspot on her cell to log on the Internet, not wanting to take a chance on the hotel's unsecured WiFi connection. She started with a few simple searches including her name and the names of a few federal agencies as search terms. Her efforts returned over a dozen hits from various news sources, but each one was basically the same story from the AP wire, repeated over and over again, with no more detail than the local radio channels she'd heard in the car.

She glanced at her cell phone, willing her father to call with some information, but she realized he'd barely had time to get to her house, let alone assess what was going on. She had no idea how she was going to endure the wait and was considering ignoring her promise to stay put when the phone rang. She looked at the screen. Meg. She rushed to answer. "What did you find out?"

"Ellery?"

"Yes. What's going on? Did you find out anything?"

"Is Gordon there?"

"Yes. I mean no. I mean he's here in town, but he's not with me right now." Ellery fumbled for words as she tried to process Meg's stilted tone. "If there's something I need to know, just tell me."

Meg sighed. "I think I should talk to Gordon."

"Dammit, Meg." She wished she could make her stop calling her father Gordon. It suggested they had a relationship outside of her. "If you know something, tell me."

"I don't, Ellery. I don't know anything about why you're in so much trouble. But I do know that if things are as bad as these agents seem to think, then you need a lawyer and anyone who touches this case is tainted. Nothing like an early morning raid to send all our clients packing. I'm going to be the laughing stock of the courthouse tomorrow."

"You? What about me?"

"What about you? You don't go to the courthouse anymore, remember? And they may be looking for files with your name on them, but I'm the one who's left behind to sort it all out. Guilt by association."

Ellery's temper flared. "Except I'm not guilty of anything." Meg's last words triggered an idea. "Can we dial this down a notch? You may be on to something with the guilt by association. Maybe they're looking into one of my former clients. Has anything they've said given you a clue about the focus of their investigation?"

"They're pretty tight-lipped. I don't know that we're going to get any information until we get the affidavit for the search warrant and it's probably under seal."

Ellery sighed. Meg was probably right. In order to get a search warrant, agents would have to swear out an affidavit to a judge stating specific information about why they wanted to search and what exactly they were looking to find. Usually, the affidavit was a roadmap of the case, but in cases like this, where national security might be involved, the affidavit was often placed under seal and only available to the accused when they were officially charged with a crime. In the meantime, she'd have to find another way to figure out what in the hell was going on.

A beep signaled she had another call coming in. She asked Meg to hold and switched over to find her dad on the line. "Where are you? What have you found out?"

"I'm at your house. They want to take your computers and the warrant allows it, but I think if I give them access, they'll copy the hard drives instead."

Ellery's gut clenched at the invasion of her privacy, but she knew she didn't really have a choice. At least if she kept her computer, she could have the hard drives copied as well to make sure she knew exactly what the feds were getting. She read off her passwords and then said, "Have you gotten any more information?"

"Not much, but they think you were a valuable resource to the group that bombed the arena. What exactly that means, I don't know yet. I'm working on it. Frankly, I think they don't really know anything and they are just fishing for evidence."

"There's nothing for them to find. I don't have a clue what they're thinking."

A few seconds of silence passed and he said, "I called Lena. I want you to see her today."

"I told you not to call her. Besides, I don't have time to meet with her today. I have a show tonight, remember?"

"I know you did, but I don't think you understand the scope of this. You're going to need an entire team in place to handle the fallout, and Lena's just one piece. I'll finish up here and then meet you at your hotel and we can make a plan."

Ellery tried to ignore the hint of excitement in his tone and gave him her room number. She switched back to the other line, but Meg had either hung up or been disconnected. Either way, she was alone and it didn't matter what her father said about an entire team, she was going to have to figure this out for herself.

Sarah burst through the double doors and practically ran down the hall. She'd been trapped in court for the last three hours, watching a young assistant US attorney haggle with a seasoned criminal defense lawyer. Liz was the agent assigned to this case, but Mason had sent her instead because he needed Liz on another project. As promised, she hadn't had to actually do anything, since the hearing was primarily about evidentiary issues, but the AUSA had wanted someone on hand just in case. Worse than realizing she'd never get back the last few hours of her life, Sarah dreaded ever having to work with this particular AUSA since she was in completely over her head and she wasn't smart enough to know it.

As she walked to her car, she switched her phone back on, relieved to be reconnected with the outside world. She had three missed calls and one voice message, all from Danny. She didn't bother checking the message, instead punching Danny's number. When she answered, Sarah said, "You must really miss me to call that many times. Aren't we supposed to see each other tonight?"

"Haven't you heard?"

"Heard what?"

"And here I thought you federal agents were on top of everything. Or are you playing dumb because you can't talk about it?"

Sarah unlocked the 'Vette and slid inside. "I give up. I have no clue what you're talking about. Care to share?"

"Ellery Durant? Search warrants? Terrorism? Stop me when something rings a bell."

The joy at hearing Ellery's name went dark at the word terrorism. And search warrants? Sarah gripped the phone tightly. "Okay, I know nothing, but you obviously do. Spill."

"Sorry, pal, I thought you would know, but I guess that's silly. It's not like all you feds work at the same place."

"Uh, Danny, get to it."

"Sorry. HSI executed a search warrant at Ellery's old firm this morning and her house. Rumor has it she has ties to the group that was responsible for the bombing."

"No way." Sarah hit her free hand against the steering wheel. "No fucking way."

"Hey, don't yell at me. I'm just telling you what's on the news. HSI is also searching some charity's headquarters, WHI, Welcome Home Institute or something like that."

"International. Welcome Home International." Sarah spoke the words as if in a trance. She simply couldn't believe all of this was going down right now.

Danny's voice switched to a softer tone. "Is everything okay? Did you really not know about this?"

Sarah switched the phone to Bluetooth and started her car. She needed to get somewhere, do something to stave off the strong feeling of helplessness she felt. The office was the obvious first place to start, but something cautioned her against it. She found it difficult to believe HSI would have suddenly developed information on who exactly was responsible for the bombing and Trip wouldn't have clued her in. What she needed was a computer where she could find out exactly what was going on. "I've been in court all morning. Didn't have a clue. Hey, can I call you back later? I have to run down some information."

"Sure. Do you think we're still on for tonight?"

The show. Damn. Was Ellery under arrest? Surely, HSI wouldn't be beating down the door of a lawyer without some very damning information to back up their investigation. "I don't have a clue."

"Are you going to call her?"

"What?" Sarah had heard Danny's words, but she was stalling. Her first instinct had been to call Ellery, but years of experience kicked in and she knew she should get more information before she talked to the suspect. Suspect. If Ellery really was a suspect, then they were done. No way could she socialize with her, even casually. She should rely on her training and steer clear of anything to do with Ellery Durant.

Except it's your years of law enforcement work that's kept you from meeting anyone in the first place. As the thought echoed in her head, Danny's voice came through on the line.

"Sarah, are you okay?"

She shook off the inner voices. "I'm fine." She was, considering an hour ago she'd been excited about the prospect of seeing Ellery again. She looked at the clock on her dashboard. It was not even noon. She had a full day to find out what was going on with Ellery before she had to make a decision about her plans for the evening. If she couldn't get the information she needed in that amount of time, she should turn in her badge. "I'll be at your place at seven. If it's a no-go, we'll grab dinner out. My treat."

After she hung up with Danny, Sarah considered her options. She was expected back at the office this afternoon. She could only imagine the atmosphere there. Despite the fact that another agency was conducting this search, the fact that there was a break in the bombing case would send a ripple of anticipation through all the federal agencies in town. That one of the suspects was a former high profile adversary would only add to the excitement. She didn't think she could handle being part of the celebration until she was convinced her own gut instincts about Ellery were wrong.

Before she could talk herself out of it, she dialed the number to the office. When Bev answered, she feigned illness, said she was headed home, but would be available on her cell. Bev seemed distracted, but said she'd let Mason know and Sarah got off the line as quickly as possible to avoid having to add details to her lie.

That settled, Sarah punched the accelerator on the 'Vette and headed for home, glad she'd had the foresight to keep her copies of the records HSI had carted away earlier that week.

The knock on the door brought Ellery out of deep thought. She glanced at her watch. She'd only been in the hotel room for an hour, but it felt like much longer. Hoping her father had arrived, she closed the distance to the door in long, quick strides.

The man standing outside wasn't her father but, judging by the nameplate, he was an employee of the hotel. She swung the door open.

"Ms. Durant?"

"Yes?"

"May I come in?"

She looked over his shoulder. Another man, one of the hotel bellmen, stood at the end of the hall, and a prickly sensation traveled up her spine. Something was up. "Actually, I was about to get some much needed sleep. I'll give you a call when I wake up." She started to shut the door, but he placed his palm against the heavy wood.

"I promise I wouldn't bother you if it wasn't important."

His tone was authoritative, but his eyes implored her not to cause a scene. Since a scene was the last thing she needed on this crazy day, she waved him in, offering a tiny salute to the bellman as she shut the door. "What is it?"

"We ran your credit card for incidentals when you checked in, but the credit card company just called back and let us know they would be declining all charges."

Ellery shrugged. She had no idea why her credit was declined. She walked over to the desk and picked up her wallet. "I have other cards."

"I'm afraid I can't—"

She cut him off before he had to deal with the unpleasantness of telling her he didn't want to run another card. "Cash then. You have an ATM in the hotel?"

"I'm sorry, Ms. Durant, but we're going to have to ask you to leave."

"Excuse me?"

"I shouldn't have booked the room. It appears there is a conflict. Again, please accept my apologies. I have a bellman waiting to help you with your things."

Ellery watched him closely as he looked around the room. She read the suspicious glint in his eyes, as he assessed that she didn't really have much in the way of "things" and she realized the only conflict about the room was the fact that he wished he hadn't given it to her in the first place. She walked over to the desk, picked up her phone and wallet, and shoved the laptop into her father's small carryon. "I think I can handle it on my own, Mr...." She squinted at his name tag. "Ross. Let your friend down the hall know he's off the hook." She shouldered past Ross and walked down the hall, past the bellman, and punched the button for the elevator. Ross and the bellman joined her in the car when it arrived and followed her to the exit. She didn't look back as she pushed through the doors, ignoring the valet who offered to fetch her car. She didn't have a car, she didn't have a place to stay, and she didn't have a clue what she was going to do next except clear her name.

CHAPTER EIGHT

S arah waited through the rings, impatiently tapping her foot on the floor, until Trip answered. "We need to talk," she said. "Is this a good time?"

"For you, it's always a good time, but I need to call you back. The battery's about to go out on my cell." He clicked off the line and Sarah went back to foot tapping until her phone rang again. She answered on the first ring. "You should keep that thing charged. Whatever happened to always being prepared?"

"My battery was fine, but I didn't trust the line. How did those names I sent you pan out?"

"One of the names, Sadeem, is a well-known commodity here in Dallas, but by all accounts he's a great guy, solid businessman and philanthropist. But obviously there's more to it than that. I was hoping maybe you'd have some intel to share."

"What makes you think there's more to him?"

"Well, he has family and business connections to a charity our unit's been looking at for potential fraud. That by itself doesn't tell me anything since my boss appears to be casting a wide net after all the crap in the news about the IRS not cracking down on pseudo nonprofits. But here's the deal. The minute I started looking closer, the files got snatched from me by HSI and I'd bet my car they think he or his cousin had something to do with the bombing."

"They may be right. What's the charity?"

"Welcome Home International. His cousin is Amir Khan."

"Holy shit. HSI is searching his attorney's offices today."

Sarah's gut clenched. "Wait a minute. Ellery Durant was Amir's attorney?"

"That's what I've been told. Was your office involved in the search?"

"Didn't even know it was going down. Since when does HSI work with other agencies? I saw it on the news, just like everyone else."

"Smart move, taking down these guys' structure first. If they didn't have help setting up networks here in the US, they'd have a much harder time getting their operations off the ground."

Sarah bristled at the idea Ellery could be involved in a terrorist plot, especially one designed to kill citizens in her own community. She had a choice to make. She could continue to let Trip believe she knew who Ellery was from local news reports or she could come clean and admit she'd actually met Ellery and had at least started to have a personal relationship with her. If she wanted the information she'd called him for, she knew she had to tell him the truth. "I know her."

"Who? Durant?"

"Yes. We had coffee Monday. I was supposed to see her tonight. I might still see her if she's not scared to come out in public after the witch hunt this morning."

"I don't want to tell you your business, but seeing her is not a good idea."

"Are you willing to tell me why? And are you willing to tell me why BAU is working on a terrorism case?"

"The director asked us to provide an assessment of the suspects."

"And Ellery's a suspect? What's your analysis of her?"

"Slow down, kiddo. All I know is what I've been told. She's listed on the IRS Form 1023 as the attorney who structured the WHI and there's a power of attorney attached, giving her authorization to make financial decisions for the organization. WHI has a wonky financial relationship with Sadeem Jafari's foundation, the Global Enterprise Alliance. Appears they dip into each other's accounts on a regular basis. HSI has traced funds from an offshore account held by GEA to an Al Qaeda training camp in Libya. Of course, it's not a direct line. The money bounced around before it got to Libya, but the working theory is that years of experience working with criminals gave Durant the perfect knowledge base to advise Khan and Jafari as to exactly what they needed to do to try to hide the money trail."

"And the other names on your list?"

"Not sure what their involvement is yet. Michael and Brian Barstow are local boys. They started volunteering at WHI a year ago and now they go by Hashid and Abdul Kamal. Their Internet postings have gotten increasingly radical, but they've made no direct threats. They were both arrested with Amir's son, Naveed, late last year, for breaking into an office building, but the case is still pending and so far we haven't been able to relate it to anything to do with the bombing."

"I can believe WHI might be supporting terrorism in general, but is there really evidence to tie them to the bombing?"

"CIA and HSI say they are close to being able to make arrests."

Sarah sank into a chair and put her head in her hands. She'd worked with Trip for years and trusted him completely. He wouldn't be passing along these accusations if he didn't have solid evidence to back them up, but she'd sat across from Ellery, looked her in the eyes, and hadn't detected a single signal of deception despite her years of training in behavioral analysis. Either Ellery was wrongly accused or she was such a cold-blooded criminal that she could fool even the best.

"Trip, I hear what you're saying, but I just can't believe it. I was with her the night of the bombing. We were only a couple of blocks away when it happened, and I've seen her since. She was as shocked as anyone by what happened."

"She was a couple of blocks away, huh? Sarah, listen to what you're saying." He paused. "Maybe you should see her tonight. Now that you know what you do, you might be in a better position to assess whether she was duped into helping Khan and his associates, whether she's in it for money, or whether she really supports their cause." He started talking faster, as he warmed to the idea. "In fact, that's a great idea. She may not lawyer up before charges are filed. If you can get close, we'll be a step ahead of the game."

"What does that even mean? You want me to develop some personal relationship with her to get her to fess up to helping terrorists? And you're crazy if you think she won't be represented. She comes from a family of lawyers."

"You'd be surprised. Sometimes lawyers are the worst about thinking they can handle things on their own. Besides, you don't have to talk to her about the case. Observations only. I just want your impression, now that you're looking at her as something besides a potential lay."

"Watch it, Trip. Not cool."

"I've seen her picture and I know you well."

"Maybe you don't know me as well as you think. I moved out here for a change. I haven't had a single one-night stand since I got here." She considered her next words carefully. "I like her. I like her a lot."

"Then check her out a bit more closely."

"How do you suggest I do that? After the searches this morning, she's all over the news. Mason would have my hide for even being in the same room as Ellery."

"I'll clear it with the director. You'll be working with me as part of the behavioral analysis he wants so badly. It's a win-win. If you're going to change your ways for a woman, you should at least find out everything you can about her first. Right?"

She couldn't deny his logic. And without agency sanction, it would tank her career to be around Ellery with all the dirt swirling around her. This way she'd get the opportunity to hang out with Ellery and make her own decision about whether she was a person capable of helping terrorists or a person with the kind of honor and integrity she was looking for. The only harm would be if Ellery figured out she had an ulterior motive, but in exchange for the opportunity to get close to her, she was willing to take that chance.

❖

Ellery looked up from her phone and told the cab driver to pull over at the end of the street. A quick glance up the road confirmed that federal agents were still hard at work sifting through her personal life. They'd already done plenty of damage, judging by the few phone calls she'd just made. On the drive over she'd called her credit card company, asking about the charge at the hotel. They'd confirmed that they'd declined the charges and that her account was suspended, but they insisted she'd have to wait until she received written notification to find out why. A quick check of her other available cards resulted in the same story. She'd counseled enough clients through the deep and violating intervention of federal seizure to realize what was happening to her now, but there was no way she could have ever prepared for the personal reality. All she could do now was find out why. She counted out the cab fare and handed it over, pocketing her last five dollars.

A few neighbors were out observing the action and she nodded to them as she passed by, but didn't engage with their curious expressions. She liked this older neighborhood for its combination of hospitality and privacy. People looked out for each other, but didn't meddle in each other's private business. Except for Leo Jacobs, the elderly vet who lived next door. As always, he was on his porch and he called out as she approached. She knew he'd have questions, and not wanting everyone to hear their conversation, she walked up the front steps so they could talk away from the action. He sat in his ancient rocking chair and the table next to him held a platter full of sandwiches and a six-pack. Clearly, he anticipated a lengthy show.

"Looks like you're in a bit of trouble, neighbor."

His words were low and gravely. Ellery shook her head in disgust. "Looks like. Seen anything interesting?"

"They carried out a few boxes from your studio, but other than that, it looks like they're mostly just digging around in there. Some fella drove up in your car. Didn't look like a fed, but he walked up to the rest of them and started saying a bunch of stuff. I couldn't make out a word. He followed them inside and I haven't seen them since."

"That would be my dad, Gordon Durant, esquire."

"Guess you'll save some pennies, having a lawyer in the family."

Ellery started to remind him that she didn't need a lawyer since she was one, but she decided not to bother. What she wanted to do was walk over and find out exactly what was going on. The only thing holding her back was not knowing if they had a warrant for her arrest. If they did, she wanted to turn herself in on her own time, especially since other than what she'd heard on the radio, she didn't know what the charges would be. If what the radio said was true, that they thought she was involved in a terrorist plot, there'd be little chance of being released on bond and she'd need time to prepare if she was going to be incarcerated. "Mind if I hang out here for a bit?"

Leo waved at the beer and sandwiches. "Help yourself."

She nodded her thanks, but decided against putting food in her swirling stomach. She settled into a chair and pulled out her phone to text her father. *Update?*

Still at it.

You should talk to the next door neighbor, Leo. He's always got some inside scoop.

A few minutes passed before he showed up on Leo's porch. If he was surprised to see her, he didn't let it show. He declined Leo's offer of a sandwich, but popped the top on one of the beers and settled in like they were old friends. "I know my daughter well. If I ask her to stay put, she'll do exactly the opposite. I should've bet on it."

"Hey, Dad, I'm right here and I can hear every word. As much as I know you love to be right, I didn't have much of a choice. The Melrose kicked me out, and it appears none of my credit cards are working. Your pals next door have any insights to offer about why this is happening?"

"Sure. They think you helped a local group fund a terrorist cell. I guess in addition to conducting these searches, they've also frozen your assets. Hope you kept some cash hidden somewhere."

Ellery stood and started pacing the porch. She looked over at her house. Twenty-four hours ago, she'd had everything she ever wanted. Work she loved, a cozy house in a quiet neighborhood, and the promise of more—a successful show and the chance to see Sarah Flores again. Now all of that was at risk. The memory of Sarah triggered a thought. "Dad, is there more than one agency at the house?"

"Just HSI as far as I can tell. At least they're the ones heading things up, but it's likely something this big would have some interagency support."

Like from the FBI. What division had Sarah said she worked for? Fraud. Doubtful her division was involved, but it was possible. She racked her brain to see if anything about their coffee date earlier in the week could be considered nefarious, but her only read was that Sarah had been genuinely interested in her personally, not as the target of an investigation. Whether that was hubris or not remained to be seen. She didn't have Sarah's number or she would've called and asked her directly. She did have another call she needed to make though, and she walked across the porch out of Leo and her father's earshot.

Karen answered on the first ring. "If you're trying to drum up publicity, you sure know what you're doing."

Ellery sighed with relief at the teasing, but friendly, tone. "If you think I'm getting a lot of press now, just wait until they carry me off to prison."

"You have to wait until after the show. I've been getting calls all morning. Seriously, I had to tell the caterers to order more wine. I think we're in for record crowds."

"I called to tell you I completely understand if you want to pull my pieces from the show."

"Not a chance. And you must be there, even if you have to bust out of jail to make it happen."

"No way. The bombing was hugely personal to so many people. My being there would be a huge distraction." Images of the wounded flashed in her mind. "It was personal to me too."

"Exactly, and that's precisely why you need to be there. You didn't have anything to do with this, so don't hole up and act like you have something to be ashamed of. Show up and embrace your new life."

Ellery had no idea how much of Karen's encouragement was aimed at making her feel more confident and how much was a mercenary means to sell out the show, but ultimately Karen was right. She didn't have anything to hide. Whatever was going on was a huge mistake, and it would sort itself out, but it had nothing to do with her new life. She'd worked hard for the recognition she hoped to receive tonight, and if she let her former life eclipse her new opportunities, she may as well never have left the practice. She knew what she had to do.

"Make sure there's lots of champagne. I'll be there."

CHAPTER NINE

Sarah pulled up to Danny and Ellen's house and parked in the driveway. When she was ready to buy a house, she might like one like this—a Craftsman with a large, wraparound porch. The neighborhood was nice. Lots of trees, close to good restaurants and bars, within walking distance of several neighborhood grocery stores. Probably way out of her price range, but maybe she could find a place nearby that needed some fixing up.

Danny opened the door before she made it across the porch. "Come on in and grab a drink." She rolled her eyes. "Ellen's still getting ready."

Sarah punched her in the arm. "Don't act like you don't like girls getting all dolled up on your account."

"Well, I must admit, I do like it. Speaking of getting dolled up, look at you."

Sarah felt the slow warmth of a blush rise through her skin. She'd changed outfits at least three times before settling on the flirty red cocktail dress with a daring side slit. She'd been told her legs were her best feature, and it would be stupid not to use them to her advantage. She feared her efforts would go to waste, though. If Ellery was even there tonight, she'd probably be too busy to give her the time of day, but if she had any chance of getting close, there was nothing like bare skin to do the trick. "Didn't you promise me a drink?"

"Don't you two dare start drinking without me."

Sarah saw Danny's wife, Ellen, walking toward her. They embraced, and Ellen gave her a long, appraising once over. "Don't let Danny tease you. The last time she wore a dress was probably at her first communion. You look amazing."

Danny nodded. "Mama gave up on me after I tore my dress playing touch football after the service. I couldn't have been happier to retire that lacy contraption. Come on, drinks are in the kitchen."

Sarah followed the couple through their living room into the spacious kitchen. "Wow, this is huge."

Ellen laughed. "You should've seen it when we bought the place. It was the size of a large closet."

"It was my have to have feature," Danny said. "My entire childhood was spent in the kitchen. Meals, homework, family meetings—it was the most important room in the house."

Sarah looked around. Everything about their place was foreign to a girl who'd grown up on navy bases. Her apartment in D.C. had looked more like a storage locker than a home. She'd hardly ever spent time there, and it seemed like a waste to decorate the place. She'd tried to make her new place in Dallas seem more homey, but so far all she'd managed were a few coordinated pieces the woman at the Pottery Barn down the street had convinced her were supposed to go together. As for her kitchen, she hoped the high-end appliances worked as well as they looked, but as long as she was within walking distance of dozens of good restaurants, she had no plans to find out anytime soon.

"So, what's this show all about, anyway?" Sarah asked as Ellen handed her a glass of wine.

"Karen Tron is a big deal in the Dallas design community," Ellen said. "She owns several showrooms in the Design District, and a few years ago she started a juried show to introduce new talent. You'll see all kinds of work on display, from furniture, to knickknacks, to light fixtures, and wall paintings. Being selected for one of her shows is quite a coup, especially for someone like Ellery who doesn't have a background in design. A lot of the other artists at the show have spent their entire lives making the rounds of the various shows, building an audience for their work."

"Do you think she'll show up tonight?" Danny asked.

"Your guess is as good as mine," Ellen said. "Probably better since you know her much better than I do."

"I'm not sure I know her as well as you think. I mean, when she was in practice I saw her at the courthouse all the time. She's a worthy adversary and I could always count on her to shoot straight with me, but I haven't had a lot of social interaction with her. On that level, Sarah here probably knows her better than the both of us."

Sarah almost choked on her wine as they both turned toward her. She'd been silently observing their conversation while she pondered her own observations. She started to say that she didn't have a clue, but both of these women knew what she used to do for a living and neither was likely to buy her "hey, I'm just a paper pusher for the FBI" routine. She cleared her throat while she considered her response. "Really good sociopaths are naturally good at it. Their lies don't always come with all the usual social cues because they don't feel any shame about lying, so there's no struggle between the message the body is delivering and what the mind knows to be true."

"Are you saying even you can't spot a sociopath?"

"Not at all. Even people with little regard for human life give signals, just not the ones you might be used to, although I'm sure you've developed a fair amount of people-reading skills in the courtroom."

"So, what about Ellery? What does your Quantico-trained gut say?"

Sarah paused before she answered, assessing whether her conclusion was more about her feelings than any empirical findings. But Danny was right. Despite the science, it often came down to gut instinct. For now, she was going to go with her gut, but she would also hedge her bets.

"I think there's a lot more to Ellery Durant than meets the eye, but I don't think she knowingly did anything to support the group behind the bombing." What she didn't say was that Ellery might well have inadvertently helped a terrorist group, which might make a difference in the investigation against her, but could still have serious consequences. It was pretty unlikely that HSI would care to parse out which was which, and she'd only been tapped with the task of giving the director an assessment of Ellery as a person, not determining whether she should be charged and with what. But that didn't mean she wasn't going to dig a little deeper.

❖

"Where do you want me to drop you off?"

Ellery pointed to a side street. "If you turn there, you can circle around and access the back of the building. It's a loading dock, and hopefully, it'll be clear."

Her dad followed her instructions and Ellery settled back into her seat, desperately trying to calm the sense of dread she had about the night's events. They were in Leo's beat-up Plymouth in an effort to hide from the crowd, but after they made one pass around the front of the building, it was clear there would be no way for Ellery to make a quiet entrance. Press had already lined the street and were taking pictures of everyone who entered the building. At least some of the other designers would be getting a lot of publicity for the event.

Not for the first time, she regretted her decision to come here tonight. It was one thing to hold up ideals, but quite another to see them through, and she feared others might be hurt by her attendance. Karen's business could take a hit from the protestors who'd lined up across the street with signs decrying terrorism, and coverage of the other designers' work could be eclipsed by new stories about how the attorney who'd helped terrorists bomb the arena had no shame about appearing in public. She couldn't win no matter what she did, but at least if she'd stayed home no one else would be smeared by the dirt the public was casting her way.

"It's not too late to change your mind."

Her dad's expression was hopeful. She knew he'd prefer it if she asked him to turn the car around and drive as far away from this disaster waiting to happen as possible. He'd probably be happiest if she would abandon this dream entirely and went back to practicing law, and she couldn't blame him for expecting her to do what he wanted. She'd followed in his footsteps most of her life without ever questioning if it was what she really wanted rather than what he wanted for her. It was expected. It was responsible. It was easy. Until it wasn't and she'd had to walk away or let it consume her. Now she'd found something that fulfilled her instead of chewed away at her soul. Would she let her chance at a new life slip away?

"I made a promise to be here, and this is the only place I want to be. You can just drop me off if you don't want to come in."

He nodded, and she detected a glint of respect in his eyes. He might not ever agree with her choices, but maybe someday he could understand that she was surviving her own way. He pulled the car up to the loading dock. As she reached for the door handle, he put his hand on her arm and gave it a light squeeze. "I'll see you inside."

Ellery climbed the stairs and knocked on the back door. Karen's assistant, Rick, opened the door and ushered her in. He was dressed in a midnight blue tux with a deep purple bow tie and he bent down to kiss her hand.

"You're not going to believe the crowd waiting to get in," he said. "The fire marshal will be paying us a visit for sure, but the show's going to be a sellout. Champagne?"

"No, thanks. The last thing I need is to pour alcohol on my already frayed nerves. Where's Karen?"

"She's up front talking to the press. Don't worry—she's making it clear all personal questions are off limits or they'll be escorted off the premises, and she hired some big hunky guys to make sure that happens."

"Sounds like she's thought of everything. Where do you want me?"

"My entire assignment for the night is to stay by your side. Let's check out the installation and then figure out the best place for you to hunker down."

He reached for her hand and she took it, clasping tightly, but not moving her feet. If she was going to do this, it was time to commit. She took a deep breath and willed her body to go through the motions until her mind could wrap itself around the chaos she was about to dive into. "Let's go."

She had to walk briskly to keep up with Rick as he led her through the showroom, but as they approached the area where her pieces were on display, Ellery slowed her pace. In the cramped space of her studio, she'd had no real concept of the volume of her work. There were close to twenty pieces of furniture crafted from other people's castoffs, saved from the ruins of time. On display with gallery accents and mood lighting, they were a breathtaking sight.

"Did we do you justice?"

Ellery smiled at the sound of Karen's voice. "I know I was there when you loaded it, but it looks like my furniture had babies since then. Was there really this much?"

"Spoken like a true artist. You were so busy with each piece you didn't take the time to look at the big picture." She pointed at the display. "If you ever had any doubt, this is your true passion. That law gig was nothing more than a J-O-B."

It wasn't that simple, but Ellery didn't bother trying to explain. She'd been just as passionate about the law even if the choice to pursue that career hadn't been her own. And she'd been just as good at it, but it was a relief to know now that she had chosen a different path, she had the potential to be just as good at something else. "I guess we'll know if I'm for real when you see how much is sold at the end of the night." She gestured toward the door. "Hopefully, the press won't keep buyers away."

"Are you kidding me? I let a few VIPs in for an early viewing." She looked around. "They're here somewhere. Don't you worry about a thing. As gruesome as it may seem, the chance to own an Ellery Durant original is now a collector's dream." Karen looked over her shoulder as she delivered the words. "I'm sorry, dear, but I have to check one last thing before the doors open. Rick will take good care of you, and I personally vetted the guest list, so don't worry."

She was gone in an instant, and Ellery stood rooted in place as Karen's words replayed in her head. If her work sold tonight was it more a factor of her current troubles than a testament to her talent? She didn't have much time to consider the dilemma before the doors to the showroom opened and the crowd burst into the room. She watched as Karen's well-trained staff handed out programs and caterers ducked in and out of groups of attendees with loaded trays of champagne and fancy finger foods. She spotted a group of women on the move toward her when she heard a voice over her shoulder.

"How's it going?" her dad asked.

"Maybe this was a bad idea."

"Maybe, but you're here now. Let's make the most of it."

He stepped in front of her to greet the approaching guests. "Hi, I'm Gordon Durant, proud father of the artist. Would you like to meet her before or after you place your orders?"

Ellery sighed and stepped up to nudge him out of the way. "Sorry, ladies. Anyone else have an overbearing parent?"

The group laughed nervously, and Ellery knew she only had a second to win them over before they finished their curious assessment of the artist turned criminal. "You all look like you have very good taste. Let me show you one of my favorite pieces." She didn't wait for them to respond, but walked across the floor to a rosewood credenza. She launched into a description of how she'd pieced the panels from wood she'd salvaged from a 1950s trailer. After she finished describing the transformation, she leaned in close. "Karen wants to keep this one for herself, but I told her it had to be in the show. Do you like it?"

As the women nodded their approval, Rick tapped her on the shoulder. When she looked his way, he made a slashing motion across his throat. She lifted her shoulders in a silent question while the women in the group crowded around the credenza, sliding open the panels and pulling open the drawers. "What?" she asked.

Rick grimaced. "It's sold."

"Let me guess. Karen pulled it."

"Nope." He glanced around the room and pointed out another group of women who were standing a short distance away. "There they are. One of them bought it. They're friends of Karen and she let them in early. I was heading over here to put up a sold sign when I saw you doing the hard sell."

Ellery shouldn't care about the identity of the buyer. She should just be grateful to sell the piece and turn her attention back to the group currently admiring her work, but she locked her gaze on the group across the room because she knew them. She watched while Danny and Ellen each took a glass of champagne from a passing waiter and toasted each other, but it wasn't them that held her gaze. No, it was Sarah Flores, looking both elegant and delicious in a deep red dress, cut to show off her long, toned, gorgeous legs. Ellery sucked in a breath, unable to look away, but sure she should run as fast as she could in the other direction. Torn between desire and danger, she could only watch as Sarah lifted her glass in the air and stared directly into her eyes.

CHAPTER TEN

From the moment they'd walked into the room, the antici-pation of seeing Ellery had Sarah on edge. Every time a person headed toward her, her breath hitched and then abated when she realized it was just a stranger and not the woman she was there to observe.

Observe. *You're only here to observe and report back.* Any spark of feeling she might have felt at the coffee shop must be put aside. She would compartmentalize her emotions and do her job tonight.

"Quit looking so serious," Danny said. "We invited you so you could have fun."

Sarah reached for the glass of champagne Danny offered and took a deep drink, enjoying the tingle of bubbles against her lips. "I'm having a blast," she said in her driest tone. "Where's your wife?"

"She's staking out her claim. We'll probably go home with half of this stuff. Why do you think we got in early and got first crack at the expensive bubbly?"

Sarah nodded. The champagne was topnotch, and she was happy to have it. She took another big swallow and glanced around the room. The gallery owner had gone all out for this show. From the dramatic lighting to the multiple staging areas, each decked out to reflect the style of the designer whose work was being displayed. No detail had been overlooked. Her survey of the room stopped abruptly when her eyes caught a block-lettered sign about thirty feet away: *ELLERY DURANT*. She finished her sweep of the room, but Ellery was nowhere in sight. Maybe she was going to make a late entrance. Maybe she wouldn't be here at all. If that were the case, she'd have nothing to report to Trip, but she knew the disappointment she felt had more to do with the prospect of not seeing Ellery, the woman, than the potential of missing a chance to observe her as a suspect.

A few moments later, Ellen rejoined them. "You two need to see the credenza I just bought. It's amazing and everyone here is going to be very jealous they weren't able to get their hands on it first."

"I hope you left something for all the other kids," Danny said.

Ellen swatted her with her program. "One piece of furniture. That's it." She turned to Sarah. "This is married life. You buy your wife an early anniversary present, but by the time you've been married for a year, she's completely ungrateful."

"Duly noted," Sarah said, joining in their laughter. "I can tell you two are totally on the skids." She watched as Ellen and Danny clinked glasses, took sips of champagne, and acted all googly. All things she wanted, but didn't have any idea how to achieve. Their happiness was at once intoxicating and painful—she couldn't decide which so she looked away.

Through the glass doors she could see the crowd forming. The police outside seemed to have the protestors under control, but in a few minutes the quiet showroom would be overrun with art collectors, press, and voyeurs. She should take the opportunity to look around. Her barren apartment could certainly benefit from an artistic touch. Her gaze swept the room, looking for something to catch her interest, but it was someone, not something that stopped her cold.

She'd expected to see Ellery here. She'd counted on it, but she hadn't expected the sudden, visceral reaction that shuddered its way through her body. Ellery was standing next to a credenza, running her hand over the surface, slowly and deliberately. Her mouth was moving, and it appeared she was talking to the women standing next to her, but her eyes were focused on the piece of furniture and all her energy went into the caress. She wore black wool trousers that draped perfectly and a cornflower blue collared shirt unbuttoned just enough to tease. Simple and elegant, she was deliciously handsome. So much so that Sarah couldn't look away in time to avoid meeting her eyes when Ellery looked her way. Caught staring, she decided to own it and raised her glass in a toast. Ellery held her gaze for a moment and then spoke to the man standing next to her. Sarah watched their exchange, not sure why she was still staring. She started to walk away, turn her back on the distraction that was Ellery, but before she could move, Ellery was striding toward her. She took a deep breath and willed her brain to take over and jump back into work mode. She finished off the glass of champagne and handed it to a passing waiter without taking her eyes off Ellery, and by the time she was within two feet, Sarah was certain her façade of professionalism was firmly fixed.

"I certainly didn't expect to see you here," Ellery said.

Sarah didn't rush to reply, instead watching for cues about Ellery's current state of mind. Although most people probably wouldn't notice, Sarah could tell by the way she ducked her head and her eyes shifted around the room, Ellery was a touch nervous. Could be she was just anxious about the show and how her work would be received. Of course, it could also be the group of protestors across the street and the police assigned to keep them at bay were an unpleasant reminder of the invasion of law enforcement into her life earlier that day. Whatever had Ellery on edge aroused Sarah's curiosity. "I guess I could say the same about you. You've had a rough day, I hear."

Ellery's laugh with mirthless. "Now that is the understatement of the year. My home was ransacked, my former firm was invaded, my bank accounts, credit cards, all shut down. If I sell anything tonight, I'm going to have to get Karen to pay me in cash if I'm going to be able to afford to eat tomorrow. But you feds don't care about the very real effects of your actions on those of us who are supposedly innocent until proven guilty, do you?"

Despite the angry tenor of her words, Ellery delivered them with measured calm. Sarah wondered if she had been as controlled in the courtroom before she made the decision to retire from her practice. Her careful manner suggested genuine thought and reflection, and if she'd projected this same demeanor during trial, she'd probably been an unstoppable force, respected by juries and her opponents alike. Sarah respected her too, but she wasn't going to rise to the bait. "We feds don't all work together, but you know that because you're smart. If you don't want to talk to me, then I'll walk away. But I'm here because my good friends asked me to join them, and I hoped to see you."

Ellery's stern expression relaxed a bit. "To tell you the truth, it's nice to see a friendly face. You look fantastic, by the way."

"Like I said, I hoped to see you." Sarah ducked her head to hide her eyes. The shameless flirting was real, but since it was also designed to disarm Ellery, she didn't want to give away any hint of duplicity that might be reflected in her gaze. "You look pretty amazing yourself."

"Thank goodness none of my clothes were seized," Ellery said with a wry smile.

Sarah returned the smile, and for a single moment, forgot why she was really here and just enjoyed the pleasure of Ellery's company.

"Can I get you another glass of champagne?" Ellery offered.

"Are you trying to get me drunk so I'll furnish my apartment with your work?"

"Now that would be the perfect revenge, don't you think?"

They laughed and Ellery stopped a waiter, picked up a glass from his tray, and handed it to Sarah. She reached to take it and their fingers touched, searing heat as they shared the weight of the glass for just a moment before Sarah broke the connection. When she finally pulled the glass toward her, the arousal she'd felt at their contact remained. She gripped the glass, willing the cold liquid to cool her libido. She was getting distracted and it felt wonderful, but she was here to do a job, not pick up a woman. Especially not this woman.

A noise sounded behind them, and they both glanced toward the front of the room. A second wave of guests surged into the room. Sarah shot a look at Ellery. Again, she appeared outwardly calm, but her clenching fists, the strain in her neck signaled she would love to run as fast and far as possible in this moment. Instinctively, Sarah reached out and squeezed Ellery's arm. "It's going to be fine."

Before Ellery could answer, a tall, ruddy middle-aged man appeared at her side. "What's going to be fine?" he asked.

Sarah watched as he placed his arm around Ellery's shoulders, but his eyes were focused on Sarah, fierce and protective. The same eyes, the same stance. Sarah took only a moment to assess his role. It was hard to miss since he and Ellery looked exactly alike. She stuck out her hand. "Gordon Durant, I'm Sarah Flores. Nice to meet you."

His eyes bored holes into her, but she could see a glint of mischief in Ellery's eyes, and he was forced into returning the polite gesture. She held his hand for a second longer than necessary. When she finally released her firm grip, Ellery said, "Just so you know, Dad, this is Special Agent Sarah Flores, FBI."

Sarah saw the corner of his mouth twitch just slightly—the only sign her title had had any affect on his composure. He recovered quickly.

"Well, Special Agent, I think you would know better than to question my daughter without counsel."

"I wasn't aware Ellery had been charged with anything."

"As if that's in doubt after the events of this morning."

"That may be, but since Ellery has her own law degree I guess I figured she was capable of deciding whether or not to talk to me on her own."

Ellery watched the feisty exchange undecided about who she was rooting for. She waited for Sarah to tell him that she wasn't here in an official capacity, that she was here with friends for a social event. At least that's what she'd assumed, but what if she was wrong? What if Sarah's open flirting was more about getting close to her as a suspect than a potential romantic interest? Had her time away from the law caused her to lose her edge?

Maybe her father was right and she needed to go on the offense. It had taken all her powers of persuasion to convince him she didn't need Lena Hamilton at her side during this show to spin her every word as part of a PR campaign. Maybe she'd been wrong to think this was just another case of the feds barking down the wrong trail as they'd done so many times in the past when it came to zealous prosecution of terrorism. Their motto was always act first, figure out the facts later, and that usually played out with full-scale raids that netted loads of discovery that might or might not lead to an eventual arrest. Since 9/11, she'd represented several clients caught in these nets. Their reputations and businesses ruined while the initial stages of the case dragged on, sometimes for years. At the end of the day, no one cared that they'd never actually been arrested or charged with anything. All anyone ever remembered was that day on the news when dozens of men and women with guns toted away boxes of "evidence."

The only thing she could do, the only thing she wanted to do, was to keep this investigation from dragging on, and she had an idea about exactly how to do it. "Dad, will you go get me a drink, please?"

"What?"

Her father looked as surprised as if she'd asked him to fly to the moon. "A drink. Champagne, water, anything. I need a moment alone with Agent Flores." She injected a stern note of authority in to the words to let him know she wasn't going to back down. He lingered for a moment before apparently deciding not to fight before he stalked off toward the bar. As soon as he was lost in the crowd, Ellery said, "Look, here's the deal. I'm here on business. It sounds like you're here on business too, but yours is getting in the way of mine. I'm going to get to work and start schmoozing people who are interested in buying my work so I can have enough money to pay my bills. I was under the impression you were here in a social capacity, but if you're really here to talk to me about why your fellow agents busted up my life this morning, then I'm happy to talk to you, but not until I'm done. Later tonight, tomorrow, whenever, but not now. Do you understand?"

"I do," Sarah said.

"Great. Now, I'm going over there." Ellery pointed at the display of her work. "I'd like it if you would find some other place to hang out."

"Until when?"

"Excuse me?"

"You said you would talk to me whenever. When does the show end?"

Ellery sighed. She'd hoped her firm tone would send Sarah packing for the rest of the night. The idea of seeing her later that night was enticing, but the idea of having to talk wasn't. "Let's make a deal. I'll meet you after, but you can do the talking this time. Depending on what you have to say, we can make a date…" She paused and winced inwardly at her poor word choice. "We can schedule a time for me to answer any questions you have."

Sarah's cocky smile told Ellery she'd caught the slip and her reply sealed it. "Sounds like a plan. Where should I meet you for tonight's date?"

Ellery shook her head, knowing it was pointless to correct her. She mentally tallied how long it would take to shake her father after the show. "Eleven thirty at Sue Ellen's. Just you. Okay?"

"Sounds very mysterious."

"The only mystery here is why anyone would think I have anything to do with what happened that night." She could feel her voice starting to rise and she took a deep breath while she sought calm. Here, in front of all of these people, was not the place to unleash her anger. She considered pointing out how she'd stuck around after the bombing and helped, but she knew enough anecdotal evidence of criminals crowding close to a scene to watch the effects of the destruction they'd set in motion to know that Sarah Flores wouldn't find that fact persuasive. In fact, this entire exercise was probably a waste of time, but she was going to push forward, and her goal was to find out more than she shared. Shouldn't be hard since she didn't know a damn thing other than Special Agent Sarah Flores was attractive and arousing.

She'd have to be very careful or she was going to be in big trouble.

CHAPTER ELEVEN

Y ou're welcome to stay here with me," Ellery said, "but I'm not leaving." She injected what she hoped was a powerful dose of authority into her voice. She and her father had been engaged in this argument during the entire drive home from the show. He kept insisting she check into a hotel and she firmly refused. What was the point? The press could find her just as easily at a hotel as they could at her house. At least if she was home, she'd have her studio, her own bed, and maybe she'd be able to deduce what the feds had been looking for based on what had been taken. Wherever she was, she wasn't going to wait around and play defense, and it would be easier to mount an offense if she was in a familiar setting.

He pulled into the driveway and put the car in park. "Fine," he said. "I know how you are once you've made up your mind."

"I hope you're not about to deny that your genes have anything to do with my stubborn streak," Ellery said in an effort to break the tension. Truth was she could use his help. As overbearing as he was, he was a fierce advocate and had a brilliant legal mind. His presence during all of this was fortuitous and, as soon as she had more information, she'd gladly take advantage of his skill. "So, are you going to stay here or check into a hotel?" It would be more convenient to work together if he stayed at her house, but if he went off to a hotel, she'd have a much easier time slipping out when she needed to without having to explain her movements. She glanced at the clock on the dashboard. It was ten thirty. She'd have to hustle if she was going to make it to meet Sarah. If her father stuck around, she wasn't sure how she was going to explain her sudden need to duck out to him.

"If you'd rather have your privacy I'll get a room, but I'd feel much better if you'd let me stay. I promised Leo a case of beer and a bottle of really good bourbon if he'd keep an eye on you."

Ellery sighed. It wasn't in her to send family packing. She clasped his shoulder. "Stay. I've got plenty of room. And thanks for everything today. I know running interference for me wasn't what you had planned for your trip."

"Not hardly, but I'm happy to do it." The expression in his eyes was distant and his words eerily hollow. "I'm always here for you. I hope you realize that."

She'd never seen him look so maudlin. Maybe he'd had more to drink than she thought. She started to ask him about the source of his angst, but decided she didn't have the energy to expend on anyone's issues but her own. No, she needed to keep her focus on whatever Sarah Flores had to say.

Once they were in the house, Ellery led him to the guest room, and within twenty minutes, the lights were out. She left a note on the kitchen counter and headed out to her car. She'd just opened the door when Leo's voice cut through the night.

"Figured you were in for the night."

She walked across her driveway and stood below his porch. "As far as anyone knows, I am." She gestured toward the house. "Whatever he's paying you, I'll double it."

"You sure you'll be able to pay up? I hear Uncle Sam's got all your money."

"Uncle Sam doesn't have anything to do with this. I'm on it."

"I got your back, girlie. If you're not home by morning, I'll raise the alarms."

She reached up and shook his outstretched hand before making her way to her truck. There were days when she'd prefer not to have all her comings and goings carefully chronicled by Leo, but it was nice to know he was keeping an eye on things.

She'd only made it to the end of the street before her phone rang. Either she'd been caught by her father or Sarah was impatient. She stopped at the sign and fished the phone from her pocket. Meg's name flashed on her screen. It was after eleven. Meg was a night owl, but as much as a pest as she'd been since Ellery had left the firm, she'd never called this late. Ellery picked up the call. "Meg, what's up?"

"We need to talk."

"Look, I know you're upset, but I'm sure everything can be explained. Maybe we can meet and go over our old client list. I'm sure this is one of those deals where they're trying to pressure us to get at a client."

"If only it were that. I'm at the place where we tried out those fake IDs our first year in college. If you leave your house now you can be here in fifteen minutes."

Ellery knew the drill. Whatever Meg had to say, she couldn't or wouldn't say over the phone and the shrill edge to her voice meant whatever she had to say was urgent. "I can see you first thing in the morning. Wherever you want."

"It won't wait. I'll see you when you get here."

"Meg." Ellery waited a few seconds before she pulled the phone away from her ear to look at the screen, but she already knew the line was dead. She'd worked with Meg for years and it wasn't like her to engage in histrionics. Whatever she wanted to talk about was not only urgent, but too sensitive to talk about over the phone. Any other day, Ellery would have declined to engage in this kind of covert drama, but today hadn't been like any other day.

She had fifteen minutes before she was supposed to meet Sarah. She couldn't call her because she didn't have her number. The only time she'd called it had been on her landline at home and the caller ID had only showed a blocked line, which was normal for a federal office. Since she was headed in the opposite direction from where Meg was waiting, there was no way she could run by, tell Sarah there'd been a change of plans and make it back across town to Meg. Not to mention, she didn't have a clue what she would tell Sarah if she could bend time and make the trip. "Hey, my former law partner, you know, the one whose office was raided this morning? Well, she has something important to tell me, but pay no attention to whatever it might be. Catch you later."

No, she really didn't have a choice. She'd go see what Meg wanted and whatever Sarah had to say could wait until morning. As she turned the car around, she tried not to think about Sarah in her captivating red dress, sitting at a bar, waiting for her. Lying in wait was more like it. Despite the palpable sizzle of attraction between them, Ellery was cool-headed enough to realize Sarah had a dual purpose for wanting to meet her that had nothing to do with sex appeal. She was probably better off postponing the meeting until she had a good night's sleep and some distance from the arousal that rested just below the surface of her skin.

Meg was seated near the rear of Snuffers, the beer and burger place they'd frequented when they were in college. The place was packed with the late night drinking crowd, and Ellery was surprised she'd managed to score a seat. She slid into the booth and launched right in. "What's up?"

Meg nodded slightly and shot a look at the young waitress approaching their table. Ellery noted Meg had a full mug of beer in front of her, and she ordered one too mostly to give the waitress something to do, far away from their table. She waited until the girl was lost in the crowd of coeds before she spoke. "At least give me a hint."

"Does anyone know you're here?"

"Besides you and the several hundred other people in this place? No." She leaned across the table. "Look, Meg, you're starting to scare me."

"You think you're scared. You weren't at the office, meeting with new clients when the feds burst in with guns drawn. This is serious."

"If anyone knows it's serious, I do. The manager at the Melrose booted me out of the place because none of my credit cards would go through. My bank accounts are frozen, and I had to sneak out of the gallery earlier because protestors had lined up across the street. I promise you, I know it's serious, but I also know I didn't do anything wrong. Now, what's so important that you had to sneak in a meeting with me this late?"

She reached into her purse and pulled out a flash drive and set it on the table.

"What's on this?" Ellery asked.

"It's a copy of the search warrant affidavit."

"I thought it was sealed."

"It is."

Ellery reached across the table and palmed the drive. She wanted to know how Meg had gotten her hands on it, but more than that, she wanted to jump up from the table and find the nearest computer. Just a few clicks of the mouse and she'd know the details of the government's case. But if what was on the drive was all she needed to know, Meg could have slipped it to her without this late night clandestine meeting. "Tell me."

The waitress reappeared and Ellery tapped her finger on the table while she carefully arranged their drinks and lingered to ask if they'd like to order some food.

"No, thanks. We're good for a while. I'll wave if we need anything." The waitress left and Ellery turned back to Meg. "Spill." She held up the drive. "What's on this?"

"I'll tell you what's on it and then I'll tell you what's not on it, but what the feds are going to find out sooner or later." She pushed aside her glass of beer. "The feds think that you set up Amir's foundation, Welcome Home International, that you opened their bank accounts, most of which are located out of country, and that you are the mastermind behind their ability to funnel money to organizations in Libya that are posing as charitable organizations but are actually terrorist recruitment centers."

Oddly enough, the sheer craziness of the allegations left Ellery feeling relieved. "Well, that's ridiculous. Talk about far-reaching. We've seen plenty of crazy accusations before, but this might top them all."

"It might, but it's not as crazy as it might sound."

Ellery tensed. "What are you talking about?"

"They have documents. A power of attorney that grants you authority to act on behalf of WHI in all financial matters."

"Wait a minute. I don't know anything about that."

"Did you know that you're listed on their IRS nonprofit filings as the attorney for the organization?"

"That's insane. And, no I didn't know anything about that. It has to be a mistake. You know I've never done any work for Amir's businesses other than to represent him at a few code violation hearings. I never had anything to do with the nonprofits."

"That's what I thought too."

Ellery stared Meg in the eyes and saw traces of doubt. "Meg, I've never lied to you and I'm not lying now." An idea popped into her head. "Wait a minute, if I was involved, my signature would be on corporate filings, right?"

"Not necessarily. The president of the organization, Amir, can sign the corporate filings on his own."

Ellery's hands shook as she tried to process this information. Knowing she was innocent of any wrongdoing didn't change the fact that someone was focused on implicating her in a horrible crime. That she had no clue why made it worse. She picked up the drive and shoved it in her pocket. All she could think about was doing something concrete and she'd start by examining whatever evidence she could glean from the search warrant affidavit. First step: get the facts. Second step: formulate a strategy. Third step: go on the offense. "I need to see all of this for myself. Thanks, Meg. I really appreciate you getting this for me. I'm sure it wasn't easy."

She stood up, but Meg's hand on her arm stopped her from leaving. "What?" she asked, dreading the answer.

"There's more. You're going to want to sit down for this."

Unable to imagine what could be worse, Ellery hesitated before finally shaking her head and sinking back into the booth. "Spit it out."

Meg sighed. "The agents took all of our files. They said I'd have to check with the AUSA assigned to the case to make arrangements to make copies."

Ellery nodded. She had no idea why Meg was telling her this, but she decided to go along. "Don't count on that being quick. Remember when they tied up that ambulance company's files for months and then they had to vet every copy service we wanted to use?"

"I do. That's why a few months ago when Jonas, our IT guy, recommended we start scanning every scrap of paper and backing it up to the cloud, I bit the bullet even though getting it done was extremely expensive."

"That's great. So you have all your files?"

"Yes. Everything including a backup of all our computer systems. I had Jonas run some searches early this evening based on what I read in the search warrant."

Ellery braced for Meg's next words, knowing she was about to drop a bomb. "Okay."

"I found the power of attorney form. Essentially the same one that was attached to the IRS filing. This one didn't have your name filled in, but it did have Amir's name on the signature block and it granted whoever was to be designated the power to deal with every aspect of the WHI's financial dealings."

"I didn't draft that. Are you saying I did?"

"I know you didn't. But I didn't either."

Meg's stare threatened to bore holes in her head, but Ellery couldn't process what she was trying to get her to understand. "But you're saying someone with access to our system did draft it." As her mind sifted through the possibilities, she checked them each off the list. A few paralegals. A few associates, but none who'd ever worked with Amir. He'd always been very particular that he only work with partners in the firm. In fact, as much as he liked her now, he'd been hesitant to take her advice in the beginning, preferring to rely on the man who'd handled his affairs for years.

"My father. Are you saying my father drafted the power of attorney?"

Meg nodded. "The metadata shows it was done on his computer. It was dated about six months before the charity was formed. There were other documents as well, documents Amir would have needed to set up the foundation. It wasn't you, but it was him. I have no doubt."

Funny she should use the word doubt, because doubt was all Ellery had now. Doubt about who she could trust, doubt about her own judgment. Meg appeared crestfallen at the prospect her mentor might have betrayed them, but Ellery reserved judgment. Simply creating documents didn't make him culpable of terrorist activity. As much as this information gave Ellery pause, she needed to know more before she could draw any conclusions. "What else should I know?"

Meg shook her head. "That's a loaded question. I'm running searches on the documents we have just so we're prepared for whatever the feds find. I can only pray there are no more surprises like this one, but you can bet there's a lot more to this. The feds executed searches using this same warrant on Amir's home and the mosque where WHI has their offices. I tried to call him to discuss it and he wouldn't take my call. My guess is he's moved on to other counsel since we're under a microscope right now."

Her words were injected with a heavy dose of anger and Ellery ducked the weight of it. She had enough of her own stuff to be angry about, but she wasn't going to vent here. She stood up. "I'd buy, but all my money's frozen." She patted her pocket. "Thanks for this. I'll find out what I can and be in touch. You do the same." She didn't wait for a response before leaving. Meg would have to find someone else to share her pity party. Ellery was going to focus her efforts on finding the truth because the truth was the only thing that would set her free.

❖

"Sure I can't get you a real drink?"

Sarah looked up from her watered down glass of tonic. The bartender was tall like Ellery and had the same color hair, but the likeness ended there. She looked at her watch. Twelve fifteen. It was time to face the fact Ellery wasn't going to show up, but the question remained: had she ever intended to? She found it hard to believe Ellery would have stood her up on purpose, but it wasn't like this was a date. Maybe her father had put a bug in her ear and convinced her a late night meeting with a federal agent was likely to do more harm than good. And he might've been right. Sarah found it difficult to resolve all of her personal observations of Ellery with her training to root out evil, but she could tell Ellery was hiding something. The question was whether that something had anything to do with the bombing, and it looked like that question was going to go unanswered tonight.

She set her glass on the bar and asked for the check. When the bartender waved her off, she tossed a ten on the bar and made her way to the door. To her it was late, but judging by the line outside, this place was just starting to heat up for the night. She acknowledged a few appreciative glances with a nod, but nothing was more attractive right now than the thought of her bed and a good night's sleep. She slid into her car, and raced the short distance home.

She collected her mail from the box and slid her key into the door, but stopped before turning it as a slow sense of dread shuddered down her spine. The door was unlocked and no way had she left it like that. She leaned close and listened, hearing nothing but the light sound of the air conditioning whirring in the distance, but she knew without a doubt someone was inside. Inside, where her weapon was locked up in the safe in her study. How quickly she'd gone from the habit of carrying her trusty Glock everywhere to hardly ever carrying it when she was off duty. Unlike serial killers, con men didn't usually pose the threat of serious bodily injury.

She paused to think the situation through. The sound of her key in the door was enough to alert anyone inside that she was home. She could turn around and leave or burst through the door and hope she was fast enough to beat their obvious advantage. The decision only took a moment. She wasn't about to abandon her home to an intruder. She calculated that if someone were waiting for her, they would be sitting in the living room that was situated directly in front of the entryway. If they were burglars, they were probably busy stuffing whatever they could find into bags. Either way, if she acted quickly, she might have a chance. In one solid movement, she twisted the doorknob and shouldered the door open, bending low to gain momentum as she dashed over her threshold and into the study to the right of the door.

She'd barely made it to the safe, when she heard a familiar voice. "You run like you're out of shape, kid. What the hell kind of work are you doing that you don't have time to get to a gym?"

Damn. Sarah bent over as the adrenaline coursed out of her body and all the exhaustion of the day came roaring back. When she finally got her breath, she stood up and faced her intruder. "What the fuck, Trip? A little warning would be nice."

"Just testing your skills. Making sure that desk job didn't make you go all soft."

She punched him on the shoulder on her way to the kitchen. Time to have that drink she'd passed on at the bar. Head in the fridge, she called out, "Beer?"

"Always."

She opened a bottle for him and fixed herself a stiff gin and tonic. As she handed him the bottle she said, "You don't deserve this. Seriously, what the hell were you thinking?"

He took a long pull off the beer and then settled into her favorite chair. "I was thinking you'd be happy to see me and glad I didn't ask you to pick me up from the airport. What're you all dressed up for?"

She looked down at her dress. She felt foolish knowing she'd dressed up for a woman who was not only not interested in her, but was in the eye of a huge shit storm. "Drink your beer. I'll be right back."

In her bedroom, she dug sweats out of her dresser drawer and tugged them on. She left her dress in a pile on the floor and stepped into the bathroom to scrub her face. Monday, she'd take the dress to the cleaners and then hang it back up in the closet where it would probably hang for months. Her brief dip into the Dallas scene was over for a while. Barefoot and comfortable, she joined Trip back in the living room.

"Now, that's the Flores I remember."

His words made her grimace. "Yep, the one who won't be getting dates anytime soon. I'm guessing you didn't fly all the way out here to toss me off this case."

"Not a chance. But you'll need to work on the down low. I told the director you already have an in with the attorney and he wants you to do whatever you need to get as close as possible, but it's important you don't tip anyone off. Pretty sure the folks over at HSI would have a hissy if they knew we were stepping on their toes."

"Wait, you're telling me BAU is officially on this?"

"'Officially' is not exactly the word I would use."

"What you mean is the director ordered it, but will deny he did if whoever is assigned to this little project gets caught."

"Exactly. But you're too good to get caught. I've already got a call in to Robert Mason. When he calls me back, I'll let him know that I need you to finish up some work you were doing on the Atlanta case. That'll give you some autonomy in the office."

"Why don't you just yank me out of my new job altogether?"

"Too suspicious. I hear that attorney's pretty smart. If you're going to get close to her, you'll need to be one step ahead."

"Hold it right there." Sarah held up a hand. It was time for her to let Trip know she had no intention of working on his little scheme. "I left the unit for good reasons and those reasons haven't changed. You're going to need to find someone else to play spy."

He cocked his head. "You're kidding, right?" He set his beer down. "Who else are we going to find? You know any other agents with your level of training who also happen to have access? Don't think I don't know where you were tonight. Look, we don't know if she's involved in the bombing or not, but we do know she was the lawyer for the folks that may have been behind it. People tell their lawyers things. Things they won't tell anyone else. She may know something even if she doesn't realize it. All you need to do is get close to her and find out what she knows or encourage her to find out what she doesn't. Piece of cake."

Still angry that he'd had her followed, Sarah stifled the impulse to tell him off. Of course, he had eyes on her. It was part of his job and Trip was all about the job. She used to be too, but look where it had gotten her—mid thirties and single with no prospect of that changing in the foreseeable future. Besides, Ellery standing her up at the bar was a clear signal she wasn't as good at this as she used to be. "If you know what I was doing tonight, then you also know Ellery promised to meet me after the event and she didn't show."

He nodded. "Something happened. She was headed your way and then she turned the car around." He showed her a picture on his phone. "She met with her old law partner at a place on lower Greenville. I hear they used to be a thing. Maybe it was a booty call."

Sarah tamped down the mental image of Ellery hooking up with the gorgeous redhead in the picture. Would Ellery really have abandoned the opportunity to learn more about the case against her for a late night rendezvous? Maybe celebrating a successful show had seemed more important than criminal charges. Sarah tried hard not to compare herself with the woman in the photo, but it was hard. "I guess whoever you had following her wasn't good enough to find out if she blew me off for business or pleasure."

"She left alone, but she hasn't gotten home yet. I called off the tail. Late night, not much traffic. No sense getting made. Besides, we have a tracker on her car."

Sarah wondered if they had a warrant for the tracker. She was definitely going soft. She wouldn't have given the method a second thought when she was at BAU. Whatever it took to bring in the bad guy was the mantra there. As long as they had enough legally admissible evidence to make the case, a few cut corners here and there wouldn't get in the way of a closed case.

"Who knows? Maybe she blew off the redhead and doubled back to meet you."

Maybe she had, but it didn't matter. Her attraction to Ellery was both strong and completely unsustainable. If she agreed to do what Trip wanted, it would have to be because of the job and not her attraction to Ellery. A good BAU agent had focus and objectivity. She had neither when it came to Ellery Durant, not to mention that diving completely into this project meant breaking the promise she'd made when she moved to Dallas.

"Trip, I care about this case, I really do, but I'm not the one for this job. I left BAU for a reason. I need a life. Not a fake, string some woman along to get information to build a case against her life, but a real life. This job can't be everything I have. I want a lover, a family, hobbies that don't include going to the range and analyzing psychos. I'm never going to have that if I keep getting pulled back in."

His eyes were kind, but his expression was firm as he said, "If I was trying to trap you in your old life, I wouldn't have let you leave Atlanta when you did. You can have all that sappy stuff, but I just need you to do this one thing."

He needn't have begged. No matter how she tried to resist, the instinct to respond to the call of duty was in her DNA, and the desire to see Ellery again, under any circumstances, was unstoppable.

CHAPTER TWELVE

Ellery rolled out of bed the moment she heard the rattle of pots and pans. She hadn't slept, and it had taken every ounce of self-control she had not to wake her father in the middle of the night to demand answers. Now that he was up, she wasn't going to wait any longer. She pulled on a pair of sweats and her running shoes and grabbed her keys.

He was standing in the middle of kitchen with a carton of eggs in one hand and a frying pan in the other. "Good morning," he said. "Please tell me you have bacon."

"Put all that away. We're going out to eat."

"Not a chance. When's the last time I made you one of my famous omelets? If you don't have bacon, I can figure out a substitute." He poked his head in the refrigerator. "Ham, or maybe—"

She cut him off. "Dad, we're going out. I have a very specific craving." She jingled her keys. "Come on. My treat."

He started to say something, but she wagged a finger at him and he finally got the hint. He put the eggs back in the fridge. "Okay, out it is. Who am I to turn down a free meal?"

When they walked out of the house, she motioned to Leo's Plymouth and unlocked the doors. Leo, who was nursing an enormous mug of coffee, stuck his head out from behind his morning newspaper and said, "Use it for as long as you need. Lord knows she doesn't get much action anymore."

Ellery smiled for the first time since the show last night, and the action provoked the memory of Sarah smiling at her from across the showroom floor, a smile that had almost allowed her to forget the horrible day she'd had leading up to the show. A smile that almost made her forget that she and Sarah were adversaries. She wondered what Sarah had thought when she hadn't shown up at the bar last night. Had she waited long? When she figured out she'd been stood up, had she found someone there to occupy her time? In that sexy red dress she'd probably had to fight off candidates for that position.

"Do you want me to drive?"

Ellery looked up at her father who was standing by the car. Time to stop thinking about Sarah Flores and focus on herself. "No, I got it."

They were several blocks away from the house before her father spoke. "I get that you didn't want to talk in the house, but I doubt anyone bugged your neighbor's car on the off chance you might be driving it around."

His offhand tone burrowed under her skin. In a few days, or maybe even today if this talk didn't go well, he would get on a plane and fly back to his carefree retirement spent regaling law students with tales of his glory days. She'd be left to face the fallout of whatever nightmare he'd created. That he could act as if she shouldn't be totally and completely on guard was galling. "I don't think you get how big of a deal this investigation is."

"What's that supposed to mean? I've handled plenty of high profile cases in my life. More than you ever will. I know exactly what's in store for you."

Ellery bristled at his condescending tone. "Is that supposed to be a jab? I made a choice to quit practicing. It was a personal choice and had nothing to do with you, so I don't understand why you continue to act like it was a personal affront that I quit the practice."

"Because it was. I spent my life building that practice and you let it go after little more than a decade. It was our legacy."

"Correction," she said. "It was your legacy."

"You were a brilliant lawyer."

Ellery sighed. "Funny, you never said that when we worked together."

"Maybe I was afraid to praise you too much for fear you'd quit striving to be better."

She could tell he was trying to buffer his remarks, but his words burrowed under her skin. "How can you still not get me? It's not in me to quit striving to be better. I'll always be a perfectionist, just like you and just like Mom, but if I choose to apply my energy in a different direction than you expect, suddenly I'm a quitter."

"There's no doubt you have many talents, I just hate to see you waste this particular one. Not everyone has the gift of advocacy."

"Well, it's a good thing I've got it because it looks like I'm going to need it now more than ever."

"You're not alone in this. I'm going to stick around, work on your case. I'll call in some favors to make sure you have a legal defense dream team."

"No, you won't. I'll be dealing with this on my own."

"That doesn't make any sense. Let me help you."

"It's true I need help, but you're the last person that can help me." She pounded a fist on the steering wheel. "You're probably the reason I'm in this mess in the first place."

"What are you talking about?"

Ellery pulled into a parking lot at White Rock Lake, and motioned for her father to follow her out of the car. When they were about fifty feet from the car and well out of earshot of the cyclists and joggers who were making their way around the lake, she told him everything Meg had told her the night before. As she spoke, he started to pace and she recognized the familiar sign of increasing agitation. He barely waited for her to finish before saying, "And you seriously think I helped terrorists set up a funding channel for their enterprise?"

"What am I supposed to think?" Ellery viewed it as an honest question rather than an accusation.

"I should hope you know me better than that. I've known Amir Khan for years. I've handled code violations for his businesses and petty crimes for various relatives, but never, not once, has he asked me to do anything illegal."

"Did you draft the filing for his charity?" His gaze was firmly fixed on the ground, and Ellery knew something was up. She pressed him again. "Dad, I need to know if you helped Amir set up Welcome Home International. Tell me."

He bowed his head for a moment and when he looked back up, she saw guilt reflected in his eyes. "You did, didn't you?"

He shook his head. "Yes, I mean no, not really. It's complicated."

"I haven't got anything better to do, so start explaining." She motioned to a bench near the lake's edge. They walked over and she sat down while he continued to pace, his furtive movements scattering the ducks that were hanging out near the shoreline. The pacing was one of his signature habits. When in trial, he always managed to cover the entire well of the courtroom when he was making arguments to a jury. She'd developed a different style, preferring to let the weight of her words speak on their own rather than reinforce them with exaggerated movements. They were so alike, yet so different in so many ways, and, although she knew he sometimes glossed over the finer points of things, she doubted he would ever purposefully do anything that placed others at risk.

But was that even true? He'd worked hard to get not guilty verdicts for people he knew were dangerous. But so had she and every other criminal defense attorney who was any good at what they did. She'd been so good at arguing away the faults of others, her talent had come back to haunt her and was the primary reason she'd left the practice. But helping someone commit a crime was vastly different from holding the state accountable to their burden to prove guilt.

"Amir came to me with one of his cousins. I don't even remember his name. They were interested in setting up a foundation, a charity for displaced Middle Eastern refugees, but they were concerned about the laws enacted after 9/11 and rightly so. I told them about the increased scrutiny that such charities faced, especially after the Holy Land prosecution, and they asked me a lot of questions about how to set up a foundation that would stay off the government's radar."

"What did you tell them?"

"I told them they should talk to someone who specialized in that type of work. A tax lawyer or someone who worked with non-profit organizations."

"But that wasn't the end of it, was it?"

"You know how Amir can be. When he decides you can help him, there's no dissuading him. Meg mentioned he insisted you meet him at the courthouse to help Naveed. It was like that."

"No, it wasn't." She was used to this refrain. For the years they'd been in practice together, his proclivity for taking on matters that were outside his specialty had always been a source of contention. Ellery steadfastly believed in referring out cases she wasn't qualified to handle, but he had always insisted on helping current clients, especially well paying ones, with whatever they chose to ask. "I'm a board certified criminal defense lawyer—more than qualified to help Naveed with his felony case. You have no experience in setting up a foundation other than knowing what to do to avoid prosecution. Did you draft their initial documents or not?"

He stared at her for a moment. "I did. It was nothing more than a draft. I told him he would need to run it by a specialist to make sure it was done correctly." He paused for a beat and then his voice got lower. "I also answered some hypothetical questions about funding the foundation's efforts. I may have suggested they select someone in the community who was above reproach to be the face of any financial dealings they engaged in, but I swear I had no idea they were up to anything other than helping people."

She knew the instant he delivered the words—he'd told Amir how he could break the law, and the expression on his face signaled he now realized the consequences of his actions. But he looked more sheepish than surprised, and she realized he'd already figured out exactly what he'd done well before his trip here. "Dad, why are you here?"

"What?"

"What prompted this little visit?"

"Can't a father visit his daughter for no reason at all?"

"If you'd ever done it before, it might not seem so suspicious. You know something, don't you?"

"Not really. When I heard about the bomb, I don't know, I just had a feeling."

She didn't believe he would have traveled back to Dallas because of a feeling and she said so. "There's something more. Something you're not telling me."

"I've told you everything I can."

"You realize you could be charged as a conspirator for giving Amir advice that helped him go against the law?" Anger rose up to burn her insides and she could hear her voice rising. She forced her next questions into a whisper, "Are you going to stand by and let me be charged too?"

He shook his head forcefully. "Of course not. It doesn't sound like you knew anything about it and the less you know, the better off you are."

"Do you really think you're protecting me by not telling me whatever it is that you know? Why did you even come here?"

He raised his hands in surrender. "I swear I don't know anything about the bombing. I was worried about you. Your mother was too. I promised I would come check in on you. I'll help you find a good attorney and then I'll get out of your hair. Believe me, it's best. If things get bad, I'll figure something out. I promise I will."

Ellery couldn't help but feel that she'd been played. She was convinced her father had used this trip to find out what he could about his own culpability and now he was leaving her to deal with the fallout. She was pissed off and had no idea what to say to him. She had no idea what to do about any of this, but she was sure about one thing. He had better leave or she would throw him out.

❖

Sarah locked the door of her apartment and walked to the Katy Trail for her morning run. The trail was tucked away behind her building, so secluded only residents and regulars even knew it was there. The urban gem was a primary reason she'd chosen this part of town when she'd started hunting for a place to live. She loved being able to walk out her front door and a few feet later start running through Dallas without having to dodge cars. It reminded her of D.C. where there were plenty of running trails situated throughout the city.

Until last night the trail was the only thing that reminded her of D.C. Now politics threatened to eclipse the fresh start she'd embarked on when she moved here. After Trip's late night visit, she'd spent most of the rest of the night thinking about the case against Amir Khan and Ellery Durant. Neither of them had been arrested, but they'd both had their assets frozen and search warrants executed on their homes and offices, or in Ellery's case, former office. She'd confirmed with Trip the night before that the tactic was to get one of them to talk and divulge what they knew that could point to who actually set the bomb. All bets were on Ellery to be the first to flip. Trip figured Ellery would hire a high-powered defense attorney to reach out to the AUSA on the case to broker the deal.

Sarah had a feeling they'd underestimated their opponent. Ellery didn't seem like the sort to rat out a client to get herself out of a jam, but maybe she was letting her increasing attraction for Ellery get in the way of her usually stellar ability to predict behavior. If Trip had known how she felt, he probably would've found someone else for this particular assignment. Or would he? Could be he thought her attraction to the suspect would allow her to get closer, have a better chance at rooting out her involvement in the case.

The only thing she was certain of was the very thought of seeing Ellery again got her blood pumping. Every night, as she'd slipped into sleep, thoughts of Ellery dominated her thoughts. The only way she was going to erase her desire for Ellery was to replace it with something or someone else. She should go back to Sue Ellen's and find a willing partner, but for now she pounded through her run, dodging dogs and parents with their running strollers on the busy trail.

Within a few moments, she slipped into a rhythm and let her rising endorphins take over. While the rush did nothing to cool her feelings, it did give her a sense of clarity, and she used the time on the path to review everything she knew so far. After ticking through the events of the week, Sarah discovered a couple of things that bothered her. She'd spent every evening this week going through the files that the agents from HSI had hauled off from her office on Monday. No one knew she had them on her home computer, and she hadn't felt the need to share that little tidbit, especially since she'd seen nothing truly remarkable other than what she'd already flagged. The connection between Amir Khan's charity and Saheed Jafari's foundation was significant, and the overseas bank account was a red flag, but none of what she'd seen definitively pointed to terrorism, and she hadn't seen anything that pointed to Ellery.

Going after lawyers was a big deal and the justice department had a reputation of treading softly in this area. Although Ellery hadn't been detained, the fact that her home and former office were searched and her accounts frozen meant someone in one of the agencies working this case had solid evidence against her. Judging by how fast they moved against her, she found it hard to believe this evidence had popped up just this week.

Two miles in now, she ached with the delicious slow burn of her muscles pulsing through the run. She kept running and used the rhythm to give her clarity. She examined every aspect of last Monday. She'd come to the office with donuts. She'd reviewed files with Liz. She'd called Ellery. They'd met for coffee. She'd gotten a phone call to return to the office. Upon her return, she'd found Liz with Mason and they'd been going through her desk. She'd given them the paper files and Liz had admitted she'd gone to Mason with her concerns about the charities. She hadn't thought a lot about it at the time, but she'd been slightly ticked off at Liz since she'd asked her to wait so she could run down the facts before she put everyone on alert. Liz had agreed on her strategy, so what had happened that day that had changed Liz's mind? And why hadn't she come to her to discuss it first?

The unanswered questions jogged her out of her rhythm and she looked up at the bright blue sky and the still rising sun. It was going to be a beautiful spring day. The kind meant for patios and beer and grilling. When she'd taken this job, she'd thought weekends like these would be hers for doing all of those things, but here she was, whirring through the facts of a case that was determined to elude her. The faster she got some answers, the faster she could resume her new life. She looked at her watch. It was just after ten. Plenty of time to go home, shower, change, and show up ready to take a certain woman to brunch and see if she could get some answers.

CHAPTER THIRTEEN

Ellery parked Leo's car in a metered space on McKinney Avenue. Before she stepped out, she pulled up the hood of her dark blue sweatshirt. Between it and her Ray-Bans, there was little chance she'd be recognized. She didn't care so much about being spotted as a suspect in the case—last night had already placed her front and center in the public eye. Her desire to be incognito today had more to do with what she had planned for this little outing.

The distance from the car to her old firm was about a quarter mile and the weather was perfect for a Saturday morning walk. Any other Saturday, she might have been in this part of town for pleasure, enjoying brunch at one of the many restaurants here in Uptown or browsing the shops. As it was, she blended in with the hipsters strolling the streets even if her plans had nothing to do with weekend leisure.

The Victorian house where she'd spent her entire former career was on a side street sandwiched between a real estate office and a print shop. She'd always loved the character of the place, despite the attendant troubles of maintaining an older building. The house had so much more charm than the many sterile skyscrapers further south, and clients had a much easier time navigating their way to appointments since it was located outside the crowded downtown area. The best thing about this place right now was that her parents had maintained ownership of the building, even after she'd left the firm.

The arrangement had been a sore spot for Meg who had offered higher than market value to purchase the building along with the firm's book of business, but Gordon had resisted selling. The building had been in the family for generations and, while he would have had no problem passing ownership to his daughter, he didn't want the house to leave the family. Meg hadn't wanted to move, so she leased it from the Durants. Before she'd put him in a cab that morning, Ellery had insisted he get her a copy of the key from the local company that managed the property in his absence, and now she stood at the back door to the building ready to unlock the door.

There weren't any cars out front or in the small allotment of spaces out back, so she was reasonably certain no one was inside. She turned the key slowly and gently pushed the door open, stepping quickly inside and punching in the code for the alarm. She walked past the kitchen, coveting a cup of coffee, but she needed to get in and out before anyone discovered her here.

The flash drive Meg had given her contained the search warrant affidavit and she'd spent the night reading the thirty-page document. A lot of it was fluff, ramblings about how the lead HSI agent had expertise in these matters and, based on his expertise, he expected to find evidence of these crimes in the following places and in the following formats, thereby justifying the warrant. The boilerplate language was followed by a series of specific allegations about Welcome Home International and a sister foundation, Global Enterprise Alliance. She recognized the name of the GEA founder. She didn't think the firm had ever had any dealings with him, but she couldn't be certain and that was one of the reasons why she was here this morning. She could've called Meg and asked her the questions that had popped up since last night, but she hadn't wanted to use the phone to ask anything about the case. More importantly, she wasn't sure who she could trust. The fact that Meg had neglected to include on the drive the forms that had been drafted by her father for WHI, gave her pause. Why would she go to all the trouble to meet her late at night with the search warrant affidavit and tell her about the other forms, but not bring them with her?

She owned the fact she might be overly suspicious, but at this point she had nothing to lose by being cautious, although coming here was the opposite of caution. If Meg or one of her associates showed up at the office right now, she'd make up some lie about checking on the property, but Meg would know better, so she'd have to work fast if she wanted to avoid detection.

She headed straight for Meg's office. When she'd moved out, Meg had taken over the space she'd inherited when her father moved to Chicago. The large office occupied two thirds of the top floor of the building. When she'd had this space, she decorated it with handmade pieces of furniture she'd created in her spare time, enjoying the juxtaposition of her hobby and her profession in the same environment. Meg, in contrast, had populated the space with more modern touches, glass and chrome, which gave the place a lighter, less substantial feel. Now, it looked more like an advertising agency than a law firm, but the office still had two perfect features: a second, private stairwell that she could use to escape when a particularly trying client was waiting downstairs and an amazing balcony that overlooked the quiet street below. Her father used to invite everyone in the office out to the balcony for drinks after a particularly good win in court. She'd continued the tradition and even added a grill.

She resisted the urge to walk outside, sink into one of the cushioned chairs on the deck and enjoy the beautiful spring day. There was no time to indulge in memories, especially since not all of them were good. Instead she sat behind Meg's desk and moved the mouse, happy to see the large monitor on her desk spring to life. The box on the screen asked for a password and she took a shot, hoping Meg's habits hadn't changed.

Within seconds, she was in. She looked around the screen for something that would give her access to the cloud where the firm's documents were being backed up to, and her eyes landed on the Dropbox icon. She put in Meg's e-mail address as the user name and drummed her fingers on the desk as she considered whether Meg would be so careless as to use the same password for these files as she used everywhere else. She held her breath while she typed in the word 1Litigator and waited while the spinning beach ball on the screen did its thing. One, two, three seconds passed and the program opened to an array of folders, all neatly labeled with the names of the firm's clients.

Ellery scanned the files and located everyone who had even the slightest connection to Amir Khan, but she didn't find anything she didn't already know. His son Naveed's case was here along with minor infractions she'd handled for his older children and his businesses. She didn't see a file folder for Sadeem Jafari, the founder of GEA, but she typed his name into the search box anyway. Within seconds, several files appeared and she clicked on the first one, labeled Certificate of Formation. She'd never seen the particular document before, but recognized it as one a new business filed with the state upon incorporating. She scanned the entire document which listed Jafari as the President of GEA, curious why Meg hadn't mentioned that she'd represented this individual who was named in a search warrant for an investigation into her.

Nothing about the filing itself raised any red flags, but she copied the document onto the flash drive she'd brought along. Next she searched for the documents her father had supposedly created for Amir. She found several versions, but all of them appeared to be drafts. None of them were signed and the space for the person appointed to hold the power of attorney for WHI was blank.

Maybe her father had told the truth and he'd merely given hypothetical advice to Amir and Amir had chosen on his own to put her name down to give legitimacy to his enterprise. Or maybe her father had given him tacit permission to do so. She knew he had a habit of not wanting to put some of his shady advice in writing. She could see him handing Amir a flash drive with the draft document on it and telling him exactly what to do to give the organization legitimacy.

But none of these speculations gave her any real insight into why the feds were targeting Amir and, by association, her as suspects in the bombing. The search warrant didn't even mention the bombing directly, but it talked about aid from the specified charities going to fund terrorist organizations and how some of those organizations had increasingly been recruiting American citizens to take part in terrorist activities both here and abroad. It had even mentioned the recent arrests of American citizens traveling to Syria to enroll at terrorist training camps. The agents who'd searched her house had as good as told her father they suspected she was involved in the bombing, but the allegations in the search warrant affidavit weren't enough to implicate her directly. Since she knew the evidence to tie her to the crime didn't exist, she would have to prove a negative if she was going to clear her name, but she wasn't going to prove anything sitting here. She copied the draft documents onto her drive with the rest of the files and signed off Meg's computer. The screen had just faded to black when she heard a door open downstairs.

"Shit," she whispered and looked around for a place to hide. Meg's office was a big open space and she'd be spotted in an instant if someone climbed the stairs. She pocketed her flash drive and walked toward the partially open door, careful to step softly on the wood floor and avoid the boards she knew would squeak. She saw a shadow pass through the hall below, but she couldn't tell who it was before the person slipped into the supply room. She considered her options. She could walk down the back stairwell, but without knowing exactly where the person downstairs was, she might be discovered. She could walk down the main stairs and bluff through some story about how she'd just come by to check on an issue the property manager had reported, or she could find a way to sneak out. The outside balcony was an option, but it was a steep drop from the railing to the ground below and she was likely to attract attention from someone passing by if she tumbled into the front lawn.

While she ran through her options, she heard a voice and she strained to listen. She recognized the male voice as that of one of the associates that Meg had hired just before she'd quit the practice, Karl Lundberg. Young and ambitious, it was no wonder he was here working on the weekend. She only heard one voice and decided he must be talking to someone on the phone.

"Are you sure you set it?" he said. "I just got here and it wasn't on…No, nothing looks out of place. Do you think the agents came back? I know they aren't supposed to come in without letting us know, but do you really think they're above coming in on their own? Maybe I should call the cops."

Ellery waited through the long pause and then heard him say. "Okay, but stay on the line while I check around."

She glanced over the railing and saw him head to the first of three downstairs offices with the phone still to his ear, apparently deciding to have a look around before involving the police. This was her chance to get away. She watched him walk from room to room, but the moment she heard him start up the main stairway, she slipped through the door to the back stairs. Thankful for her soft soled running shoes, she took the steps two at a time until she reached the first floor. She leaned against the door to the kitchen, but she didn't hear anything on the other side. Ready to risk it, she gently pushed open the door and looked around the room. Karl was nowhere in sight, but she could hear his voice and it sounded like he was still upstairs. Praying she hadn't left anything out of place, she tiptoed her way out the back door, shutting it carefully behind her before speed-walking back out onto the street, in the opposite direction of the house.

Once she was several blocks away, she breathed a sigh of relief. Funny how she could get so worked up about visiting a place that had been her second home for so many years. Her feelings were mixed. Being back in the office was disconcerting, but she'd experienced melancholy as well, and she had to admit she missed some aspects of her former life. Her hand-crafted furniture made people happy, but it didn't change lives. She'd represented so many people whose lives and liberty hinged on her ability to do her job. By sheer advocacy, she'd been able to help them get back on track—from the falsely accused to the ones who'd strayed and just needed a second chance to find their way. Overall, the work she'd done had been fulfilling, but the toll it took on her day in and day out had been consuming.

She shook away the thought. All her energy had to go into her own defense right now, not on revisiting the decisions she'd made in the past. She should go straight home and start analyzing the documents she'd lifted from Meg's computer, but as she walked down the street, the smells of Saturday morning brunch emanating from the local restaurants distracted her from her task. She'd never gotten around to eating breakfast, and now it was almost time for lunch. She could grab something and take it home, but as the adrenaline rush from her break-in wore off, she realized she was completely worn out. She needed to sit down, eat, and rejuvenate. With her hoodie and sunglasses, she should be able to take in a meal on the patio without attracting any attention. Besides, if for any reason, someone later should question why she'd been in this part of town at the same time the office had been broken into, brunch could be her alibi.

She looked around, considering her options. Breadwinners was just across the street, and a heavy dose of carbs was just what she needed. She crossed the street and peered in the window, assessing the possible wait time. The place was packed, but it was late enough that many of them might be leaving soon. She started toward the front door, when a familiar face caught her eye. Seated smack in the middle of the front dining room was Sarah Flores. Even in casual clothes with her hair pulled back through a ball cap, she looked amazing. Ellery looked to the other side of the table. Sarah was joined by another woman, attractive, but not stunning like Sarah. The other woman looked familiar, but Ellery couldn't place her. She watched for a moment, but couldn't tell the nature of their interaction. Who was she kidding? Weekend brunch was a dating gig, not a business thing. Whoever this woman was with Sarah, she was definitely interested. She leaned close and hung on Sarah's every word.

Ellery knew she should turn away, but she couldn't break the spell caused by the surprise of seeing Sarah. She removed her sunglasses to get a better look. A moment later, when Sarah looked up and caught her staring, she regretted giving in to temptation, but she stayed rooted in place, unable at first to turn away as Sarah's eyebrows rose in question. Ellery's breath quickened and her heart threatened to pound its way out of her chest as it powered her instinct to move. She took two steps, while watching Sarah's questioning glance turn into a frown, but she didn't stick around to see what happened next, choosing instead to stalk off in the opposite direction. Weekend brunches and the women who shared them weren't in her future. Not until she cleared her name.

❖

Sarah knocked on the door and listened to the sound of someone rustling around inside. It was possible Liz was still asleep, but unlikely based on the fact she usually showed up at the office super early. It also occurred to her Liz might have company. She hadn't called her because she wanted to catch her by surprise. If she wound up being the one surprised, she'd just beg off and find another way to determine the extent of Liz's involvement in the bombing investigation.

Seconds later, Liz flung the door open and didn't even try to mask her surprise. "Sarah, what are you doing here?"

Sarah gave her a broad smile, poked her head in the door, and started talking in a fast ramble. "I was out exploring the city and remembered you said you lived around here. I don't know a lot of people here, but I hear brunch is the thing to do on a pretty day like today. Someone said Breadwinners is a good place. I put the address into my GPS, but I don't want to go alone. I'll buy. All you have to do is tag along. Cool?"

She paused to breathe and prepare for any excuse Liz was prepared to offer. She didn't hear any other sounds in the apartment so she assumed Liz was alone. Her hair was combed, she smelled of soap, and she was dressed, so she didn't have the I-can't-possibly-get-ready-in-time-to-go-anywhere excuse. "Mind if I come in?"

"Uh, sure." Liz stepped back to allow her in. Sarah wandered into the space, casually examining every surface. Liz was a neatnik, something she already knew from her desk at the office. "This is a beautiful apartment. Do you rent or own?"

"Rent. Dallas real estate is a bit steep on my salary."

"I hear you. I'm renting too. In Uptown, I like it because there are so many restaurants nearby and I can't cook my way out of a paper bag." Sarah edged into the kitchen. "Do you cook?" She didn't give a rat's ass about Liz's culinary habits, but she did want to see if she was cooking now since she might use that as an excuse to beg off on going to brunch.

"Sometimes. Hey, I actually had some stuff I was going to work on. Maybe we could do brunch another time. Would that be okay?"

Sarah faced her square on. Liz's eyes twitched and she tapped her forefinger against her thumb in a nervous gesture, and Sarah could tell she really wanted her to leave the apartment. Sarah cocked her head, trying to get a better read as to what was causing the edge. As she stared at Liz, she noticed she kept shifting to the side. "What are you hiding?"

"What?"

"You're hiding something." Sarah stepped around her and spotted a plain cardboard box sitting in the corner of the kitchen. She walked over and looked down at it. The top was open and it was stacked with papers. She recognized the ones on top. "Why do you have WHI's records at your apartment?" She managed to summon a healthy dose of incredulity to go with her question even though she felt a bit like a hypocrite since she had her own copy of the very same documents back at her place.

"I have a good reason."

"Does Mason know?" Sarah saw the immediate surge of fear in her eyes. Whatever Liz was up to, she was acting on her own. "When did you know that Ellery Durant was involved with the WHI?"

"What?"

Sarah had surprised herself with the question. She hadn't meant to lead with that. "Let's back up. I have a lot of questions. I need you to answer them and I need you to trust me when I say everything I'm going to ask is important. If you don't want to talk to me, tell me now and I'll leave, but I will call Mason and let him know that you have these documents at your house. Understood?"

Liz nodded in defeat. "I'll talk to you, but not here. My daughter is coming over later and she doesn't need to hear any of this."

"Then how about that brunch I mentioned. I can drive and bring you back after. Deal?"

"Fine."

The drive to Breadwinners only took a few minutes, but Liz's silence made it seem like much longer. Sarah found street parking several blocks away and they walked in silence until they reached the restaurant. After a short wait, they were seated and Sarah tried to make small talk while they waited for someone to take their order. "How old is your daughter?"

"She's seventeen. Going on thirty."

"Mature for her age or just thinks she is?"

"Mostly the latter. I love her, but her high school years have been trying."

"Where does she live?"

"She spends most of her time at her dad's place in Highland Park, but I see her on weekends. Most weekends anyway."

Liz's tone was wistful and her seemingly straightforward statements were weighted with innuendo. A custody battle, a wealthy ex who'd been able to afford better attorneys, a rebellious teenager who didn't mind her mother. All of these were possibilities, and Sarah couldn't help but feel that something about Liz's personal life factored into the decisions she made on the job.

After they ordered their food, she launched right in. "You said you would tell me about the bank records."

"There really isn't much to tell. I was just being thorough and there's not enough time during the day to get everything done."

"You're lying." Sarah watched as Liz reacted swiftly to the accusation.

"I didn't come here to be chastised by you. You may have forgotten, but I have seniority."

"In this particular unit, maybe, but I'm sure you know that my experience with the Bureau outweighs yours." Sarah delivered the words as gently as she could, but she knew they would rankle.

"You think you're better than the rest of us because you worked BAU? I've spent years running down people who cheat, lie, and steal. What we do here is important, and if you don't want to be a part of it, you should leave. Don't think I don't know you're working behind the scenes on the bombing investigation."

Sarah tried not to show her surprise at Liz's revelation. It had been a little over a week since the first call from Trip, and even then she hadn't been officially working the investigation until he'd shown up last night. Liz had to be guessing unless she had some other source to find out what she was up to. Sarah made a split second decision. "You're right. I'm working with BAU regarding possible suspects. If you know something you haven't reported yet, now's the time to spill it."

The appearance of their waiter stopped Liz's response and they both exchanged stares while he placed their food on the table and topped off their coffee. Liz waited until he was across the room before she started talking. "I've been digging on my own. Amir Khan is one of those untouchable types. He does such good things for the community, creating jobs, running a charity, that no one questions his dealings are aboveboard. My daughter, Hannah, goes to school with his son, Naveed."

"Are they friends?"

"I think so. She's mentioned him, in passing. Frankly, my relationship with my daughter is sketchy at best. Between the acrimonious divorce and the fact that she's a typical teenager, I'm lucky to have any conversation with her at all. She's been dating someone, but I can't get any information from her about it other than 'he doesn't go to my school' and 'you wouldn't know him.' Her father seems to like her aversion to communication. It fits right in with his head in the sand lifestyle, which is why she spends most of her time with him. She makes me out to be the bad guy since I'm the one who pulls her phone records to see who she's talking to and texting."

Sarah found the personal insight intriguing. "I wish I'd had parents who were remotely interested in my whereabouts when I was a kid." The subject made her wistful, but there wasn't time to dwell on her own feelings. To get back on track, she asked, "Did you find something about Amir Khan that concerned you? I mean, beyond the bank records?"

"Sorry, I'm not telling this very well. I did find something. I have a friend who works in the Dallas County Probation Office. They send some of their probationers to do community service, mostly Muslims, to the WHI. They pack care packages, print brochures, stuff like that. He gave me a log of volunteers."

"Uh huh." Sarah took a sip of coffee while she waited for Liz to get to the point. Liz sat hunched forward in her chair, her eyes big and her voice low. Whatever she was about to say, she thought it was extremely important and Sarah leaned close to hear.

"One of the volunteers signed in with two names. I'm guessing he added his Western name only because that's the name on his record in Dallas county. He's on probation for burglary and he picked up a new case."

It was Sarah's turn to get ramped up. She rolled her hand at Liz. "For God's sake, what's his name?"

"His real name is Brian Barstow, but he goes by Abdul Kamal."

It wasn't breaking news since Trip had already told her that the Barstows volunteered with Amir Khan's charity, but Liz was still holding something back. "What are you not telling me?"

"I managed to trace Brian to a website, it's called Take Back the Homeland, and it's filled with radical propaganda. He posts there as Abdul Kamal."

"And you told Mason about it and that's why HSI came and grabbed the records from us, right?"

"Yes, but there's more. Something I haven't told anyone."

Sarah reached a hand across the table. Liz was visibly shaken. Whatever she had to say was private, personal, and Sarah sensed she's been holding the secret too long. "Tell me. Whatever it is, I'll help you. I promise."

"My daughter. If she finds out I've been spying on her, she'll never forgive me, but if I didn't do something, I'd never forgive myself."

"What is it? What about your daughter?"

"Brian Barstow's brother, Michael. He goes by Hashid Kamal. I think he's the man Hannah has been seeing. I think she's been dating a terrorist."

Sarah squeezed Liz's hand, offering what comfort she could while trying to process Liz's revelation. What she wanted to do was insist they leave now and go find Hannah so they could debrief her about the Barstow brothers, but she knew she needed to tread lightly here. The good news was if Brian had a record in Dallas County, she should be able to have Danny pull the case file for her. She should have thought of that when Trip first mentioned the boys had been arrested last year, but she'd figured if there was anything to find, HSI would have found it. Mistake. From here on out she'd only rely on information she had the opportunity to analyze on her own.

In the meantime, Liz was sitting across from her, looking more like a grief-stricken mother than a federal agent. "Have you discussed this with Hannah?"

"No, she's been on a trip for spring break. I've been waiting until she got home today."

"You didn't tell Mason about your daughter, did you?"

Liz, to her credit, looked her straight in the eyes. "No. Are you going to report me?"

"For what, being a concerned mother? The only thing I want to do right now is talk to Hannah. Didn't you say she's coming to your place today?"

"No way! I haven't talked to her about this. You think I'm going to let you?"

Sarah softened her voice in response to Liz's panicked reaction. "You're going to have to let me. Better me than a crowd of HSI agents out for blood, don't you think?"

"I don't know." Liz looked down at her hands in her lap. "I just don't know what to do."

Sarah knew she'd come around. Liz hadn't gotten to where she was in her career without learning how to be objective, although this was probably the first time her objectivity had been tested to this extent. She looked away to give her a moment with her thoughts. The street was busy with people enjoying the early spring day. Couples walked, hand in hand, laughing, talking, doing things that people who don't let their jobs consume them do on the weekend. When she met someone special again, she'd be like that, but she couldn't help but think that she'd never meet someone special again until she was like that.

She reached for her coffee and then looked back at the window, sucking in her breath when she saw the one person she had met who made her wish she worked a different job. Ellery's eyes were trained on her. Curious, wistful. Sarah raised her eyebrows in question, but seconds later, Ellery broke their gaze and started to walk away. Sarah glanced at Liz. She should stay. It was important she seize on the opportunity to talk to Liz's daughter as soon as possible, but talking to Ellery was just as important. She pushed her chair back, preparing to tell Liz she'd be back as soon as she could, but Liz spoke first.

"Okay, I'll let you talk to Hannah, but only if you let me talk to her first. I'll call you. I promise."

Sarah relented. "Fine, if you don't call, count on me showing up on your doorstep again. I need to run to the restroom. Get the check and I'll be right back." Sarah didn't wait for Liz to answer before taking a circuitous route and doubling back out the front door. Once she reached the sidewalk, she paused to look around, finally spotting the dark blue hoodie in the crowd. She strode briskly, not wanting to attract attention by running down the street. She quickened her steps and pulled right up alongside, sliding her arm to hook through Ellery's. Ellery stopped abruptly and looked over at her, a frown on her face.

"Don't do anything to draw attention to us," Sarah said. "I just want to ask you something."

"They have phones for that."

"I'm thinking you probably don't trust your phone right now, am I right?"

"That would be correct. I don't trust you either, so that puts us at a bit of an impasse."

"I figured as much when you didn't show up last night." Sarah resisted sharing that she knew where Ellery had actually gone the night before. No sense scaring her off by letting her know her every move was being watched. "Look, I meant what I said about wanting to talk to you with no strings attached. Are you still up for that or is daddy dearest going to object?"

"Leave my father out of this." Ellery barked the words. "If you want to talk, start talking."

Sarah looked over her shoulder, wondering how much time she had before Liz started getting anxious. "I can't right now."

"Because you're on a date?"

"What? Oh, the woman at the restaurant? She's a colleague." Sarah peered into Ellery's eyes and the skeptical look she saw there surprised her so much she didn't catch her next words in time to keep from blurting them out. "You're jealous."

Ellery's eyes widened. "You've got to be kidding me. I'm in the middle of a crisis and you think I have a thing for the person who put me here?"

Sarah started to protest. She hadn't put Ellery in this position at all, and she certainly wasn't responsible for Ellery's choices about which clients to represent and what advice to give them, but none of that really mattered. No matter how much she denied it, Ellery was jealous and Sarah liked it. She leaned closer. "You may not like me now, but last week when we met for coffee, if we hadn't been interrupted, you would have asked me out on a real date. Am I right?"

She watched as Ellery opened her mouth and then quickly shut if before speaking. Frustration, confusion, aggravation took turns toying with Ellery's expression, but still she didn't say anything. Meanwhile, Sarah was laser focused on her lips. They were full and beautiful, and she imagined they were both soft and strong. If she moved forward just a bit more, maybe she could run her tongue along the edges, inviting a slow, delicious, lingering kiss.

"We can't do this."

Ellery's breathy words shook her out of her kissing fantasy, but the haze of desire remained, shooting sparks of heat throughout her body. She met Ellery's eyes, almost black with arousal and realized how close they'd both come to succumbing to want over need. No matter how much they shared the desire, Ellery was right. She had a job to do and getting close to the suspect didn't mean getting in her pants. She pulled a card from her pocket and handed it to Ellery. "You're right, but we still need to talk. Call me when you're ready."

Ellery slid the card into her back pocket without giving it a glance and slipped back across the crowded street. Sarah had no idea if she would call, but as she walked back into the restaurant, all she could think about was how once again her job had robbed her of the chance to have a personal life.

CHAPTER FOURTEEN

Sunday morning, Ellery trudged outside to retrieve the paper from her front lawn. It was still dark outside, but she hadn't been asleep for hours. Dogged by thoughts of the things that had gone wrong in the last two days, she'd given up around four a.m. and spent several hours examining the files she'd downloaded from Meg's computer. She wondered if either Meg or Kyle had figured out they'd had a breach yet. More likely some poor cleaning lady would get in trouble for forgetting to lock the rear door and set the alarm.

She'd read through the files several times. Sadeem Jafari ran a foundation called the Global Enterprise Alliance. The paperwork for the foundation made it sound a lot like the charity Amir Khan had discussed with her father. She'd Googled both organizations and they appeared to be connected to a lot of the same work. Amir and Sadeem ran in the same circles, but ostensibly those circles were respectable. She found it hard to believe the Amir she knew would have anything to do with the bombing or any of the acts of violence associated with Al-Qaeda or ISIS.

"Hey, girl, you going to read that paper or just stand there holding it?"

Ellery looked over at Leo. He was propped up with his own copy of the *Dallas Morning News* spread out on his lap, drinking from a glass of orange juice that was probably spiked with vodka. "You're up early."

"Can't get a jump on things if you spend your time sleeping in."

"I'm ready for things not to be so jumpy. Hopefully, circumstances have calmed down for a bit. You can be sure the government will take their time combing through all my files before they decide what to do to me."

"Pretty odd no one's claimed responsibility for the bombing, don't you think?"

"I guess." Ellery had given the same fact considerable thought. She knew it was likely the government knew more than they were letting on, but unlike the Boston Marathon bombing where the suspects were arrested within days, several weeks had passed with no definitive statements from any federal agency other than the searches executed on Friday. Did they really not know anything? If so, that meant they were definitely on a fishing expedition with their searches. *If you'd agreed to hear what Sarah had had to say, you might have a better idea of what's going on.*

Sarah. She flashed back to Sarah accosting her on the street the day before, looking every bit as gorgeous in jeans and a T-shirt as she had in her fancy red cocktail dress on Friday night. She'd seen a lot of her this weekend, but none of it under the circumstances she would have preferred. She'd run the whole gamut when it came to Sarah Flores, from thinking she was just another annoying, know-it-all federal agent to being captivated by her charm over coffee. Now Sarah was solidly defined as adversary.

But, adversary or not, Sarah had information and right now, information was power and Ellery was sorely lacking in that particular commodity. She'd stalked off yesterday morning, fueled, she realized now, by pride, but she'd kept Sarah's card, just in case. The card was sitting on her kitchen counter, the front a sterile recitation of Sarah's official contact information, but on the back in perfect cursive, the words "Call me" written above a number. She'd tossed the card on the counter when she got home yesterday and tried to avoid looking at it the rest of the day, but if she was being honest, she'd have to admit its presence, its possibilities, were part of the reason she'd been unable to sleep.

"I think they know more than they're letting on," Leo said. "Probably think if they rattle enough cages, they can distract from the fact they're hiding the truth."

Ellery nodded. Leo's assessment might not be far from the truth. And caged was a good word for how she was feeling right now. Without access to funds other than the money Karen had fronted her from Friday's sales and without access to the facts of the case the government was building against her, she was trapped.

Call me. She'd stared at the card for so long, she could recite the number on the back from memory. Would contacting Sarah be a trap or a way out?

❖

Sarah knocked on the door again and resumed pacing. She'd waited all night for the call and now that she'd gotten here, she was chomping at the bit, certain she was on the edge of breaking a piece of this case wide open. She'd about decided to bust in, when the door swung wide open and she was standing face to face with a young blond woman. "Hannah?"

The girl nodded and motioned for her to come inside. Hannah Dawson was very pretty, but the dark circles and puffy skin around her red eyes signaled she had probably been up most of the night and had spent a lot of it crying. Sarah could only imagine the heart to heart she and her mother had had. Liz had been worrying about her daughter being involved with someone capable of committing horribly violent acts in the name of some crazy jihad for almost a week. That worry had probably burst forth like a volcano erupting when she saw Hannah for the first time since she returned from spring break.

Sarah wondered what would have happened if she hadn't called Liz on her actions yesterday. Would she really have confronted Hannah at all or would she have just tried to overlook her daughter's transgressions? From a clinical perspective, she knew it was hard to see fault in the people you care about.

You don't see fault in Ellery.

But that's not because I care about her. It's because my trained eye doesn't detect any sort of deception when it comes to her.

You almost kissed her on the street yesterday.

So what if I did? That wasn't about caring. It was pure attraction.

Right.

Sarah took a deep breath. She needed to shut down the argument in her head, compartmentalize her thoughts about Ellery, and focus on the girl in front of her. With any luck, she would have details that would not only lead them to more information about the bombing suspect, but would clear Ellery. And then what?

"You must be Agent Flores."

"Just call me Sarah. Where's your mom?"

Hannah pointed inside and led the way. Sarah followed, using the time to take in more details about the apartment than she'd garnered the day before. The living space was nice with family photos and personal mementos scattered about. It definitely had a more homey feel than her place. Liz was sitting at the kitchen table, reading through what looked like a diary. She looked as Sarah approached. "Thanks for coming. Can I get you anything? Coffee, OJ?"

"Coffee would be great." Sarah watched Liz nod to Hannah who responded to the silent order with no sign of teenage rebellion.

"Sugar and cream?"

"Just cream, thanks."

As Hannah prepared her drink, Liz pushed the journal she was reading across the table to Sarah. "You're going to want to take a look at this. I've flagged the important dates."

Sarah opened the journal and read the inside cover. *This diary belongs to Hannah Dawson. If that's not you, then get out.* The writing was surrounded by drawings of horse heads, flowers, and butterflies. Not your typical girlfriend of a terrorist kind of stuff. Sarah shot a look at Hannah who met her eyes with a slight grimace. As much as she hated violating Hannah's privacy, she wasn't about to get in between mother and daughter. She flipped to the first entry Liz had flagged.

I don't get what he sees in me. Lacy says there's something off about a college guy who wants to date someone in high school. She's jealous. I can tell. And she should be. Her boyfriend, Jason, is a dick, like most of the guys at our school. Besides, Mom always says girls mature faster than boys, which means me and Michael are really about the same age.

The entry was dated eight months ago. Sarah thumbed through the journal and noted the last flagged entry was two months after that. She knew without asking that the Michael in the journal was Michael Barstow aka Hashid Kamal. She'd looked up the origin of the name last night. Hashid meant one who rallies people and Kamal meant perfection. Interesting choice.

She shut the journal and looked up at Liz and Hannah. She wasn't here to read lines on a page. She wanted to hear what Hannah had to say about her involvement with Hashid and learn what she could from her expressions during the telling. "So he went by Michael when you first met him?"

"Yes."

"Were you still dating him when he changed his name?"

"For a while. He'd been acting strangely. I know he went by the name Hashid in some circles, but he didn't ask me to call him that until just before we broke up."

"Who broke up with whom?"

"It was kind of mutual. He got arrested. He was charged with a felony. He said it was just some prank, but I explained to him that my mom was a cop and if she found out, she'd kill us both."

"What was his response?" Sarah watched while Hannah darted an anxious glance at her mom. Sarah could tell she had something else to say, something she didn't want to say in front of her mother. Well, the time for secrets had passed. "It's important that you tell me everything. Even things you think might not be important."

"He said my mother had no power over me because she's a woman. And then he said that if I was going to be with him, I would need to obey him."

Sarah held back a laugh at the absurdity of a twentysomething boy trying to subjugate a teenage girl. The look on Hannah's face told her that Michael/Hashid's request had shaken her up. "And what happened next?"

"We had a fight. I told him that was bullshit and he told me there were plenty of young blond girls who would do whatever he said because…because…"

"Because what?"

"Well that's when it got kind of crazy. He said other girls would do what he wanted because he was headed for glory."

"Glory? He used the word glory?"

Hannah nodded. "He'd started talking weird, you know, like about the afterlife and stuff."

Sarah looked at Liz who appeared to be growing increasingly uncomfortable with the conversation. "Okay." She decided to take a different tact. "Do you know what he was arrested for?"

"He broke into a building with his brother and some of his friends. That's pretty much all I know about it."

Trusting that people usually knew more than they thought they did, Sarah pressed for more. "How about the friends—do you know who they are?"

"Some guy named Akbar, they go to college together, and Akbar's cousin, Naveed Khan. He goes to my school."

Sarah instantly recognized the name of Amir Khan's son. She could tell by Liz's expression she did too, but she did her best to mask her response. "Uh huh. How well do you know Naveed?"

"Not well. He's a senior. He's really popular and I think he's going to Princeton next year. That's about it. Michael never really introduced me to his friends, and Naveed and I don't really run in the same crowd."

Something she'd said earlier about Michael kept bothering Sarah. "Did any of these other guys act like their girlfriends were supposed to obey them?"

Hannah cocked her head. "Brian had a girlfriend, but I never met her. I don't know about Naveed. If he was seeing someone, she probably went to another school. Akbar was going with this girl, but she didn't act like the type who obeyed anyone. I only met her once, but she was kind of a bitch." Hannah shot a look at her mom who sighed. Sarah was glad she didn't have to stick around for the aftermath of this conversation.

She spent the next hour asking Hannah everything she could think of about her relationship with Michael Barstow until she was satisfied that if Michael had been involved in the bombing, Hannah didn't know a thing about it. If it turned out Michael was involved, Hannah would face much more aggressive questioning from other agents, but Sarah was satisfied she'd learned all she could.

When she signaled she was ready to leave, Liz walked her out of the apartment. "What do you think?" she asked.

"I think you have a very normal teenage daughter who was smart enough to stop seeing a kid who got in trouble with the law and tried to boss her around. Not sure you could hope for better than that."

"I suppose. But now what?"

Liz was smart enough to know it wouldn't end here, not since she'd stirred the pot by alerting Mason and subsequently HSI to the records they'd found. "I'm not sure, but I think it's best if Hannah stays with you for a few days. Until we get things sorted out."

"She's supposed to go to her father's, but I think I have some leverage here."

"I'll call you later. Let me know if she thinks of anything else."

Half an hour later, Sarah was back at her apartment, agitated and alone. She was convinced Hannah had been dating a terrorist wannabe if not the real thing, and the prospect made her glad she didn't have kids of her own. Oh sure, they were cute when they were tiny, sucking their thumbs and crawling around on the floor, but teenagers were a force to be reckoned with. If anything, it was even harder as a single parent.

At the rate she was going, single was all she ever would be. The entire purpose of moving to Dallas and taking this job had been to get the rest of her life on track. She had a plan. Meet a gorgeous, smart woman. Date for a respectable amount of time. Get married and move in together, not necessarily in that order. Children were a definite maybe.

So far, she'd met the gorgeous smart woman, but unfortunately, Ellery Durant was also a suspect in a case, and although she knew deep in her soul that Ellery couldn't be responsible for what happened the night of the bombing, she knew that by accepting Trip's request to investigate her, she had killed any chance she had for something romantic with Ellery.

She walked into the kitchen to make a drink. Just because she had to work on the weekend, didn't mean she didn't get thirsty. A stiff vodka tonic would make the computer work she was about to do a little more palatable.

She'd just squeezed a lime into the glass when her phone rang. She picked it up off the counter and stared at the screen. Ellery's home number blinked with each ring. She took a deep breath to calm her racing heart and answered. "Flores."

"What are you doing?"

"Truth?"

"Of course."

"Making a stiff drink."

"Sounds professional."

"It's Sunday. What should I be doing?"

"Depends. Do you still want to talk?"

"Yes."

"Two conditions."

Sarah took a deep breath. "I'm waiting."

"You come over here. You come alone and you talk, I listen."

"That sounded like more than two conditions."

Ellery sighed. "Are you coming over or not?"

"I'm on my way."

CHAPTER FIFTEEN

S arah parked her car in front of Ellery's house and started to walk to the front door, but she was stopped by the sound of a sharp whistle. She looked around, finally spying an old man peering at her from the house next door. He was drinking a beer and rocking back and forth in a chair on his porch. She nodded and waved.

"Nice car, girlie."

"Thanks."

"You're a fed, aren't you?"

She cocked her head. Nothing about her right now should signal federal agent. She was dressed for Sunday brunch, not a day at the office and her badge was in her purse, not strapped to her side. She smiled and said, "It's Sunday. I'm not anything on Sundays."

He threw his head back and laughed, a gravely rumble of a laugh, part humor and part edge. "Right. Whatever you say." His laugh stopped abruptly and the smile disappeared from his face. "Tell you what, though." He waggled a finger, motioning her over. She took a few steps until she could hear the sound of his harsh whisper. "I don't care who you are. You hurt that girl, you'll answer to me. You understand?"

Sarah held back a sharp retort. Everything about this old man's posturing was born of genuine concern for Ellery, and she couldn't help but admire his nerve and loyalty. This wasn't just a neighbor; he was a good friend. On instinct, she stuck out a hand and clasped his firmly in her own. "I understand."

When she turned around, Ellery was standing on the front steps of her house, grinning. Sarah walked over to meet her. "Just getting to know the neighbors."

"He threatened you, didn't he?" Ellery asked.

She shrugged. "A little bit."

"Leo's a former Marine. He's our entire neighborhood watch and he fancies himself my personal bodyguard."

"Have you needed a bodyguard before?"

"Matter of fact, I have."

Sarah stared for a moment, but Ellery didn't volunteer more. She got the distinct impression the subject was off limits, which was fine since she'd come here for a very specific reason. Ellery had called to say she was willing to hear whatever Sarah could tell her about why she'd been caught up in this mess, and Sarah was prepared to tell her everything she knew. Probably not what Trip had in mind when he tapped her for this job, but at this point she cared more about getting to the truth than dancing around it. Ellery struck her as the kind of person who would know right away if she was being disingenuous, and she was willing to risk divulging some key facts in order to get some in return.

She followed Ellery in, observing every detail of the tidy, but comfortable space where Ellery lived. From the original art on the walls to the photos arranged on the mantel, Ellery's house had all the trappings to signal a real person lived here, unlike her own sterile apartment. She stopped in front of a beautiful wood cabinet with leaded glass doors. The shelves were lined with an odd mix of objects: a Cleveland Indians ball cap, a set of trading cards, a hardhat from a local business, and a male action figure with hooks instead of hands.

"That piece was once a barn door," Ellery said. "The glass is from a church out in Cleburne. They replaced all the windows with energy efficient ugly ones and I lucked out by picking up a bunch of their castoffs."

Sarah ran her fingers along the side of the cabinet. "It's beautiful. Pine?"

"Yes."

"I'm curious about the contents."

Ellery opened the cabinet doors and touched each object as she explained the significance. "No, I'm not a Cleveland fan, but I did go to a game when I was there trying a federal bribery case. We won the case, so the hat has good mojo." She pointed at the hard hat and trading cards. "Two other companies we represented that avoided prosecution."

Sarah pointed at the action figure. "This is the one that really has me stumped."

"One of our clients didn't think the investigator we hired was aggressive enough so he hired this guy." Ellery picked up the action figure. "His name is Jay J. Armes, and according to his autobiography, he's 'the World's most successful private investigator.' He rescued Marlon Brando's son from kidnappers, he owns pet tigers, and he has tons of attachments he uses in place of the hands he lost when he was a kid playing with explosives. An associate at the office found this vintage action figure on eBay and I had to have it for my collection."

"Wow. Pretty sure you can't top that as far as souvenirs go. Is that why you quit?"

"You want something to drink? Beer? Wine?"

Sarah didn't miss a beat. "Whatever you're having is good." She followed her into the kitchen and pretended to look at a cookbook sitting on the table while Ellery reached into the refrigerator and fished out a couple of beer bottles. She hadn't really expected Ellery to answer her question when she'd already ducked it once before, and she wasn't quite sure why she was fixated on the reason Ellery had left a lucrative law practice to make furniture for a living. It wasn't that she didn't understand the lure of a simpler life, but Ellery had seemed so enthusiastic about describing the souvenirs of her former life and Sarah thought she'd detected a trace of wistfulness.

Ellery watched Sarah with a careful eye. She was standing in the kitchen, pretending like she wasn't watching her every move, but Ellery knew better. She doubted there was a single thing this woman missed and, as much as it aggravated her, she had a grudging admiration for her too. She grabbed two bottles of beer, twisted off the tops, and handed one to Sarah. A tiny test really, since she figured she would want a glass. Would she ask?

Sarah took the bottle and read the label. "Local. Nice. I haven't had as much time as I would like to try out some of the local breweries. Would you mind if I had a glass?"

Ellery smiled, happy with the honesty. She reached into the freezer and pulled out a well-chilled pint glass and handed it to Sarah who handled the pour like a pro. "I didn't figure you for a beer drinker."

"Why? Because I had a mixed drink the first time we met?"

"That wasn't the first time we met." She grinned. "Unless you were drinking at Danny Soto's office."

"I might start drinking if I had to work for the county. But as for your assumptions, I like to drink a lot of different things. I picked a clear drink that night because the odds of someone bumping into me and spilling it were pretty high."

Ellery motioned to the table and they sat next to each other. "It was pretty crowded. I guess we're lucky someone didn't target the hotel for the bombing." She was instantly sorry for her careless words and she quickly pivoted. "Although I guess you probably think that the reason they didn't choose the hotel is obvious, since I was there and I'm involved."

"I didn't say that. I didn't even think that."

"Then why are you here?"

Sarah looked taken aback by the question, but she recovered quickly. "Here's the truth. I don't think you had anything to do with the bombing, but I do think that maybe one of your clients did. You probably had no idea what they were really up to, but you might be able to help us get the truth."

"If you've been doing this for any length of time, you know that I can't talk to you or anyone else about things my client has told me without his express permission."

"I get it, but there are ways around it. The fraud exception for example. If you—"

Ellery waved a hand to stop her. The fraud exception to the attorney client privilege could be used to allow her to divulge otherwise confidential information if her client's action had implicated her in a crime and she needed to defend herself, but as far as she was concerned, they weren't there yet. "You're assuming there was some wrongdoing and that I know anything about it."

"Well, here's the deal. There are documents filed with the IRS that have your name on them. Those documents make you a party to whatever Amir Khan's charity was up to, no matter what your intentions."

Ellery had a choice. If she told Sarah her name had been added to those documents without her permission, she'd be implicating her client of forgery. *Former client.* Hell, it didn't matter if Amir was a current or former client, the privilege survived the relationship. It was important to her that Sarah not believe she was responsible for something she hadn't done, but her hands were tied until she knew more. She stalled. "You still haven't told me what the charity was up to that has HSI crawling all over themselves. I thought that was the purpose of this little talk."

"You're right." Sarah looked around the kitchen. "Do you have something I can write on? I think it would help to have a visual."

Ellery pulled a pad of paper out of a drawer and shoved it and a pen across the table. Sarah drew a triangle and began labeling the three points. She tapped her finger on the one labeled WHI. "Welcome Home International is Khan's claim to fame. It started out as a legitimate nonprofit, established to provide assistance to refugee immigrants from the Middle East."

"That much I already knew."

"Okay, but there's another organization." She pointed to the label, GEA. "Global Enterprises Alliance. It's another nonprofit, not as well known as WHI, and you'll be happy to know your name isn't anywhere on their filing documents. Their board president is a guy named Sadeem Jafari."

Ellery nodded, schooling her expression into what she hoped was nonchalance. She recognized Sadeem's name from the search warrant affidavit, which of course, Sarah didn't have a clue she had, but she also recognized it and GEA from the documents on Meg's computer that she now had on a flash drive in her study. She felt a tinge of guilt at not telling Sarah what she knew about GEA, albeit limited, but then she reminded herself this meeting was about getting, not giving information. Instead, she asked, "What's the connection?"

"The most obvious one is money. Seventy percent of WHI's funds are deposited into bank accounts held jointly with GEA, and all of that money is held offshore."

"You know it's not illegal to have an offshore account. If it was, most US corporations would be in a world of hurt."

"It may not be illegal to store funds offshore, but it's where the funds went after they got there that's the problem." Sarah put her finger on the last point of the triangle that simply said "Terrorism."

"Don't tell me there's a group actually called that."

"Very funny. It's shorthand for the several groups that the WHI and GEA money is funneled to, all of which aid terrorist training camps in Libya and Pakistan under the guise of charitable pursuits in the Middle East."

"This sounds a lot like the Holy Land case." Ellery referred to a recent high profile case where supporters of a Dallas charity, the Holy Land Foundation, had been accused of sending money to Hamas sympathizers who'd been included on a terrorist watch list.

"Because it is a lot like the Holy Land case. The Holy Land defendants are doing serious time. Do you really want to go down with your former client?"

Ellery shook her head. It wasn't that easy, but she didn't expect Sarah to understand. The Amir Khan she knew appeared to be a patriotic American. He'd moved here years ago, and he spent considerable time and resources making his part of it a better place for both his family and the rest of his community. But there was no denying her name had made it onto that IRS filing somehow. If Amir didn't have anything to hide, then why use her name? Who was he covering for and why?

"I don't think it's as simple as you're making it sound," Ellery said. "Before I agree to anything, I'd want to see proof that the money from WHI is being used for terrorist activity and that Amir knew about it."

"You know I can't tell you specifics. Some of it's classified."

"But you know for sure that some of this terrorist activity can be tied to the bombing?"

"There are connections. That's all I can tell you right now."

Ellery sensed Sarah was equivocating. Chances were the investigation into Amir's charity was part of a scorched earth campaign to rout out suspected terrorists whether they had anything to do with the bombing or not. She tried again. "I know that if we go to trial, the AUSA will have to turn over what they know."

"You really want to take it that far? I'm giving you an out. Tell me everything you know and help us prosecute these guys." Sarah leaned in and placed a hand on her arm. "Come on, Ellery, you were there. You saw what they did."

Ellery flinched at the raw edge of emotion in Sarah's voice. The sights and sounds of the bombing's aftermath flooded into her consciousness and the memory of what she'd seen that night made Sarah's request seem not only reasonable, but the right thing to do.

But she wasn't just a witness to a horrible tragedy. She was a lawyer who'd taken an oath, part of which was maintaining her client's trust. Until she knew for sure that Amir himself had done something to violate that trust, she wasn't going to say a word. "I'll make you a deal. Get me whatever information you can about a direct connection between Amir Khan and any terrorist activity and give me the week to think it over."

Sarah took a drink from her beer and set the glass on the table. She folded her hands and stared at Ellery as if she was trying to read her mind. Seconds ticked by with neither one of them saying a word as Ellery did her best to mask her thoughts. Finally, Sarah spoke. "I'll give you until Tuesday. I can't hold them off any longer."

She didn't need to say who "them" was. Didn't really matter. Ellery knew no one had a real case against her, but fighting Homeland Security was a David versus Goliath endeavor. "And the information?"

"I'll do what I can."

"Fair enough," Ellery said, but she didn't mean it. Nothing about this was fair, not the least of which was the fact that she wished she were meeting with Sarah under vastly different circumstances. She flashed on the memory of watching Sarah through the window at Breadwinners. She assumed she was there enjoying the day with brunch and a pretty woman. She'd wanted to be that other woman. Weekend brunches, dinners out, even the simple act of drinking beer here at home without the pressure of giving up her former client to law enforcement—those were the things that she wished she were doing with Sarah instead of sitting here negotiating the terms of a surrender.

She looked up from her beer to see Sarah staring again, but this time her eyes signaled compassion. She locked onto her gaze as if she could morph this whole ordeal into a completely different situation. Like the night of the bombing, at the reception, when Sarah had flirted with her, but she'd been stuck with April. Or the night of the show, when Sarah had appeared in that mind-blowing red dress, but the only date they could make was to discuss the case. What she wouldn't give to have both those chances repeated so she could get to know Sarah under different, better circumstances. The heat of her desire suddenly felt suffocating and she pushed back from the table and stood up. "Do you want another drink?"

Sarah stood up too without ever breaking her gaze. "Are you okay?"

She took a step toward her and Ellery backed up into the counter. "No. I mean, I don't know."

"This is a lot, I know." Sarah's voice was tender, soft. "You've probably helped dozens of people navigate these waters, but I imagine it's different when it's you."

Ellery felt the touch before she saw it. Sarah's hand on her arm again. Gentle, yet strong. Reassuring, but something else too. She should pull away now, before she drowned in the possibility of the something else. But she was frozen in place. She opened her mouth to speak, but slowly shut it before she could spoil the moment with words. Sarah's eyes, dark and dangerous, pulled her in like a tractor beam, and she didn't even try and resist as her body leaned forward and she gave in to the urgent need to kiss her.

Sarah's lips were silky soft, the hint of the malt from the beer only adding to their deliciousness. She responded to the kiss with a soft groan, and Ellery circled an arm around her waist and pulled her closer, while Sarah reached up and curled her hand around the back of Ellery's head. Her eyes were black with desire and Ellery deepened the kiss, heady with want.

The next few seconds or minutes or however long was lost to raw feeling. Pushing hard, landing soft, tasting amazing. Ellery lost her breath, her head, her way and, in those moments, she'd never felt as close to someone as she did when she surrendered to their kiss.

And then it was over and it was Sarah who broke the embrace. One second their eyes were locked and the next Sarah's head ducked and she pulled back. Gently, but her tenderness only made the separation more stark. "I'm sorry."

Ellery started to respond in kind, but she wasn't sorry. It may have only been a fleeting moment, but it had been incredible and she wasn't sorry. Not now anyway. Tomorrow, or the next day when Special Agent Sarah Flores was trying to get her to rat out a former client, she might be sorry, but right now she regretted nothing. "I'm not. Do you want to talk about it?"

Sarah smiled. "You sound like a shrink."

Ellery smiled back. The moment might be gone, but if she tried hard, she could keep from dirtying it up with reality. "Takes one to know one."

"True. I've spent my life analyzing other people's behavior, but for the life of me, I have no idea what got into me just now."

Ellery nodded, but Sarah's comment pierced her gut. *You're being silly. Just because you felt something intimate, doesn't mean she did. And it's pretty clear she didn't.* It was a kiss. A searing, toe-curling kiss, but she knew better than to mistake physical arousal for something more. She couldn't help but feel Sarah wasn't being completely honest, but she didn't want to hear more about her regrets. "Don't worry about it." She meant the words as much for herself as Sarah.

"Seriously, that was completely out of line." Sarah's eyes, still dark and dangerous, darted around the room as if she was jonesing to get far away as fast as she could. "If you want, I can give you someone else's number to contact."

"What?" Ellery had no idea what she was talking about.

"When you're ready to talk. You can call another agent. He's someone I trust."

Ellery reached out and grabbed Sarah's arm and fixed her with a stare. "Stop it. It was me. I kissed you, not the other way around. There's no need for you to act like you violated some silly federal agent code of ethics." She didn't release her until she saw Sarah beginning to relax. What she'd said was only partly true. She'd initiated the kiss and Sarah had kissed her back, but she was so shaken up about it, all Ellery wanted to do was comfort her, even if it meant glossing over that part of it.

"I should go." Sarah's word held a trace of regret.

"If you need to."

"Yes."

"I'll walk you to the door." All she wanted to do was sweep Sarah up into another kiss, longer and slower this time, but instead she led the way to the door. She paused on the doorstep, toying with the words she wanted to say, certain they would be futile. "You don't have to go."

"I do."

"Okay."

Sarah took a step through the doorway before turning back. "Can I ask you something without offending you?"

Ellery laughed. "As if you hadn't already? The whole idea that I might be involved in a plot to bomb innocent people is pretty offensive on its own, don't you think?"

Sarah cracked a tiny smile. "Yes, but this is personal."

"Shoot."

"April Landing. I don't get it."

Ellery sighed. "The short version is she's a remnant of the kind of life I used to have."

"And the long version?"

"I guess the long version is the story of why I left that life, but it's definitely not the kind of story you tell standing in a doorway saying good-bye to a beautiful woman."

Sarah blushed. "You shouldn't say things like that. You're killing my badass FBI cred."

"Oh, I doubt that." For a split second Ellery considered telling Sarah everything, baring her soul. She'd never told anyone the real reason she'd left her law practice, and the very idea she would choose this woman, her adversary, to share her story was mystifying.

It was the kiss. Every electric sensation of the kiss lingered, shocking the good sense right out of her.

"I should go," Sarah said again.

Ellery nodded. Sarah was right. Their attraction was a powerful force, but while Sarah held the key to whether or not she would be prosecuted, it was too dangerous to yield. She should let Sarah go now, before she lost her head and her heart along with it.

CHAPTER SIXTEEN

Sarah jerked upright as her eyes tried to focus. Her room was dark, but the sounds of the city trash truck told her Monday morning had arrived. She hadn't been able to fall sleep until just before dawn, and even then her memories of Ellery and their unexpected kiss had morphed into a series of crazy dreams.

In the first dream, she'd been in D.C. with Trip and the rest of the BAU team. They'd just returned after closing the Atlanta Strangler case with an arrest. They had a DNA match for the suspect, and they'd found souvenirs from each of the victim's homes in a chest in the suspect's attic. The team was celebrating their victory when a call came in about a new victim. Same M.O., but the death occurred after their suspect was already in custody, casting doubt on their entire investigation.

In the next dream, she and Ellery were at the basketball game the night of the bombing. Ellery left their seats in the arena to get them something to eat. Moments later, the blast from the explosion tore through the arena in the direction of the concession stand. Sarah raced through the crowd toward the rubble. She had just begun digging into the debris with both hands when the loud beeping of the city trash jerked her from sleep.

The painful sense of loss she'd felt in the dream clung to her as she stumbled into the kitchen and punched the button on her Keurig. She'd made a huge mistake letting Ellery kiss her, and an even bigger one returning it. She should never have agreed to Trip's plan to get close to Ellery, especially since she seemed incapable of setting aside the attraction she'd felt from the moment they'd met. She didn't care that Ellery was a person of interest, that her accounts were frozen, that she was infuriatingly loyal to her former clients to her own detriment. Despite of all those things, Sarah wanted her. She was handsome, smart, loyal, and passionate. The memory of the dream echoed, and Sarah had no doubt if Ellery were trapped in a burning building, she'd rush in to save her.

She sipped her coffee and contemplated what the revelation meant in terms of her job. What dumb luck. She'd gotten this transfer so she could have a life and she'd wound up investigating the one woman who'd captured her interest. Was she doomed to have only small pockets of personal life sandwiched between cases? Was the point of the first dream that the job would always come first? That its pull was never-ending?

She cared as much as anyone about finding the people responsible for the bombing, but all they really had were allusions to activity, but no actual proof. No one group had taken responsibility, and any evidence that Ellery's client had supported a terrorist group, while illegal, didn't automatically translate into any tangible acts. Just because Ellery was associated with the organization didn't necessarily mean she knew where the money was ultimately going after it left WHI. But she had to admit, it looked bad. Suddenly, Sarah wished she were tracking serial killers again. Dead bodies equaled bad acts—there was no gray area. Were the nightmares of her former life more palatable than the murky questions of moral turpitude she currently faced?

An immediate solution would be to tell Trip she was done with this little side project. She'd continue her regular work at the fraud unit. Surely there were some straightforward schemes she could investigate, shady real estate investments, doctors ripping off Medicare. Something, anything that didn't put her in such close proximity with a woman she couldn't have. And later, after Ellery's case played out and she was absolved, they might be able to explore finishing what they'd started yesterday in Ellery's kitchen. Deep, slow kisses without the added dose of conflict.

Heat flooded her at the memory of Ellery's lips on hers and she made a snap decision. She picked up her phone and dialed. Trip's outgoing voice mail greeting played after the first ring and she was forced to leave a message. "Trip, it's Sarah. Call me. Today. It's important."

She hung up the phone, decidedly unsatisfied. Her plan consisted of getting Trip to share what he could, giving Ellery enough information so she could make an informed decision, and then bowing out of the work side of the equation. She might not be able to see Ellery while the case was pending, but she didn't have to be in the position of prosecuting her. Unwilling to wait for Trip's callback to move forward, she dialed Danny's number.

"Hey, we were just talking about you."

"All good things, I hope."

"Just wondering how your meeting went after the show Friday night."

Friday night seemed so long ago. Sarah remembered she'd mentioned to Danny and Ellen that she was meeting with Ellery after the show in response to their request to take her out for a drink. "Didn't happen. Besides, it was all about business, you know, if it was even going to happen."

"Shame. The two of you would make a striking couple."

"Lay off, Soto. You know better."

"I get it. Dating a potential witness is oh so taboo."

Sarah couldn't help but laugh. Danny had met her wife Ellen during their investigation of a serial murder case the year before. Ellen had been not only a witness, but for a short period of time, a potential suspect. "This is different, pal."

"Why don't you come over for dinner this week and explain it to us?"

"I'll do you one better. I need access to a file from your office. How about I swing by this afternoon? Are you in trial this week?"

"We're picking a jury this morning, but we're not starting evidence until tomorrow. Come by anytime after three. And I was serious about dinner. Ellen thinks you're lonely."

Damn. Ellen was perceptive, but Sarah wasn't sure her loneliness would be fixed by watching Danny and her wife act all lovey-dovey. The very prospect made her feel lonelier still. For a second, she let herself imagine a double date with Danny and Ellen, but the only person she wanted to round out the foursome was the one woman she definitely could not have. She spent a moment reliving the achingly tender, way-too-short, but way-longer-than-it-should've-been kiss, and her knees went weak from the memory. But crazy high levels of attraction weren't enough to erase all the things standing between them. No, she was going to have to find a way to fix her loneliness without the likes of Ellery Durant.

An hour later, she strolled into the office, doing her best to act as if this was just a normal day. As far as everyone else knew, everyone on their team was back to working regular cases since HSI had scooped up any files related to the bombing.

"Hi Sarah, what did you do this weekend?" Beverly asked as she passed by her desk.

She pulled up short at the question, completely unprepared to respond to the casual remark. She'd gone to Ellery's show, gotten stood up after. Had brunch with Liz who spilled secrets, and run into Ellery. And the kiss, the kiss she hadn't been able to forget for a single second since she'd left Ellery's house the day before. Everything led back to Ellery.

As she fumbled for a response that didn't include any detail about what she'd actually done over the weekend, she heard Liz call out, "Sarah, can you come help me real quick?" She looked across the room and saw Liz waving at her from the door of the conference room. She mouthed "sorry" to Beverly and rushed over.

Liz ushered her in and shut the door. "She's sweet, but you have to watch out because she's a bit of a gossip," Liz whispered.

"Who, Beverly?" Sarah didn't try to hide the incredulous tone in her voice.

"Yes, Beverly. She's stealthy about it, so you'd never know, but most of the rumors around the office? All her."

Sarah raised her eyebrows. "Seems like something you could've told me before."

"Takes me a while to trust someone. Don't judge. We all have our issues."

"Fair enough. So, you trust me now?"

"No one's shown up on my doorstep trying to question my daughter."

"And no one will if I have anything to do with it. She didn't do anything wrong. She seems like a pretty good kid."

"As far as teenagers go, I suppose she is. I wake up thankful every day that she isn't pregnant or in rehab."

"High standards."

"I'm kidding," Liz said. "Mostly. She is a good kid. I wish I saw her more, but it's easier to miss her than to have her hate me for dragging her away from the life she's always known."

Sarah thought about her own mother who'd found it easier to ditch her family than stick around and make things work. Sacrifice had never been a word in her mother's vocabulary.

"So, what do we do now?" Liz asked.

"Sorry, what?"

"You're obviously going rogue on this. You know, showing up on my doorstep over the weekend, questioning my daughter."

"Takes one to know one. You still have all of those records at your place?"

"Let's just say I'm not big on trusting agents outside the Bureau to do my work. Mason's an easy boss, but when it comes to drawing a line in the sand, he has no sense of territory. He'd just as soon give everything over to HSI than be responsible if something goes south. Besides, I heard you asked for the scanned copies of the documents. I'm willing to bet you have a copy at your house right now. Am I right?"

Sarah offered a grudging smile. "Let me guess, Beverly?"

"One and the same."

"Okay then, I have a question."

"Shoot."

Sarah considered carefully. Her gut told her to trust Liz with the information her question would convey, but if she was wrong, she could wind up causing even more trouble for Ellery. She decided to go with her gut. "Why doesn't the scanned copy contain any of the records that have Ellery Durant's name on them? The search warrant references a couple of documents, but I haven't seen them in any of the papers we had."

"I don't know. The IRS form was in the box I gave to HSI, but it was only a page or two. Could be that part of the form just jammed up in the scanner and didn't go through. Wait a minute, how do you have a copy of the search warrant? Do you have an inside connection with HSI?"

Sarah could hear Trip's voice in her head, telling her to keep quiet, but again her gut told her to trust Liz. If she wanted to get any information, she was going to have to give some. "BAU has been asked to assess Ellery Durant, and since I'm the only agent in the area with their particular training, they asked me to see what I could find out. They gave me a copy of the warrant Friday. Needless to say this is all on the down low."

"Got it. Have to say I was surprised to see her name come up. She's an aggressive son of a bitch in the courtroom, but she's always been very professional when we've met before. I figured her for a straight and narrow type when it came to her own affairs."

Sarah couldn't help but be pleased to find Liz had essentially the same impression of Ellery she did. Well, except for the aggressive part. To her, Ellery seemed pretty unassuming. Well, unless she counted that kiss and how could she not count the kiss since the memory of it had lingered in her conscience the entire night and was the reason for what she had to do now. "I'm finishing that project up today and then I'll be available for the most boring assignment you can muster up."

"Wait a minute, you have a perfect in to work on the bombing case and you'd rather review files?"

Sarah nodded. "There are good people on the case. I know that for a fact. I just don't need to be one of them." She spoke the words as if she meant them, hoping if she just kept thinking that way, the tinge of doubt telling her she was going to miss out on something exciting would subside.

The only really exciting thing that had happened to her lately had been Ellery's kiss. She might not be able to have more of that, but it was time to quit putting her life on hold for her job.

❖

Ellery got out of her truck and looked around until she spotted the dark sedan parked near the end of the street. She waved at the car. If the federal agents watching Amir's house were taking pictures, she wanted them to have a good shot for their files.

She had taken a chance coming here, but she'd called his office and they said he was home. She rang the doorbell and waited, hoping Amir would let her in. He was probably busy trying to console his family after the invasion of privacy he'd suffered on Friday and she only hoped he didn't attribute any of his misfortune to her. Yet.

The door swung open and Amir's wife, Fara Khan stood in the foyer. "Ellery Durant. I couldn't believe it when I saw you through the peephole."

"Mrs. Khan, I'm sorry to just drop by, but—"

"But you weren't sure you'd be welcome otherwise, right?"

"That's about the size of it. Is Amir in?"

"He is. Come with me."

Ellery followed Fara through a large living room into a study.

"Have a seat. I'll go get him for you."

While she waited, she looked around the room, which was apparently Amir's home office. A large computer monitor sat on the desk, but the shelves were practically empty.

"They took almost all of my papers. Those shelves were full of binders. A lot of them old and worthless information, but they just kept grabbing and grabbing."

Ellery stood and reached out a hand. Amir looked at her outstretched hand for a moment before he shook it. "Same thing happened to me, Amir."

He nodded. "Sit, sit. Do you want some coffee? Fara makes the best coffee."

Ellery hesitated before deciding that sharing coffee would be a good way to make this visit as friendly as possible. "That would be great."

While Amir asked Fara to make them drinks, she took in the rest of the room. One wall was a photo gallery, featuring some local celebrities who had worked with the WHI to raise money. She imagined every one of the people featured in these photos wished they could go back in time and make a different choice rather than be associated with someone accused of terrorism. Then she realized Amir might not know he was being accused of terrorism since he wouldn't have access to the search warrant affidavit. Should she share that with him? That hadn't been part of her plan when she came here, but it might be the out she needed.

The coffee was wonderful, dark and delicious, but no matter how hard she tried to forget, she wasn't here for a friendly visit. "We need to talk."

"My lawyer says I shouldn't talk to you, but then again I only met him a couple of days ago. Certainly not long enough for me to know if I should trust him."

The words "my lawyer" sounded weird coming from Amir, especially since she realized he wasn't talking about her or her former firm. "Who did you hire?"

"Robert Novak. As I said, I don't really know him, but he was recommended by a friend."

Ellery wondered if the friend was Sadeem Jafari. It would probably be in Jafari's best interest to arrange for Amir's representation so he could have inside knowledge about anything he said to law enforcement. "In the abstract, he's probably giving you very good advice, but in reality things are more complicated."

"I have known you and your father for a very long time. You have always done right by my family, but it seems we are both under a microscope right now, although I do not know why. I would never turn you away from my home, but you probably should not have come here."

Ellery set her coffee cup down and contemplated her next move. She could get up and walk out, choosing not to consult with Amir before she made a decision about whether or not to give the feds what she knew. Or she could give him a chance to explain. Technically, what he had done didn't fall into the realm of attorney client privilege, at least not as to her. He'd used her name on documents that implicated them both in potential federal crimes. The fraud released her of her duty to him.

But it wasn't that easy, especially since it was highly likely her father had been the impetus behind Amir's action. As frustrating as her father was, was she willing to implicate him as well? And she felt she owed it to Amir to tell him exactly what he was facing since neither he nor his new lawyer would have any way of knowing the full detail until the warrant was unsealed.

Not for the first time she considered the balance between her duty as a lawyer and what she owed strangers who might be harmed by the secrets she kept. She'd never violated a client's confidence and she'd take many awful secrets to her grave, but she'd never had her own liberty at stake. Was it selfish to think she should break the rules to save herself or was it merely practical? She decided to start by seeing if he would even admit what he had done. "The government thinks your charity is a front, a way to funnel money to terrorist groups."

"It isn't true." He straightened in his chair and slapped the arm to emphasize his point.

"They say they have money trails to prove it."

"They can't because it isn't true."

"Who is Sadeem Jafari?"

"He is family, my cousin. Why?"

Ellery watched him carefully, but he didn't show any visible surprise that she'd asked about Jafari. "His foundation, Global Enterprise Alliance. What do you know about it?"

"I know we have many of the same interests. We have worked together many times."

"And you give WHI money to his foundation?"

"Yes. It's part of our outreach. We work together."

"I've read both of your mission statements and they are essentially identical, which makes me wonder why Sadeem even bothered to start his own foundation. Why didn't he just use his resources to bolster WHI?"

"He's very independent, younger, with new ideas. We are a more conservative organization. I think he fancies himself the modern Muslim. He felt he could reach a different donor base than that of WHI."

Yeah, the radical extremist Muslims. She took another sip of coffee and considered Amir's measured reactions to her questions. He seemed genuinely puzzled at any suggestion he or his cousin, Sadeem, might be doing something wrong, but she'd lost count of the amount of times she'd had a client lie to her face. As well as she knew him, she wasn't confident she would be able to tell if he was dissembling or not.

She decided the best way to judge was to catch him completely off guard so she spat out the question she really wanted answered. "Why did you put my name on the IRS forms for WHI?"

Amir closed his eyes and shook his head. "He said it wouldn't matter, but I worried about your reaction. I promise you, I meant you no harm."

"He? My father?"

Amir nodded. "This work is very important to me, but there is so much scrutiny. I thought if they ever asked any questions, I would tell you about it, but until now, no one has raised any issues. I suppose you have told them that I lied."

"No, I haven't, but I need to. My accounts are frozen and I may face criminal charges for whatever activity the government suspects you of. Protecting a client's information only goes so far, but I wanted to come to you first before I tell anyone anything."

Amir reached out a hand. "You do what you must."

"How can you say that, Father?"

Ellery looked up to see Naveed standing in the doorway to the study. "Hi, Naveed. How are you?"

"I will be fine, no thanks to you. Are you really going to turn my father in?"

She'd never seen him angry and his demeanor surprised her. "Well, I'm not sure what you heard, but it's not that simple. Maybe I should leave you two to discuss it."

"First you abandon me and my case and then you betray my father. He has done nothing wrong and he never will."

Naveed's voice carried a distinct edge that had been absent when she'd met with him at the courthouse a few weeks ago. "Naveed, I'm sorry I couldn't do more for you on your case, but I left you in good hands with Meg. It wasn't personal."

"Naveed, apologize to Miss Durant. It's not her fault you followed the careless whims of your cousin and his fanatic friends."

The look Naveed shot his father was piercing, but his words were light and casual. "You're right, Father. Ms. Durant, I'm sorry. I get agitated when I think about the police pawing through our things, but that's no excuse for taking it out on you."

"Apology accepted." Ellery stared at Naveed's eyes as she spoke. The sharp edge was still there. No matter how nice and polite his words were, he was still angry about something. She couldn't really blame him. The crime he'd been charged with was small change compared to the possible indictment his father faced. Even if nothing came of the government's investigation, just by virtue of the asset freeze and search warrants, Amir would likely suffer setbacks to all of his business interests. She made a quick decision.

"Amir, if you come clean about the IRS application, it will be better than if I tell the feds about it. Talk to Novack and see what he says. If you want, I'll talk to him directly, but it will need to be fast—there's a short window here for cooperation. If you ever trusted my advice before, trust me now when I say you will be in a better position if you go to them first."

"I will talk to Mr. Novack and have him call you."

"Thank you, Amir." Ellery stood up, ready to leave, but she realized she had one more question. "Your cousin, Sadeem, did he use my father to advise him as well?"

"No, your father was retired by the time he established his foundation." Amir looked sheepish. "He went directly to your former partner, Megan Patrick, to do the paperwork, because he'd heard she was not as thorough as you. He thought she wouldn't ask many questions. As far as I know, he just made up a name of an attorney for the application, thinking she wouldn't check."

His words were a blur as she realized how deeply Meg had betrayed her. She must've doctored the paperwork to make it look like her father had drafted it, but why hadn't she mentioned it when she'd handed over the search warrant affidavit that contained Jafari's name along with Amir's? As for the contents of the application, she hadn't checked Jafari's paperwork or she had and she hadn't cared.

The very idea she'd been deceived by both her father and her friend and former law partner was suffocating. "I should go."

"I'll show her out," Naveed volunteered.

"Thank you, son."

Ellery followed Naveed to the door, but she paused in the entryway. "Your father is an honorable man."

"My father is a weak man. He will take the easy way out. He hasn't done anything wrong. If you both keep quiet, they would never be able to prove otherwise."

His tone was casual, but Ellery could hear the undercurrent of judgment. "I believe your father is not a terrorist, but he did do something wrong. He lied on a document filed with the government. The good news is the falsehood is a minor crime compared to the allegations of terrorism. If he admits the one, he might be able to avoid the other. Besides, are you really being fair? Just a few weeks ago, I was in court trying to get you a deal rather than have you fight charges."

"That was different."

Ellery waited for him to explain, but he didn't elaborate. The old her would have asked what he meant. The old her would have pressed Amir for more detail about Sadeem, since his foundation information was in her old law firm files. For a second, she wondered about Meg and whether she had been duplicitous, but then the second was over and she decided she didn't much care. None of these people and their decisions were her problem anymore. If Amir didn't do the right thing, she would. If it meant implicating her father and Amir both, she didn't care. She'd lived too long with the guilt caused by keeping confidences. The personal cost was too high and she was done paying for other people's mistakes. The only way to truly break free from her old life was to cut all ties completely.

As she walked out the door, she met a young blonde walking up the sidewalk, toward the Khan's front door. She smiled and the girl smiled back, but she looked more nervous than happy and Ellery noticed she quickened her pace. When Ellery reached the street, she glanced back at the Khans' door and caught a few words of the whispered conversation as Naveed ushered the girl into the house.

"Jasmine, you shouldn't have come here." "I didn't have a choice."
After those few words the voices were jumbled until she heard the
door shut behind them as they entered the house.

Something about the exchange bothered her, but she shrugged
it off and climbed into her truck. Amir had likely told Naveed not to
have anyone over while they were in the middle of this mess, but the
pull of teen drama often outweighed parental caution.

As she drove away, she waved at the occupants of the sedan still
parked at the end of the street, imagining the surprised expressions
of the agents behind their dark sunglasses. She wondered how long
it would be before Sarah knew she'd visited Amir. She had until
tonight to give Sarah her decision, but part of her wanted to call
her now and tell her she'd made up her mind. But she'd promised
Amir she'd give him a chance to do the right thing, and as much as
she wanted this over, she felt compelled to keep her word even if it
meant another twenty-four hours before she could see Sarah again.

CHAPTER SEVENTEEN

The hallways of the Dallas County courthouse were dead compared to the last time she was here. Sarah found Danny sitting in her office with two guys, one of whom she recognized from her visit there several weeks ago. Before the bombing. The day she'd first met Ellery.

"Hey, Sarah. Come on in." Danny waved. "We're just finishing up."

"You get your jury squared away?"

"For what it's worth. Not the greatest bunch, but we got to keep a few of the ones we wanted. We start opening first thing in the morning."

"You ever think about doing something different?"

"Like what?"

"I don't know. Maybe work at a big firm, tax law or some crap like that."

"Crap is a good word for it. You know the big firm lawyers have no life."

"And you do?" Sarah asked. "I'm betting you were working on this case all weekend."

"Yes, but the difference is I'm doing something that matters. Kind of makes it worth all the work." Danny frowned. "What's all this about? You suddenly regret leaving BAU?"

"No. I mean I don't know. I don't regret leaving the unit or moving, but I'm not sure I landed in the right spot."

"You're not stuck. I'm sure you have options. You've been doing this a while. Any unit would be lucky to have you."

"I think I'm just feeling unsettled. I need a real life and this job is the perfect way to get one. I just have one thing to do before I can get back to it."

"I'm not following."

"My old supervisor, Trip, has me doing a side project for him. I'm sure that's what's got me messed up."

"Care to share?"

"Has to do with a certain local attorney and a couple of charities. Do you follow?"

"I do. Is that why you were flirting with her at the show on Friday night?"

"I wasn't flirting."

"Whatever."

"I wasn't."

"Not that you noticed," Danny said. "But there were plenty of eligible women there. Hot ones. But you only had eyes for one. Don't even try to deny it."

"It was work."

Danny grinned. "You're really good at your work."

Her protests weren't doing any good, so Sarah tried to change the subject. "Speaking of work, I came by to see if you could help me out with a couple of files. I wrote down all of the names." She reached into her purse and pulled out an index card. "Here."

Danny took the list and studied it for a moment. "I know these guys. It's all one file. They were all indicted as parties to the same offense."

"What was it?"

"Burglary of a building."

"Sounds kind of dumb."

"Maybe. It doesn't look like they took anything, but it was kind of weird for that reason."

"How do you mean?"

"Well, it was an office building. I mean sure, there are computers and stuff, but it just didn't strike me as the kind of place a bunch of kids would think of breaking into without a good reason. The fact they didn't take anything, makes me curious about what they were really doing there. Ellery said they were just messing around, but usually when we get cases with a bunch of kids fooling around, they choose someplace more interesting—warehouses, malls, music venues."

"Wait a minute, did you say Ellery?" Sarah sat forward in her chair.

"I did. You remember the day you came by? She was here for Naveed Khan's first court appearance. I think she was just filling in for her old law partner, but she was pretty adamant that the whole thing was nothing more than a bunch of kids goofing off."

Sarah remembered the meeting well. Ellery, looking sharp and handsome in lawyer clothes, had been annoyed with her for butting in on her talk with Danny about the fate of her young client. Sarah hadn't meant to get on her bad side, but she hadn't been able to help herself. Now she wished she'd listened more closely to the details of Ellery's discussion with Danny. "Don't you think it's odd that Amir Khan's son was facing felony charges just days before a bomb goes off in the city?"

Danny frowned. "What makes you think the two things are related? Naveed was arrested over six months ago. Our grand juries have been backed up and these punk cases got pushed back a bit. The fact that his court appearance happened the week of the bombing was a coincidence. Besides, you feds seem to think Amir is a felon, so why would you be surprised to find out his son is a member of the same club?"

"I'm not sure what to think." That much was true. Sarah couldn't put her finger on it, but she didn't believe in coincidence. There was more to this story, and she was convinced there were connections even if no one had figured them out or even noticed their existence yet. "How fast can I get the file?"

"If you have a flash drive, I can download the police report and indictment for you right now."

While Sarah waited for Danny to copy the file, her mind raced back to the first time she'd met Ellery. She'd seemed like a fierce advocate for her client, not at all like someone who was passing a case for a colleague. She'd been invested in the outcome of Naveed's case. Was that because she had something at stake in getting a good result? What had she said about her client, Naveed? He was in the top of his class and he'd been accepted to an Ivy League school. What was a kid like that doing hanging around punks like the Barstow brothers who were on a CIA watch list?

Every nerve ending was on high alert. When Danny finally handed her the flash drive, she practically grabbed it out of her hand. She was halfway out the door before she registered Danny asking her a question.

"Want to come over for dinner tonight? You can help me brainstorm my opening statement for tomorrow."

Dinner with friends. She should say yes because that was the kind of thing normal people did, but until she closed this case, she wouldn't get back to normal. She'd started this day intending to tell Trip she was done working on this case, but she should've known better. Digging deep, doggedly pursuing leads, those tasks were the things that had always defined her and moving across the country and working as a paper pusher hadn't changed who she was. "I'll have to take a rain check. Give my best to Ellen."

An hour later, she'd examined every aspect of the file Danny had given her. She was no closer to a solution, but she had a hunch. She picked up the phone and dialed Trip's number, happy to hear him answer on the first ring.

"Whatcha got?" he asked.

"Not sure, but I need your help."

"Shoot."

"If I give you an address for an office building, can you have Peter run down a list of every business in the building, rosters of employees and whatever else he can dig up?" Peter was the resident computer genius in the BAU and his information gathering skills were unparalleled.

"Mind telling me what you've got in mind?"

"I'd rather wait until I have more info."

"I can have him start right now."

"Faster the better."

"On it. Anything else?"

"Not yet."

"Did you talk to her? I know you were at her place yesterday."

"I'm trying not to let it bother me that you know my every movement." Sarah blushed when she remembered how yesterday's visit with Ellery had ended, the memory of her claiming lips, her strong arms. Thank goodness whoever the agency had watching could only see what went on outside Ellery's house.

"You know it's not you we're watching."

"Still."

"We need to move on this."

"Tomorrow. Give me a day."

"Done. And, Sarah?"

"Yes?"

"You were meant for this. You have the right instincts. It's in your blood. You don't have to come back to BAU, but don't waste away in the fraud unit."

When she hung up the phone, Trip's words echoed and she knew he was right. Now she just had to figure out what to do about it.

❖

Ellery didn't recognize the phone number, but she was done hiding out. Holding out a fraction of hope the caller was Sarah, she answered the line. "Hello."

"Ellery, it's Bob Novak."

"Hey, Bob, good to hear from you." She was surprised to hear from Amir's new attorney so soon, but she'd known Bob for a long time. More than likely he'd called to discuss the proposition Ellery had given Amir that morning before he contacted the AUSA handling the case. "I guess Amir told you I came by."

"He did." Bob cleared her throat. "Look, we've known each other a long time and I know you wouldn't purposefully do anything to get a former client in trouble, but as long you're both in the spotlight, I think it's best if you keep your distance."

His words were like a punch in the gut, and any hope she'd had that Amir would do the right thing faded fast. She forced herself to remain calm. "I'm guessing Amir didn't give you a lot of detail about why I showed up to visit him."

"He said you wanted to touch base, wish him the best, see if there was anything you could do. I told him not to talk to you anymore, but to let me be the bad guy about it. I'm sure you realize the feds probably have him under surveillance. Pictures of a co-defendant showing up at his front door doesn't help either of you."

Ellery seethed. Apparently, Amir hadn't bothered to mention his transgressions or made any overtures toward clearing her name. He'd made her next decision an easy one. "Bob, I'm only telling you this because I respect you. I've seen the search warrant affidavit and I know exactly what I'm accused of doing and what Amir is accused of doing. Your client is not being entirely truthful with you. I just don't want you to spin your wheels looking for defenses that don't exist."

"I don't suppose you'd care to clue me in."

She considered his request. She could share the copy of the affidavit, but she had no idea what Meg had done to get it and, as angry as she was with her right now, she didn't want to compromise sources she could use to help other clients. Disseminating a sealed document in violation of a court order was pretty serious stuff. Besides, if Amir didn't want to keep his new attorney in the loop, that was his business. She'd given him an opportunity to do the right thing, but she couldn't make him take responsibility.

She could do one thing, though. "Tell you what. Talk to Amir again. Remind him I said he had until tonight to consider doing what I asked. If I don't hear from you by seven tonight, I'll do what I need to."

"Sounds ominous."

"Just talk to your client, Bob. If you can get him to be honest with you, it'll help in the long run."

"Who are you hiring? I heard your dad was in town. Is he going to represent you?"

Ellery laughed both at the idea she could ever put her destiny in her father's hands and at the fact she hadn't even considered hiring someone to represent her. "Let's just say I'm still exploring my options."

"Don't try and do this yourself. You know what they say, an attorney who represents himself—"

"Has a fool for a client. I know, I know. Trust me, I have it covered." Ellery's mind flashed to an image of Sarah leaning close as they kissed. She harbored no illusions that their kiss, no matter how electric, would sway Sarah's mind if she decided she'd broken the law. Sarah was all about law and order, as she should be. But she'd also be fair. If Amir didn't own up to implicating her in his activities, then all she could do was hope Sarah would believe her side of the story.

After she hung up with Bob, she contemplated her next action. She had hours before she expected to hear back from him about Amir's decision and to let Sarah know whether she would cooperate. The time stretched before her like an empty canvas and she knew exactly what she wanted to be doing. Within a half an hour she was in her studio, music blaring, working on new pieces to replace the sold out inventory. She may not be able to fix everything that had gone wrong in her life, but she could make something special in the time she had.

❖

"I just sent you the list. Check your e-mail."

Sarah smiled at the sound of Peter's voice. Always brisk and efficient, he couldn't be bothered to say hello before launching in. She clicked open her e-mail account and scanned the inbox. "I see it. Thanks."

She waited for him to say good-bye, but instead he said, "I went ahead and cross-checked all the names with the current investigation."

It would take her hours to do the same. "And?"

"See the entry for Chavez and Hamilton?"

"I see it. Sounds like a law firm."

"Try architects. Want to guess what one of their big projects was back in 2001?"

She didn't want to guess. She didn't want to know her earlier hunch was right on target, that Naveed and his friends didn't break into that building just for fun. But she had to know the truth. "Tell me."

"They designed the arena."

"Damn."

"What do you want to do?"

"Hang on a sec." She put the phone between her chin and shoulder and jabbed at her keyboard, pulling up the police report from Naveed's case. While Peter waited, she scanned it, line by line. "Nothing was taken."

"What?"

"The boys who broke in, they didn't take anything."

"I'm guessing the police didn't search their cell phones when they were arrested, or even if they did, they didn't have a clue what they were seeing."

"You think they took pictures of the plans for the arena?"

"I don't know, but the timing's right since the break-in occurred about six months before the bombing. Plenty of time to strategize. I'm sending you the contact information for the named partners of the firm now. I'll send you the rest of the info on the building occupants, but I think this one's your best bet."

"I think you're right. Go ahead and send the rest, but I'm going to head there now. Let Trip know what I'm up to, will you."

"Will do. Hey, Sarah?"

"Yes?"

"We miss you around here."

She started to stay she missed them too, but it was more complicated than that. She did miss this adrenaline surge, but she knew the after effect was chilling. Hunting down bad guys was definitely a charge, but in this case, it was looking like the bad guys were tied to Ellery, and she'd give anything if that weren't the case.

She sighed. Maybe she was jumping to conclusions. After all, it was a big leap to assume that because Naveed was one of the boys who'd broken into the same building that housed the architectural firm that designed the arena, he'd been responsible for the bombing. Like Ellery had said, he was a smart, up-and-coming kid. What would his motivation be to engage in such a vicious act of terrorism? But her gut was rarely wrong, and she knew without a doubt the two things were connected.

The drive to the building didn't take long, and within the hour, she was standing at the reception desk at Chavez and Hamilton Designs.

"I'm sorry, neither Mr. Chavez nor Ms. Hamilton have any available appointments this afternoon."

The middle-aged, front desk power broker didn't look sorry at all. Sarah pulled out her badge and dangled it over the counter that separated them. "I think they'll see me. Would you mind double-checking?"

The woman picked up the phone and whispered into the line. Sarah watched as the woman's smug demeanor deflated. When she hung up the phone, she said, "It looks as if there's been a cancellation. I can show you in to see Mr. Chavez."

Sarah greeted the news with an exaggerated smile. "Thank you so much."

Carlos Chavez was waiting at the door to his office when Sarah approached. He invited her in, shut the door behind them, and motioned for her to have a seat. "Linda said you're with the FBI?"

"Yes. I'm following up on an investigation by the Dallas Police Department. Were you aware this building was broken into about six months ago?"

"No, I wasn't, but we only lease space here. I guess if nothing happened to our offices, the landlord didn't think it was worth mentioning."

"So, you don't recall noticing anything unusual or out of place around that time or after?" She glanced around the office as she asked the question. Stacks of paper covered every available surface.

He laughed. "As you can see, I'm not big on tidy, but trust me, I know what every single slip of paper means and where it is. I just work better surrounded by chaos."

Sarah smiled. "And your partner?"

"Hard to believe, but Victoria is messier than me. They say you should find a business partner that complements you, but we decided having double the creative energy was more important than good organizational skills. Mind if I ask why the FBI would be interested in a break-in at a private office building?"

She weighed her options. If she told him the truth, she risked compromising the investigation, but she had to find out if her hunch was correct. "I understand you designed the arena downtown. Do you do a lot of jobs like that?"

"If only there were a lot of jobs like that. We've worked on some amazing projects, but, like many architecture firms, our mainstay is office buildings." He dipped his head slightly and narrowed his eyes. "Are you investigating the bombing?"

"Yes, and as I'm sure you can imagine, it's a delicate matter. Whatever I say to you, whatever you say to me—it's important that you not discuss it with anyone else. Do you understand?"

"Of course. Ask me what you really want to know."

"Do you keep copies of the plans for the arena here at your office? If so, where specifically, and can I see them?"

"Yes, we have them and you can see them. They're in Victoria's office." He stood up. "Come with me and I'll show you."

They walked through a door in the back of his office down a small hallway to another large door and went inside. Victoria Hamilton's office was lighter, more feminine, but in an equal state of disarray. Carlos walked to the back wall that was lined with cabinets and pulled out a sheaf of papers. He spread them out on a nearby drafting table and waved Sarah over. "Here they are."

She looked down at the blue lines on the paper. Her mind whirred as she imagined two of the boys holding down the corners of the paper and the other snapping pictures with his cell, while Naveed waited in the car. She pointed at the paper. "What exactly am I looking at here?"

"This is the overall design scheme, complete with suggestions for the landscaping. When you move to the next page," he flipped the paper, "that's when you get into the showplace itself. The arena is designed to hold twenty-one thousand people." He pointed to the right side of the page. "This is where the explosion went off. I don't know what kind of explosives were used, but they had an extra boost of impact because of the way this area is structured. See the supports here? Each one of them came down, which caused this entire area to implode and block all the exits on that side of the arena."

"You've obviously given this some thought. Has anyone else talked to you about this?"

"Victoria and I discussed it in the days after the explosion. It's a bit disconcerting to see something you designed be damaged by such a violent act. But, no, I haven't discussed it with anyone from law enforcement if that's what you're asking. The plans are on file with the city, so I'm sure if one of your colleagues wanted a copy, it would be easy to get one."

Sarah looked around the room. She didn't see any locks on any of the cabinets. "Do you have an internal security system of any kind?"

He shook his head. "We lock up at night at the front door to the reception area where you came in, but other than that, nothing. There's a security guard in the building, and I always figured we were at low risk for theft. The other businesses in the building are all professional offices, real estate, mortgage lender, a psychologist. Probably the only things worth taking in the whole place are computers. Thieves would be better off breaking into a Best Buy if that's what they're after."

He was right, which gave her additional confidence in her theory that the boys were after something very specific when they broke into this building. The problem would be proving it. If they had taken photos of the plans, in all likelihood, the photos had been destroyed by now. She supposed there might still be fingerprints on the plans themselves, if the boys had slipped up. She pointed at the plans. "I'm going to send someone to pick these up. In the meantime, can you make sure no one else touches them?" She gave him her business card and urged him to call her directly if he thought of anything else. She walked to the door to leave, but paused before she opened it. "One last question."

"Sure."

She pulled up a copy of the indictment for the burglary case on her phone and handed it to him. "Do you recognize any of these names?" She watched while he scanned the screen and knew the second she'd hit gold because his back stiffened and he sucked in a deep breath. "Who is it? Who do you know?"

"Akbar Jafari. He's a college kid. He interned for us last year. Great student and a hard worker. Are you saying he broke in? Why would he do that? If there was something here he wanted, he could have gotten it during the time he worked here."

Sarah didn't have the answer to his question, but she knew without a doubt she was one step closer to figuring out who was responsible for the bombing. Naveed Khan's cousin Akbar, Sadeem Jafari's son, had worked for the architect who had designed the arena. The boys, along with two brothers whose terrorist leanings had drawn the attention of the CIA, had broken into a building where the plans for the arena were kept about six months prior to the bombing, plenty of time to plan and execute their fatal plan. These facts tied Naveed directly to the bombing, but still raised lots of questions. How had they managed to pull off the act? At least some of these kids were already on the CIA and HSI's radar. Seems like someone from one of those agencies would have checked their whereabouts for the night of the bombing. What was Naveed's role?

And the most important question of all, to her anyway, what did Ellery know?

CHAPTER EIGHTEEN

L ooks like you have company."

Ellery looked in the direction of Leo's beer bottle and watched as Sarah's Corvette pulled into her driveway. For the second time, she wondered how a government agent could afford such an expensive car, but she had bigger worries right now. She'd been sitting on Leo's front porch for the past hour, contemplating her next move. Seven o'clock had come and gone and, with no further word from Amir or his new attorney, she had some decisions to make. She'd hoped to have a bit longer to figure out her next move, but Sarah's arrival signaled time was up.

She raised her beer bottle as Sarah looked their way. Sarah's smile was reserved, reminding her of the serious talk ahead, but she also couldn't help but notice how good she looked in jeans, loafers, and a cherry red sweater that hugged her chest. She remembered how April had shown up for their chili dinner, looking awkward in jeans instead of a cocktail dress. Sarah, on the other hand, made every outfit look as if it was a second skin. She sighed. If only they'd met under different circumstances.

"Sorry I didn't call first," Sarah said as she climbed the steps. "I was hoping I'd find you home."

"Where else would I be?"

"And it's not like you folks wouldn't know if she was out gallivanting," Leo said.

Sarah smiled. "Good point." She looked at Ellery. "If you're busy, I can come back later."

Ellery could tell she was only offering to be polite, but she wasn't in any hurry to respond to Sarah's ultimatums. "Sit down and have a beer with us."

Sarah looked between them and Ellery was certain she was trying to find a way to assert her authority without rising Leo's ire, so she was surprised when Sarah said, "Sure, I'll take a beer."

Ellery reached into the bucket full of ice and bottles near Leo's feet and ignored his scowl as she pulled out a bottle and handed it over. Sarah twisted the top and took a deep drink before leaning back against the railing and crossing her feet. To a casual observer, she didn't look like she had a care in the world.

And she probably didn't. Sarah would close out this case and move on to the next. Her reputation, her livelihood would be completely unaffected by the outcome despite the huge cloud of dust she'd kicked up as she moved along. In contrast, no matter what Ellery did to clear her name, people would always have doubts. One accusation, even unfounded, could tank a name, a career, a life. She drank from her beer because she had nothing to say.

Leo, though, had plenty to talk about. He pointed at Sarah's Corvette. "That's one of the anniversary cars, isn't it?"

"Yes, sir."

"Got the extra package?"

"Yes, sir."

"Not cheap."

"No, sir."

Ellery watched the ping-pong conversation for a moment before butting in. "What are you talking about?"

Sarah shot Leo an expectant look, as if deferring to him. He wiped beer off his lips with the back of his hand and said, "That there's a 2013 Anniversary edition Corvette. Chevy made three hundred of those beauties to celebrate the model's sixtieth anniversary. She's driving a seventy thousand dollar car, she is. Pretty fancy stuff for a government employee."

Ellery nodded. "Some people might think she was doing something illegal to have the money for that kind of car."

"That's for sure, but then again, she might have some good explanation."

"Like she won the lottery?"

"Or she found it alongside the road and no one showed up to claim it."

Sarah shook her head. "You're both hilarious. And subtle." She looked at Leo. "I'm sure you would agree that the easiest explanation is usually the right one."

"Mostly."

"I bought the car. Spent the last ten years working a job that took every minute of every day. My social life consisted of a few drinks in bars and late night rendezvous. No wining and dining. You save a lot of money that way. Sold the house my grandfather left me, put the money in the bank and watched it grow. Between that and my savings, I was able to get the car of my dreams, since driving is one of the few pleasures I've had time to enjoy. I also have a weakness for expensive shoes." She stared at Ellery. "Are all of your entanglements so easy to explain?"

The undercurrent of anger was impossible to miss, and Ellery saw Leo start to rise out of his chair in challenge. She waved him back, sending him a look designed to say she could fight her own battles. "I think we should adjourn to my house. Leo, thanks for the beer."

He frowned as he looked between them, but he finally said, "You know you're welcome here anytime. And you know what to do if you need me."

Sarah thanked him as well, but Leo only grunted. Ellery walked Sarah back to her house and led her into the kitchen. Sarah didn't sit at the table this time. Instead she paced the floor, a frown on her face. "Should I bill the government if you wear out my wood floors?" Ellery asked.

"From the start I couldn't believe you would be involved in anything that had to do with terrorism, let alone the bombing."

"Obviously, you've changed your mind."

"Do you even care what I think?"

Ellery stared at Sarah, trying to cipher the source of her angry tone. "I can't believe you're asking me that, but the truth is it doesn't matter what you think. I know the truth."

"I wish I did."

"I wish you did too," Ellery said. "So, we're back to the bombing now. You and I both know the basis for the searches last week weren't linked to the bombing. It's a witch hunt. HSI has information that Amir Khan's charity raised money that ultimately went to a group that may or may not have ties to a terrorist group. The proof isn't concrete and the search warrants were a fishing expedition. The truth is there is nothing that ties Amir to the bombing, right?"

"You have a soft spot for Naveed, don't you? I remember you advocating for him the day we first met. Ivy League bound, star student, never been in trouble."

"What does Naveed have to do with this?"

"I'm guessing the plan was for Naveed to fade the heat. Because if he says their plan to break into an office building was just a silly prank, then people would believe it. What I don't get is why you quit practicing right around the time they all got caught? Maybe you were having second thoughts about representing young terrorists, which makes me wonder why you were with Naveed in court on his first appearance?"

Ellery watched Sarah grow increasingly agitated as she ticked through her thoughts. She'd expected Sarah to show up and pressure her to make a decision about flipping on Amir, but her persistent focus on Naveed was completely unexpected. Well, when it came to being aggravated, she could join the club. "I have no idea what you're talking about. Would you like to fill me in or would you rather keep making these vague references to whatever it is that's got you so riled?"

Sarah stopped pacing, but she remained standing, staring. Ellery didn't have a clue what message she was supposed to be getting from the silence, and she'd just about decided this entire meeting was a waste of time, when she saw Sarah's expression settle from skepticism into resignation. She wanted to say something to urge her to speak, but decided to let her talk on her own time. When Sarah finally spoke, Ellery was surprised by her first words.

"I'll take a beer if you're offering."

"Of course." Ellery pulled a bottle and a cold glass from the fridge and set it on the table in front of her.

"What, you're not going to join me?"

"Seems like I might need to keep a level head to deal with whatever it is you've got in store for me. Besides, I'm already one ahead of you."

"Good point." Sarah took a deep pull straight from the bottle. Ellery watched her drink, remembering the heat of Sarah's lips on hers, wishing this exchange were taking place under very different circumstances. While Sarah drank, she allowed her mind to wander into a fantasy full of wishing Sarah's visit wasn't about terrorism, bombings, and crime. She'd walked away from a life where her days were full of the drama that accompanied the push and pull of prosecution and defense. The fact that these very things were dogging her chances to get close to the one woman who'd captured her interest in years was cruel irony that clouded her thoughts to the point she almost missed Sarah's next words.

"Naveed was one of the bombers."

"Excuse me?" Surely she hadn't heard her correctly. "You've got to be kidding."

"I'm not."

Ellery did her best to shift focus. Despite Sarah's earlier comments about Naveed, she'd been completely unprepared for the harsh accusation. "You have proof?" Sarah's expression was pained and she pounced. "You don't have proof, do you? This is another one of those throw something against the wall and see if it sticks tactics, isn't it?"

Sarah shook her head, but instead of triumph, Ellery read pain in her eyes. "I don't have everything I need to prove it to a jury, but I have enough to know I'm right. The rest will come."

Ellery sank into one of the sturdy wood chairs and leaned her arms on the kitchen table that she'd crafted from remnants of an old barn. Seemed she could remake anything except her own destiny. "Tell me."

Sarah walked over to the fridge and pulled out a beer bottle, twisted the cap and placed it in front of her. "I will, but you're going to want this." She sat at the table and sighed. "One of the tenants in the building that Naveed and his friends broke into is an architectural firm that designed the arena. Naveed's cousin, Akbar, interned at the firm last year. I've confirmed that the original blueprints for the arena were present at the office at the time of the break-in."

"A little attenuated, don't you think?"

"Spoken like a true defense attorney. There's more. Michael and Brian Barstow, the two other boys who were with Naveed and Akbar that night, have been going by Hashid and Abdul Kamal for the better part of the last year. Michael's got a very interesting blog site, all about the evils of America and the glory of Islam."

Ellery didn't bother to try to hide her surprise. She hadn't met the other boys, but she'd taken Naveed at his word that the break-in had been a stunt, boys' play. The potential impact on his future was the primary reason she'd turned down Amir's request that she represent the entire group, and because the case was still lingering through the system when she'd left the practice, she'd left it to Meg to determine if talking to the other boys was even necessary in formulating Naveed's defense. "Are you saying they were all involved in the bombing?"

"I believe that's true, but I don't know everyone's role yet."

"You said Naveed was one of the bombers."

"If he was involved at all, he was in it all the way. And I know he was involved."

"It doesn't make sense. You said yourself, Akbar used to work at that firm. Why didn't he take the plans for the arena when he worked there? Were the plans even missing?"

"No, but someone could easily take a picture with their cell phone. The police didn't search any of the boys' cell phones at the time of the arrest, by the way. As for why Akbar didn't take the plans when he worked there, I don't know. Maybe this scheme was hatched after the fact, but if that were all I had, I would expect you to be able to tear it apart."

"What else?"

"I just talked to my contact in D.C. Did you know Naveed has a girlfriend?"

"What does that have to do with anything?"

"Doesn't matter if you knew. The point is she's a pretty blond thing. Petite and feminine. You know the type—a wink and a smile and she gets whatever she wants."

Ellery's mind flashed to the girl she'd seen on Naveed's doorstep the day before and the furtive, whispered conversation they'd shared. Suddenly, Sarah's slow and deliberate storytelling gnawed at her nerves. "What's your point?"

"I guess he thought his files would be safe on her computer. I mean, nobody ever thinks the Barbie doll is guilty of anything, right?"

"You must have one hell of a warrant if you're tapping into communications by people not even covered in your original warrant."

"I'm not supposed to talk about a sealed FISA warrant. Wait a minute, how do you know what's in the original warrant?"

Ellery smiled at the gotcha. "You have no reason to know this, but I was a big deal in this town before I quit. I still have friends who are willing to look out for me."

Sarah looked her up and down as if appraising. "I have no doubt."

Ellery locked into her gaze and lost track of the amount of time they stared at each other as she pondered the attraction. It wasn't just that Sarah was beautiful, charming, and a clever adversary. They were more than adversaries. At the root of it all, she believed they both wanted the truth, even if they took very different routes to get there. Sarah was trained to suspect everyone and whittle down from broad generalizations to a narrow truth. On the other hand, she'd learned to start by looking at her one client and then finding a host of other options to create doubt. Her way had failed her before, once with devastating consequences, which made her question if she'd missed something critical when it came to Naveed.

"Tell me what you know," Ellery said. "I need to hear it and I give you my word, if I can help you, I will." She willed Sarah to hear the weight of the promise behind her words. After a moment, Sarah started talking.

"All of those boys have girlfriends. Young, pretty, blond, girlfriends. Don't you think it's odd that a group of Muslim extremists would have the most Western looking girlfriends they could find?"

"I guess so. What exactly did you find on the computer of Naveed's girlfriend?"

"Photos taken with a cell phone. Photos of the arena blueprints."

"What else?"

"You don't think that's enough?"

"You and I both know it isn't. What aren't you telling me?"

"Truthfully, we haven't found anything specific yet. There are a ton of messages between them, but they're still being sorted out. I imagine most of them are coded."

"You really think they would be careless enough to have the plans for the arena where they can easily be found, but have some kind of sophisticated code for communicating about a plot to bomb the arena?"

"They're terrorists, but that doesn't make them smart."

"Naveed is."

"Exactly, which is why the plans aren't on his computer."

Ellery wasn't convinced, but she moved on. "So, what are you doing next?"

"We have agents checking to see where each of them was the night of the bombing, checking cell phone records, etc."

"You obviously don't want to tip them off that you think they were involved."

"No, we don't want another Tsarnaev."

Ellery shuddered. She, like the rest of the country, had followed the trial of the one surviving Boston Marathon bomber. The story of the bloody shootout that preceded his apprehension, including the fact he'd run over his own brother while trying to escape the police, had been horrifying. "So, here's what I don't understand. Why are you telling me all of this?"

"Naveed trusts you. That's why you were with him in court, right?"

"His attorney wasn't available. I was just standing in."

"She could've gotten anyone to cover, but she picked you because that family looks to you for guidance. They always have."

"More information you gathered from e-mail?"

"It's true. And I think you care about them as well. Certainly enough to pay them a personal visit this morning."

"Someday you should try living under a microscope and see how it makes you feel. For your information, I went to Amir to discuss the only case I knew about at the time. You know, the one where you and your friends accused us both of conspiring to send money overseas to support terrorism. The one where you purposefully placed me in an adversarial position to my former client in an attempt to get me to reveal confidential information. If Naveed was involved in the bombing, I don't know a damn thing about it."

"Would you even tell me if you did?"

Caught up in the heated exchange, Ellery said, "I—", but then she stopped. She couldn't answer the question because she wasn't entirely sure. In her line of work, the good of the one, the defendant, outweighed the good of the many, society. She'd always accepted the truism, and for years she never allowed herself to question the consequences, but last year, when the consequences became truly real, she had been forced to face the dark side of the work she did, and in this moment, it all came rushing back.

She leaned forward and put her head in her hands. "I can't talk about this right now. Go away." She listened as Sarah's footsteps echoed across the wood floor and she heard the sound of a glass clinking against the metal of her kitchen sink. In a few minutes she could be alone and then she would find a way to shake off the memories and ease back into the life she'd made for herself. A life where there was no room for a woman like Sarah, who would never be satisfied until she knew every little thing about her and then be horrified at what she found.

❖

Sarah set the glass down, leaned against the sink, and looked out the window. The solar-lit backyard was serene, complete with a swinging chair and a gazebo filled with flowers. The large building to the left was probably Ellery's studio, and she imagined it was as beautiful inside as out. She wondered if she'd ever be invited in to see the place where Ellery created the stunning pieces she'd seen at the show.

Trip wanted her to get Ellery to talk about her former client. She was highly trained in questioning people from all walks of life, but everything about Ellery's demeanor, her reactions, told her there was something complex at play and she wanted to get to the root of it, not because of what it might mean for the case, but as a way to understand this strong and complicated woman. She was convinced that whatever had Ellery so agitated had nothing to do with this particular case.

She could be wrong. It was rare, but it happened. If she pushed now, Ellery might shut down and close her out completely. Trip would be upset if she lost access, but his feelings had nothing to do with her hesitation. Any pause on her part was personal. She finally settled on being as non confrontational as possible, and she didn't even turn around as she spoke. "I'll go away if that's what you really want."

Silence.

She waited, resisting the urge to turn around, to plead with Ellery to open up to her. Years of training and experience told her the fastest path didn't always lead to the truth, but the patience she usually possessed was nonexistent, and she knew it was because she'd let herself get too close. She should walk away, call Trip and tell him to assign someone else or bring charges and let the chips fall where they may. She'd done the best she could, and if there was ever a sign she should no longer be doing this kind of work, her inability to crack Ellery's impenetrable shell was it.

She pushed back from the sink and walked alongside the table, so close to Ellery she could reach out and touch her shoulder, but uncertainty about whether the touch would be about comfort rather than attraction told her to resist the urge. As she crossed from the kitchen to the living room, Ellery raised her head.

"Wait."

She turned slowly as if any sudden movement might scare Ellery back into silence.

"Stay."

She walked back into the room until she was standing on the other side of the table, but she didn't sit down. "We don't have to talk about it."

"Maybe I want to."

"If it's what you want."

"Sit down. You're making me nervous, towering over me like that."

"I'm guessing a lot of people don't look down on you."

"Are you trying to be funny?"

Sarah pulled out a chair and slid into the seat. "I was trying to add some levity to the situation. We haven't had a lot of that in our short relationship."

Ellery straightened up in her chair. "Relationship? That's an interesting word. I'm thinking you mean it strictly in the context of your behavioral analysis background, since when I kissed you, you ran out of here like the place was on fire."

As if that was the only thing on fire. Sarah cleared her throat. "We shouldn't have…I should've stopped you."

"What? Before I even did it? As I recall, you kissed me back."

"I did."

"But it meant nothing to you."

"Did you ask me to stay so you could grill me about my feelings or because you had something else you wanted to say?"

"I suppose both is not an acceptable answer."

"It is if it's true. How about we start by talking about the case and then we can talk about the rest?" Sarah made the offer expecting Ellery to continue to resist. What she hadn't expected was for Ellery to start telling a story completely unrelated to anything to do with the bombing or the unspoken attraction between them.

"A year ago a man came to me for help. He was a family man." Ellery spoke in a matter-of-fact tone. "Good job, at least until he was arrested, and no prior record. He was on his second attorney and his case was set for trial in a month. I am, I mean I was, always leery about defendants who'd gone through a couple of lawyers, because, you know, the common denominator is the client. He was charged with murder. I called his prior attorneys before I took on the case. The first one was a family friend who vouched for the guy. He had bonded him out of jail, but the most serious criminal case he'd handled was misdemeanor shoplifting and he wanted no part of a murder case. The second attorney was a guy I detest. Blowhard, all flash, no substance. I wouldn't hire him to represent my worst enemy."

"I've been up against that type in court. It's no fun, especially if they win."

Ellery nodded. "The timing was a problem. The judge had continued the trial twice to let this guy settle on the attorney he wanted, but she runs a very strict docket and she'd already made it clear she thought the guy was beginning to think he could delay trial forever if he just kept switching counsel. She gave him a choice. Forfeit his bond or be ready on the special setting."

"He was out on bond on a murder case?"

"High bond, but yes. His employer posted it. Like I said, he had a good job. Everyone who knew him raved about him, talked about how he had to have been falsely accused. The state was crazy to think he was guilty."

"What kind of evidence did they have?"

"The usual. All circumstantial. The victim was his neighbor. He was the last one to see her alive. Neighbors heard them fighting several times. An eyewitness saw a car that looked like his near where her body was discovered."

"Sounds a little lame, even from this jaded FBI agent."

"Except something similar had happened before. In another state. Neighbor lady turned up dead. He'd been the last one to see her and they'd argued."

"Okay, so he doesn't get along well with his neighbors."

"Exactly. The only physical evidence the state had were some fingerprints in her house, but nothing that couldn't be explained by the fact he'd been there several times. I had a great time making them look crazy for suspecting the head of the homeowner's association, a successful local businessman, and a loving parent."

Sarah noted the bitter edge to Ellery's voice, and she was certain she knew where this story was going, although she wasn't sure why Ellery had chosen to share it with her. "What was the result of the earlier case?"

"State didn't have much in the way of evidence except a witness who'd seen him at the house the day of the murder. The witness disappeared before trial and they didn't have enough to go forward on. They dismissed the case without prejudice."

"Meaning they could refile if the witness ever showed back up."

"Right, but that was ten years ago and they never refiled."

"So, here he was in Dallas charged with a similar crime and he hires you. What did your gut say?"

Ellery stared hard. "Doesn't matter. It's all about the evidence."

Sarah heard the edge in her voice, bitter and ironic. She didn't want to stop the flow of Ellery's story, but she desperately wanted to expose the source of Ellery's obvious distress. She was convinced that was the only way it could be resolved. "What happened?"

"Exactly what should've happened. The jury found him not guilty. The state's case was weak and they didn't meet their burden. Another victory for me and he got to resume his life."

Ellery's clipped tone signaled her win wasn't a true victory. At least not in retrospect. She could wonder or she could ask. Time to jar Ellery out of this vague retelling. "Are you going to tell me what really happened or just dance around the subject?"

"I've never told anyone. I have a funny habit of taking my oath to keep my clients' confidences seriously."

"Like I haven't noticed." Sarah smiled to lighten the mood. She reached a hand across the table and curled her fingers into Ellery's, happy when she didn't draw away. "You started telling me this story for a reason. Can you tell me the reason without telling me details?"

"It's hard to distinguish between the two. I've already told you enough that you could look up the case if you were interested."

"I'm interested, not because of what you might say, but because of why." She drew a finger across her lips. "I get you may not be inclined to trust any government agents right about now, but I promise you I have no desire to look past whatever you tell me."

"You may not be able to keep that promise once you hear what I have to say. I haven't told anyone this."

In the long pause that followed, Sarah wasn't entirely sure Ellery was going to finish the story. She'd just about decided to try to gently change the subject, when Ellery cleared her throat and resumed her telling.

"This guy, I'll call him John, he wouldn't accept no for an answer. When he first came to me, I tried to turn him away. I had a lot of other cases pending and I knew this particular judge was unlikely to give us a reset on his case. He said he'd take his chances. He wanted me. When I heard his story and looked at the evidence, I thought I was taking on a sure winner. Even if he hadn't offered to pay me a small fortune, I would have taken his case for the sheer justice of it. Justice. That's a good one." Ellery laughed and the sound was hollow and hard.

Sarah listened as Ellery relayed the story of the trial. How the judge had not allowed the prosecution to introduce anything related to the prior case. How the state's key witness got cold feet and took off after sending a letter to the prosecutor recanting his story. How Ellery won by doing nothing more than cross-examining the state's remaining witnesses without calling any of her own, and how she delivered an indignant closing argument that shamed the prosecution for putting her client through the trial in the first place.

As she listened she could imagine Ellery standing in the well of the courtroom, capturing the attention of the jurors with the combination of her intense likability and commanding presence. They probably nodded right along with her as she pointed out the holes in the state's case and then demanded they do the right thing and let her client go. She almost caught herself nodding along as Ellery replayed every detail.

"A week later, I called to tell him I had the expunction paperwork ready for him to sign. I explained to him how the charges would be wiped from his record and all evidence in the police reports that was related to him would be destroyed. He asked if I could meet him at a job site and he gave me the address."

Sarah leaned in closely now as the tension in the room sucked away the air and she hung on Ellery's next words.

"It wasn't a job site. It was just a desolate piece of land in the middle of nowhere. Dirt and rocks and the occasional patch of wild grass. No fences, no houses, no barn. Just the two of us standing out there all alone." Ellery took a long drink from her beer and then set the bottle down softly on the table as if she didn't want to break the mood, but the disconnect of her next words shattered it entirely. "You want to know the number one question I get asked?" She didn't wait for a response before saying. "It's how can I represent a guilty person."

"I can only imagine."

Ellery's smile was mirthless. "Thanks for not asking, but my stock answer is unless I was an eyewitness, there wasn't any way for me to know for sure if one of my clients actually did what they were accused of doing. Innocent people sometimes confess. Bad guys sometimes get falsely accused. It's a jury's job to decide if a person is guilty according to the law, and my only role is to make sure my clients don't get railroaded by the system."

The shifting tense of Ellery's speech signaled she had one foot still in the profession. It was obvious whatever Ellery believed about her role in the justice system before had changed drastically, but Sarah didn't need to hear the details to accept that whatever it was affected her ability to cooperate in the case against Naveed Khan. "I get it. You don't have to tell me anymore."

Ellery squeezed her hand and kept talking. "So, John and I are standing in this field and after he signs the expunction papers, he thanked me for my work. He said he'd had every confidence in my abilities during trial, but he'd wanted to help out along the way. He pointed to a ravine in the distance. It was the perfect place for a witness to stay out of sight, he said. Six feet under, he said. He handed me the paperwork, walked over to his car, climbed in and drove away."

Sarah forced a calm expression, but she wanted to say holy shit.

"When I got back to the office, I mailed the paperwork back to him, unfiled. I enclosed a letter saying I was phasing out my practice and I wouldn't be in a position to help him anymore. The next day I told my law partner I would be gone as soon as I could wrap up my pending docket."

Sarah took a deep drink from her beer, her other hand never letting go of Ellery's. She could only imagine the effect of her client's confession. She had a million questions, but this was Ellery's story to tell, so all she did was offer a slight prod. "Did you ever see him again?"

"No. I heard he took a transfer with his job and lives somewhere on the West Coast. And I never told anyone what he told me." Ellery's voice cracked. "Until now."

Sarah cut off the whispers in her head that questioned Ellery's judgment. She'd listened to dozens of horrific confessions in her time at BAU, but she'd always been the adversary, not the advocate of the confessor. Lawyers didn't rat their clients out. She might not like it, but it was the law and she'd sworn to uphold all of the law, not just the parts she didn't like. Besides, this wasn't just some random lawyer talking, it was Ellery, and she was witnessing firsthand the devastating effect keeping secrets could have. She shuddered at the very idea of having to hold inside the horrible things she'd heard over the years, never being allowed to sort through them with another person or even speak of them.

She let go of Ellery's hand, stood up, and walked around the table. She knelt by Ellery's chair and placed her hands on Ellery's knees. "It's okay."

"It's not okay. Nothing about it was okay."

"Surely you've represented people you were pretty sure were guilty before."

"Absolutely, but this was different. I was absolutely certain he was innocent. I'm sure I've been wrong before, but this guy was a monster and I didn't have a clue. Where was my barometer? How had I gotten so far off track? And, before you ask, of course I thought about telling someone. I examined it from every angle. He'd hired me to defend him in the case of the murdered neighbor. At first glance, the case of the murdered witness fell completely outside the scope of my representation. But it didn't. They were linked and if

I divulged one, it necessarily opened up our communications about the other.

"I'd spent my entire professional life parsing questions like this, but it all boiled down to one big question. What the hell was I doing? I stood in a field with a stone cold killer, and for the very first time in my career, I felt danger. If he could kill a complete stranger and a neighbor he'd known for years, he could kill anyone. What was I doing with my life? What if I'd had a family at home that he could threaten? I obviously sucked at detecting danger before it got close."

Bam. Sarah instantly got it. Naveed, son of a prominent businessman, exemplary student, pristine record. Ellery had even emerged from isolation to plead his case and here she was back again, facing the same situation. Danger had crept up on her and there was nothing scarier than a threat disguised as a friendly. Whatever was between them, the last thing she wanted to do was be another friendly that really wasn't and she made a snap decision. Trip and the other agents working this case were going to have to work a little harder. She wasn't going to be the reason Ellery had to relive the kind of betrayal that had caused her to leave her practice.

She stood up. "You did what you had to do. I get it." She took a step back as if the slight distance could make it easier to say her next words. "I'm going now and I'll do everything I can to make sure you aren't bothered again."

Ellery stood and took a step toward her. "I want to help you with your investigation, but the only thing I know is that Amir Khan put my name on a tax filing to gain credibility for his organization. I confronted him about it today and he admitted the truth. As for the rest, I don't know anything. I swear to you, I wasn't involved in any of it—the money, the explosion. Nothing."

"I know." The heat of Ellery's gaze set off alarm bells telling her to get out now, but she was rooted in place. Ellery took another step closer and their stance was now intimate, with almost no space between them. She reached up and stroked Ellery's face, gently at first and then pulled her closer, her entire body quivering with anticipation. Ellery's lips were as strong and soft as she remembered, and she groaned as their kiss deepened. She slid her hands around

Ellery's waist, beneath her shirt, and stroked the tensed muscles of her back and abdomen. Soft, smooth, strong. Her body sagged at the intensity of sensation and she pulled Ellery closer as her mind swam toward clarity in a sea of confused thoughts. Her work, her duty, her loyalties. How important were any of these compared to the rush, the righteous feel of this tender woman who'd bared her soul and offered her a glimpse at what something deeper could be like? She was falling fast, and she only had a split second before she let her feelings trump her obligations.

"Stop thinking."

Ellery's voice cut through the clouds of her haze. She'd never stop thinking, analyzing, because that was who she was, but in this moment all her thoughts had a singular focus. She wanted only Ellery and she had to have her right now.

CHAPTER NINETEEN

Ellery tugged Sarah's hand from her waist, pulled it to her lips, and kissed her knuckles. Sarah's head tilted back, her eyes dark with need and her gaze unfocused, signaling she was every bit as aroused as Ellery hoped. She'd told her to stop thinking, but as much as she wanted this, she had to know Sarah wanted it too. "I want to take you to bed."

Sarah didn't speak at first, and the second of hesitation robbed her courage. Ellery started to turn away, unwilling to see the expression on Sarah's face as she made an excuse for not giving in to her feelings. But a hand on her arm pulled her back.

"Don't pull away. I want you too."

"But?" She searched Sarah's face, still flush with arousal. "Nothing's stopping you from giving in to what you want."

Sarah closed her eyes and stepped forward. Before Ellery could process what was happening, Sarah's lips were on hers, hungry and willing. She parted her lips and moaned as Sarah's tongue gently stroked hers. "This is what I want," Sarah whispered, her voice urgent.

Ellery took her hand and led her down the hall to her room. A vision of Sarah, naked on her back on the bed she'd made with her own hands left her breathless. She sped up, barely able to wait for the real thing. She paused in the doorway and urged Sarah to step inside ahead of her, and then she watched expectantly as Sarah's gaze swept the room.

"Wow. Let me guess, you made all of this?"

"I confess I've kept my favorite pieces all to myself." She circled her arms around Sarah's waist and pressed close to her back. "Do you want me to tell you about them?"

Sarah leaned back against her. "Yes, but not now. Just show me your favorite."

Ellery smiled and led her to the edge of the four-poster bed. She eased Sarah's sweater up over her shoulder and sucked in a breath as she admired the swell of her breasts tucked tight into a sleek black brassiere. "Beautiful," she murmured as she traced a finger along the edge of the bra.

"I have a habit of spending too much money in the lingerie department. Shoes, cars, and lingerie. My top three vices."

Ellery ducked her head to hide a grin at Sarah's rambling that she suspected was the symptom of a slight case of nerves. She never suspected this supremely confident woman would be bashful when it came to intimacy. While the polite thing to do was proceed slowly, Sarah's shyness merely stoked the fire.

She unhooked the pretty bra with one hand and tossed it on the bed. "I wasn't talking about the bra." She cupped Sarah's breasts. "This is what's beautiful." She bent down and teased her tongue around first one of Sarah's nipples and then the other as Sarah arched toward her. "And speaking of shoes, don't you think it's time to lose those fancy loafers?"

Sarah responded by kicking off her shoes and pulling her into a deep and consuming kiss. When they came up for air, Sarah had apparently decided to assume control. "Time for you to start losing some clothes too," she said as she ran a finger down the front of her shirt, ticking her nails against the buttons. "Strip or be stripped."

Ellery didn't try to hide her grin this time. "Both of those options sound pretty amazing." She slowly unbuttoned the first two buttons of her shirt, watching Sarah's eyes cloud with what she hoped was desire. She'd only just started on the third button when Sarah grabbed her hand and said, "At this rate, I'll explode before you're done."

Sarah worked swiftly through the rest of the buttons and tossed the shirt to the floor. She stepped closer until their naked breasts touched and Ellery groaned as the sensation ripped through her to the gathering wet between her legs. As if she could read her mind, Sarah unbuttoned her jeans and slid her hand deep inside and drew lazy circles on her soft cotton briefs. Each pass of Sarah's fingers brought her closer to climax, and she was torn between giving in to the sensation and wanting to feel every inch of Sarah's naked body against her skin while she came.

Painful as the pause was, she reached down and stilled Sarah's hand. Holding Sarah's gaze, she stepped out of her jeans and then tugged Sarah's jeans and panties down to the floor, pausing on her way back up to kiss the inside of her thighs. Sarah bucked against her lips and she knew losing the clothes had been the absolute right decision. She lowered Sarah onto the bed and eased in beside her.

Sarah lay against the soft down pillows and shuddered from the aftereffects as Ellery teased her way up her thighs with insistent lips. She stretched her arms above her head and moaned as Ellery ran her hands along her side and began stroking and pinching her breasts. Her first instinct was to roll on top of Ellery and direct the action. Lying back and letting someone else please her was a foreign concept, but Ellery's touch was magic, and she sensed she'd only ruin the effect if she tried to take control. Besides, Ellery could use some time back in the driver's seat after all that had been taken from her lately.

"You're thinking again," Ellery whispered, her voice husky with desire.

"I'm sorry."

"Don't be sorry." Ellery drew a finger across her stomach and Sarah shuddered again. Ellery smiled in response, but the expression was tempered with cautious reserve. "Do you want me to stop?"

Sarah opened her mouth to say I want you on top of me. I want you to ride me. I don't want you to stop until we're both screaming so loud your nosey neighbor knows exactly how many orgasms we've had, but the words faded at the tentative look in Ellery's eyes, her tender kisses, and the incredible heat stoked by even her lightest touch. In the face of Ellery's vulnerability, the most precious gift she could give was control, and surprisingly, she realized she didn't want to be in charge. She knew exactly what she wanted. "I want you to make love to me."

No sooner had she said the words than Ellery's hesitation vanished, and Sarah relaxed into the rhythm of her searing strokes. When Ellery dipped back between her legs and teased her tongue across her clit, Sarah rocked against her and cried out in pleasure as the first waves of orgasm surged through her body. Losing control had never felt so right, and through the blur of climax she had a moment of clarity—Ellery was the reason why.

Ellery opened her eyes to complete darkness. Her first instinct was to sit up and snap on the bedside lamp, but as the blur of sleep gave way to intense memories of the last few hours, she resolved she was in no hurry to return to the harsh light of reality.

She inched her hand across the covers until she found Sarah, curled up next to her. She propped up on her elbow and waited impatiently for her eyes to acclimate to the dark. Sarah's hair fanned out across the pillow, and Ellery longed to reach out and curl her fingers through the dark waves. Instead she closed her eyes and let her mind retrace their lovemaking.

"Who's thinking now?"

Ellery opened her eyes and smiled at the beautiful woman staring up at her. "I promise my thoughts were relegated to things like will the delivery guy bring the pizza into the bedroom because no way am I ready to leave your side."

"You lawyers say the sweetest things. And here I was assuming you were thinking lewd thoughts."

"Who, me?" She blocked Sarah's mock jab and grabbed her hand. "Oh my, look how weak the big, strong FBI agent is. I wonder what she's been doing." A second later, she was laughing as Sarah rolled over on top of her and pinned her arms above her head. "Please, Officer. Don't stop."

Sarah dipped down and ran her tongue along her neck to her lips. Ellery lifted her head to meet her in a blistering kiss. As spent as they'd both been an hour ago, she was surprised how quickly her body lit up at Sarah's touch. She curled a leg around Sarah's and slid her slick center against Sarah's thigh.

"Oh my God, you feel amazing." Ellery's words were punctuated with heavy breathing as Sarah used her leg to stroke her with ever increasing intensity while she licked and sucked her sensitive breasts. It seemed like only seconds before the rising tide of orgasm rushed through her and she arched off the bed and into Sarah's tender embrace.

Sarah held her close, leaving light kisses on her forehead, her cheeks, and her lips while she rocked through the receding waves of her climax. Finally spent, she opened her eyes and met Sarah's intense gaze. "That was incredible." She looked down at Sarah's thigh, still between her legs, and she felt another shudder surge through her body. "Truly incredible."

"Yes, it was. Maybe even a bit beyond incredible. Like make me completely forget about pizza, incredible."

"Well, I don't know about that." She laughed as Sarah playfully twisted her ear. "Cut it out. You're ruining the mood."

"Oh, I bet I can get it back."

"I have no doubt, but if I don't have something to eat soon, I will die."

"Die, huh? Well, we wouldn't want that."

Ellery watched as Sarah extracted her leg and leaned down to the floor beside the bed. "What are you doing?"

"Saving your life." She crawled back up onto the bed and flashed her cell phone. "Name your favorite delivery. I'm buying you dinner."

Ellery started to reply, but the phone in Sarah's hand started emitting a sharp ring. Sarah looked at the phone, shook her head, and frowned. Ellery willed her not to take the call, not to let anything shatter the playful mood, the breathtaking intimacy of their evening, but she wouldn't ask.

The phone kept ringing.

"I'm sorry. I have to take this."

Ellery could only manage a nod as Sarah answered the line with a sharp, "Flores here."

Resisting the urge to listen in on whatever was so important it was worth interrupting what they'd shared, Ellery climbed out of bed, grabbed her shirt and jeans, and walked out of the room. She dressed in the hall and then made her way to the kitchen. She put a kettle of water on the stove burner to boil and measured out her favorite grind for the French press. While she waited for the water to get hot, she leaned against the sink and stared out the window. It was pitch-black outside, but it felt like morning, or at least it had a few moments ago. Waking up with Sarah, even this late at night, felt like a new beginning, a new day. The orgasm was wonderful, but it was just a bonus. The intimacy of the night had started when she shared her story, her secret, and Sarah, instead of turning away, had pulled her closer. But she couldn't help but think the phone call broke the spell.

"Hmmm, coffee. You sure do know the way to a girl's heart."

Ellery kissed her lightly on the lips and started to back away, but Sarah pressed closer. She held up a hand. "Water's boiling." She could feel Sarah's eyes on her as she pulled the kettle from the burner and poured it over the grinds. She pumped the press, staring at the floating grinds as they settled into place, captured and contained. "Do you want your cup to go?"

"I'm sorry."

"Don't be. Cream and sugar?"

"Cream."

Ellery nodded. She walked to the refrigerator. In a few minutes, Sarah would be gone, back at work, and she wished she didn't care.

"Are you going to talk to me or just be my barista?"

"I don't know what to say."

"I think you do, but you're pissed because I'm leaving."

"I'm not pissed. I'm..." Ellery didn't know what she was, but whatever it was jammed up her feelings and scattered them all over the place. A little bit hurt, a little bit disappointed. Oh hell, maybe she was mad, but she sure as hell wasn't going to admit it now. "I assume you wouldn't leave unless it was important."

Sarah walked over and stood a few inches away. She didn't duck away as Sarah put her hand behind her neck and pulled her close. Her kiss was gentle and lingering.

"Being with you like this was amazing."

"I hear a 'but.'"

"But I do have to go and it is important."

Ellery heard the undercurrent. Whatever it was would always trump anything personal between them. Of course it would. Sarah was a natural adversary. A cop investigating a defendant. Funny, she'd left a job that put her at odds with people like Sarah, only to fall for someone who put her right back into the same situation. Rough luck.

Fall for. In that moment, she realized how hard she'd fallen. The old her never would have let her guard down, no matter how attracted she might be to someone in Sarah's position. Could she really blame Sarah for keeping her distance?

Yes. Because if anyone had any reason to keep their distance, she did. She stood to be hurt the deepest. But Sarah's career could be at risk, her conscience argued. *Just because you were willing to walk away from yours, doesn't mean she's willing to put hers in jeopardy over what may only be a fling.* But it wasn't a fling. She'd felt more in one night with Sarah than she'd felt over a lifetime with a string of other women.

"Are you okay?" Sarah asked.

Ellery struggled to recover. Sarah was on her way out the door. She should tell her how she felt, she could ask her to stay, but she didn't have a strong enough handle on her own feelings to share them, let alone convince Sarah to share hers.

She leaned back in and kissed Sarah, hard and long, enough to leave her gasping for breath and weak in the knees. When she finally found the strength to pull away, she handed her the coffee mug. "Go. I know wherever you have to be is important. But I want you to know that this"—she pointed between them—"this is important too."

CHAPTER TWENTY

Sarah drove straight to the airport with the windows down and the radio blaring, but neither the wind nor the loud music could drown out her thoughts. Trip had called to say he would be landing at the airport in an hour, but he hadn't offered any other details about why he was showing up again. As for Ellery, all she knew was she hadn't wanted to leave, but she'd been relieved not to have to engage in the after sex discussion of what it all meant because she didn't have a clue.

More easily than she'd thought possible, she'd crossed a line. No matter what she felt in her gut, Ellery was a target of a federal investigation, and the intimacy they'd shared could easily be grounds for termination. In the moment, she had cared more about the electric pulse of Ellery's touch than the career she'd always put first. Now that she'd fled Ellery's magnetic presence, she'd expected her good sense to take over, but she wasn't sure she knew what constituted good sense anymore. The job was fulfilling, but it didn't stand a chance against the rush she'd felt as Ellery stroked her to orgasm and then cradled her tenderly. She had never experienced such intensity, and she'd never felt so vulnerable after a sexual encounter.

Traffic was light and she made it to the airport in record time. She parked the car, used her badge to speed through security, and made it to the gate with thirty minutes to spare before Trip's flight was scheduled to arrive. She settled into a seat, leaned back, and closed her eyes, too exhausted to people watch. She'd barely hit the fuzzy edge of sleep before Trip's gravelly voice roused her.

"Some cop you are. I could've had your gun and taken out half the people in this terminal while you were snoring."

"If I was carrying." Sarah instantly regretted her words, certain he would never let her hear the end of it. She wasn't disappointed.

"Going soft. Seriously, Flores, you may not need firepower while you're working a desk, but as long as you're on this assignment, I expect you to be prepared for anything. You understand?"

This was the perfect opportunity to tell him why she was no longer right for this assignment, but instead she said, "You really think I need a gun to get close to Ellery Durant?"

He stared at her for a moment and then shook his head. "I think you used other ways to get close to Miss Durant. We need to talk." His eyes held a mix of compassion and something else. Disappointment?

He knew. She had no doubt, but her mind scurried to comb through the details of the last six hours to figure out how she'd given herself away before she realized what she'd taken for granted. Trip had asked her to get close to Ellery, but she'd been foolish to think she'd be the only one watching her. Another thought occurred to her and she had to know. "Is her house bugged?"

"No, but you were there for six hours. For all those damn HSI agents know you're just one helluva interrogator, but they don't know you like I do."

"Is that why you're here?"

"Don't be silly. Like I'm going to fly across the country to lecture one of my best agents. I'm here because some major shit is going down and the director wants me to make sure the agency's interests are looked after. Getting to scold you for going off book is just a bonus." He lifted his carry-on bag. "But I can do that in the car. Where's that fancy ride of yours?"

True to his word, Trip didn't mention the subject again until they were on the road and, even then, not until Sarah brought it up. "Go ahead," she said. "Let me have it."

"What's your take on her?"

"Does it matter? I can tell you right now that you need to yank me off this detail. I'm not objective."

"You're never objective. If you think you are, you're fooling yourself. Every interrogation you've ever done, you've come at from a point of knowing how you feel about the perp and what he did. It's your angle and it's never objective."

"Ellery Durant is not a perp."

"Says you."

"That's what the agency pays me for." She sped up to pass a car and then settled into the fast lane. "You spent years training me to construct profiles, read people, and make assessments, and I'm one of the best. I'd bet all the salary you've ever paid me that Ellery not only had nothing to do with the bombing, but she didn't have a clue Naveed Khan was anything other than an honor student on his way to a good college. You saw the report I sent. No one had any idea what these kids were up to. If Ellery were really involved, why would she have quit her practice before the case was resolved? She would've done everything in her power to make sure those boys weren't even indicted."

"Are you willing to throw your entire career away for some woman you barely know?"

It was a valid question, but Sarah wasn't prepared to make a choice. *Which is probably why you ran out the door before Ellery could force you to talk about what happened between you.* If she couldn't even have the conversation about whatever it was that was happening between them, was it worth risking everything?

She'd spent her entire career taking chances, hunting killers with little regard for her own personal safety. This kind of risk, putting her feelings on the line for a woman who gave her the biggest rush of her life, was what she should be living for. There was no comparing the two. "I know her well enough. And for the record, whatever happened between me and Ellery wasn't a method of interrogation."

She felt Trip's eyes on her and imagined what he must be thinking. To him, the work would always come first, and under his mentorship, she'd never expected to feel any different. He'd been surprised when she requested a transfer and more than a little disappointed to discover she was moving from his elite unit to Dullsville as he liked to call the fraud unit. He'd pulled her back in, knowing she couldn't say no, but now he probably wished he'd chosen an agent with better judgment. "I'm sorry."

"Sorry you slept with her or sorry I know about it?"

It was a complicated question, but she didn't have the energy or desire to sort out her feelings until she had more time, so she settled on the simplest possible response. "Sorry I didn't quit this investigation first."

"Don't be. You're the best agent I've ever worked with. It's not in your blood to quit anything, and I know you well enough to know you have to see this thing through. And I know you well enough to know that you wouldn't have risked everything for nothing. All I need to know now is that I have your full focus. You can sort out your deal with Durant later. Understood?"

"Understood. What's the plan?"

"Based on the information you sent to Peter about Naveed Khan and his pals, HSI got a handful of material witness warrants."

"So, what? We pick them up, spirit them away, and hold them until we get some answers?"

"I wish. HSI is picking them up, but there'll be no spiriting away. They'll be questioned here, and you and I will take turns observing. They'll be treated like detained suspects with all the usual rights and warnings."

"This from the director?"

"Pretty sure the chain of command goes all the way to the top on this one. The trial, when it happens is going to be the center of national attention, and they want everything leading up to it to be as transparent as possible."

"Got it. Where is this going down?"

"Division headquarters. I got them to agree to use our facilities since the local HSI office isn't really set up for observation. You up for this?"

Sarah glanced in the mirror. What had been sleepy, post-sex bliss, now looked like full-scale exhaustion complete with dark rings under her eyes and hair that resembled a rat's nest. "I came straight here when you called. Any chance I have time for a shower?"

"If you have any food in that pristine apartment of yours, absolutely."

She knew he wouldn't consider the yogurt and blueberries in the fridge real food, but she really needed that shower. She could always run down the street and grab him a burger if he balked. "Absolutely."

Trip slept the rest of the drive, and Sarah spent the time sorting through her thoughts. Her only regret of the night had been the abrupt way she left Ellery's house. Ellery had been right. What had happened between them was important, but she wasn't sure they meant the same thing by the distinction.

The next morning, Ellery sipped from a blazing hot cup of coffee in between yawns and pondered the fact that no amount of caffeine was a substitute for a good night's sleep. After an evening of incredible sex, she'd expected to fall into a deep and satisfying slumber, but Sarah's abrupt departure had left her feeling empty and restless. She'd finally rolled out of bed at dawn, and after a few hours listlessly puttering around the house, all she wanted to do was go back to bed.

She knew the reason for her malaise, although she was reluctant to admit it. The entire evening had been intensely intimate, from her confession about her former client to the several orgasms they'd shared. She'd bared her soul to Sarah in a way she'd never done with anyone else, and when Sarah rushed out the door, it was as if she was stealing away with her heart.

"I'm making way too much of this," she said to the air in the room. They'd been thrown together by circumstance, and faced with the revelation about Naveed, she'd been feeling vulnerable. It didn't hurt that Sarah was fantastically sexy, but the sex was nothing more than a by-product of ramped up, misplaced emotions.

CARSEN TAITE

Maybe if she kept repeating the thought she would believe it, but the sharp ring of her cell phone would keep her from testing that theory. She looked at her phone and was instantly disappointed. "Meg?"

"Have you heard from Naveed?"

"You really need to break this habit where you think we still work together."

"Seriously, I was at the courthouse from eight thirty to just now and he never showed up. And Danny Soto, who's usually pretty reasonable about these things said if he didn't check in by noon, she was filing a motion to hold his bond insufficient. I've left him about a dozen messages, but I figured you might have talked to Amir recently since, well, you know."

"What? Since Amir and I are suspected of colluding to defraud the IRS and send money to terrorists?"

"Funny. And you should probably be careful since you never know who's listening."

Ellery laughed. If only Meg knew she'd slept with an FBI agent working the case mere hours ago. "That ship has probably sailed, but just in case any government agents are listening, I unequivocally deny any involvement in any schemes, foreign or domestic, to either commit fraud or support or engage in terrorism."

"Like I said, very funny."

Meg didn't sound amused and Ellery couldn't care less. She hadn't forgotten the files that she'd found on Meg's computer related to Sadeem Jafari, but she wasn't going to be careless enough to confront her about it on the phone. She wanted to see her face when they had that little discussion. "I do have some information for you, though. Why don't you swing by and we can talk about it?" She waited, hoping her deliberately vague reference would be enough to convince Meg to show up.

"I can come by, but it'll have to be later this morning. I've got to find Naveed and I've got a hearing set in Collin County I've got to get to."

"Fine, I'll be here. Just come by when you can, but make sure you do. It's important."

• 234 •

After she clicked off the line, she realized it was the second time in the last twenty-four hours she'd told a woman something was important, but her meanings couldn't have been more different. Seeing Meg was important because she needed to know why Meg had lied to her. Seeing Sarah again was important because the life had been sucked out of her when Sarah ran out the door. No matter how important the two things, she wasn't going to get what she needed from either Meg or Sarah for a while. She picked up the mug of coffee and walked out to her studio, where she had total control over outcomes.

CHAPTER TWENTY-ONE

Sarah led Trip into division headquarters and stopped at Beverly's desk. "Are they ready?" Bev nodded and pointed at an office door down the hall. Sarah hid her surprise. She'd walked past that door dozens of times since she'd started here, and she'd never suspected it was an interrogation room.

She hoped the chairs inside were comfortable. It was eight a.m. She'd left Ellery's house just after one. Since then she'd picked Trip up at the airport, gone home to shower and change, and then spent the next several hours reviewing every scrap of information any government agency had on the suspects. She'd done her best to convince Trip her presence at the interrogation wasn't necessary, but he insisted she join him. She suspected he wanted a show of force to let HSI know they weren't the only ones with a vested interest in the outcome of this investigation. She'd resigned herself to the fact she was in for a long day of watching someone else conduct an interrogation. The prospect was both aggravating and exhausting.

She motioned to Trip to enter the room first so she could hang back and observe. There were four other agents in the room. Way too many. While Trip introduced them around, she zeroed in on the one other woman in the group. Her olive complexion, long dark hair and dark brown eyes suggested she was of Middle Eastern descent, and her firm handshake and confident bearing said don't be fooled by my petite size. Sarah liked her instantly.

"Aadila Rashed, HSI, Office of Intelligence."

Sarah took note of the way Aadila didn't lead with a title like the other agents had. She gripped her hand. "Nice to meet you." She looked around the room. "Looks like it might get a bit crowded in here."

"You have a good point," Aadila said. She pointed to one of the other HSI agents. "Shirani will be staying to observe with you and Agent Sandler. Daniels and Avery were on their way out to help look for the two witnesses we haven't managed to locate yet."

Sarah cringed at the term witnesses. She'd been a witness to the bombing, or at least its aftermath, but as far as she was concerned, the term was too watered-down for the guys they were about to grill. They were suspects, plain and simple. "Who's questioning the 'witnesses'?" Sarah asked.

Trip spoke up. "*Assistant Director* Rashed will be handling the interrogation."

Sarah looked at Aadila with a new sense of admiration for both her and the agency. It wasn't easy to climb the ranks in the intelligence community, and she gave kudos to the agency for sending one of their higher-ups to deal with this particular task. "Do you want to discuss anything in particular before you begin?"

Aadila motioned for them to sit. "Absolutely. I would like to get your perspective. I assume you've read the dossier we put together?"

Sarah nodded, hoping she looked more awake than she felt. The file ICE had sent over had been a surprisingly thorough compilation of information about Naveed, Akbar, and the Barstow brothers, especially considering they hadn't had much reason to suspect Naveed and Akbar at all until her discovery of the architectural firm break-in. She'd reviewed all of the information and found it to be heavy on facts, but short on substance. Luckily, she had some insight to offer, at least as to Naveed, although she felt a bit like she was betraying Ellery by speaking up. "The information you have is a good start, but I'd like to talk about how to dig a little deeper."

"I think Naveed is a sociopath and, although he's the youngest, he's the ringleader of the group. The others defer to him because of his family's standing in the community and his future aspirations. Top of his class, popular at school, accepted to several top colleges, these things give him credibility with the others, especially his cousin Akbar, whose successes must have been purchased by his father."

"How do you know this about Akbar? I don't recall seeing anything about that in the file?"

"Simple. His grades and résumé alone weren't good enough for him to get into SMU. The fact he didn't have to earn what he has will make him feel more entitled, but it will also cause him to be insecure, and that's probably how Naveed convinced him to break into his former employer's office and get those plans."

"You are attributing a lot of authority to a high school senior."

"I am and I could be dead wrong, but my gut tells me I'm not and I've been doing this for a long time."

"With a great deal of success, I'm told."

Sarah glanced at Trip who shrugged and said, "Don't look at me. I didn't tell her anything."

"Your reputation is well-known," Aadila said. She waved at Trip. "If he leaves the room, I'm going to steal you from the Bureau."

"Thanks, but I'm out of the biz. This is just a one time thing." Sarah did her best to ignore Aadila and Trip as they exchanged knowing looks without any consideration for the fact that she was standing right there. "Are we going to get started?"

"Sure, who should we start with?"

"If Naveed is here, you should start with him. Act like you don't know much at first. You're relying on him to fill you in. Approaching him that way will feed his pride and ego. He won't tell you much of anything, and he may even attempt to send you in a completely different direction. Act as if you believe what he has to say, no matter how absurd and then take a break. After the break, you can act as if you have spoken with the others and now you have the real facts. Once you crack his ego, by convincing him that his followers have turned on him, you can wedge it open to get him to confess. Push him to take all the credit. He'll want to do that anyway." Sarah stopped abruptly. "I'm sorry. This is your show. I didn't mean to take over." She looked over at Trip, who was smiling indulgently and she could almost hear him thinking "see, this is in your blood."

Aadila smiled as well. "No need to apologize. I appreciate the insight. Very thorough. You'll watch and signal if I get off track?"

"Uh, sure." Once she'd snapped out of the realization she wasn't actually running this interrogation, she felt a growing sense of agitation. To combat the desire to escape the small room where she was relegated to waiting, Sarah leaned back in her chair and watched Trip and Aadila make small talk. She paid little attention to their words, instead slipping into a hazy state of wishing she were back home in bed. Make that back in Ellery's bed. Had it really only been hours since she'd left Ellery's house? It seemed like days. Long, lonely days. She hadn't hesitated to take Trip's call, pick him up at the airport, do her job, but the easy way she'd slipped back into work mode was disturbing. Maybe she just wasn't cut out for anything but the job. For all her desire to find something satisfying outside of work, it was entirely possible she simply wasn't built for anything but dedication to her career and a personal life that was transient at best.

A few minutes later, the phone on the wall rang. She watched as Aadila answered it and told whoever was on the other end she would be there soon. When she hung up, she opened the curtain to the two-way window and they could all see Naveed, seated at a table in the center of the room. He wasn't handcuffed and he was alone. He looked casual, bored even.

"How long should I wait?" Aadila asked.

"If his demeanor doesn't change in about fifteen minutes, go on in," Sarah said. She didn't think it would, but it wouldn't hurt to observe him for a bit.

The time dragged by. Sarah figured they were all anxious to hear what he had to say, if he would say anything at all. When fifteen minutes had ticked away, Aadila stood. "I'll take a break to check in with you in a bit. There's a button on the wall. Use it if you think I'm off track."

When she left the room, Trip spoke. "Would you rather it was you in there?"

Sarah looked over at the HSI agent, Shirani, who was still in the room. He didn't look remotely interested in their conversation, but it still made her uncomfortable to talk about this in front of him. "I don't know."

"That's not an answer."

"It's the best I have. I know you or I could do this as well or better than anyone else, but she's smart and I'm sure she's capable of getting what she needs. And she's objective. You know it's not just what we talked about before. I was there, only blocks away. I heard the bomb go off. Maybe this is all too personal for me."

"Objectivity isn't all it's cut out to be. We all tend to fight harder for things when we have a stake in the outcome. That's not necessarily a bad thing."

"Maybe you're right." Sarah knew he was still talking about the bombing, but her mind wandered to Ellery and the very real personal connection they shared. From the night of the bombing to last night, their lives were intertwined in ways they could have never imagined.

She turned her attention to the two-way glass and watched as Aadila calmly lobbed questions at Naveed aimed to loosen him up. He answered lazily, as if this meeting had no potential consequence, and he responded to queries about his grades, extracurricular activities, and plans for college with seeming nonchalance.

After what seemed like forever, Aadila finally broached the first subject of substance and Sarah stood at the window, intent on not missing a single detail of Naveed's demeanor.

"I'm sure you're wondering why you are here," Aadila said.

Naveed shrugged. "I suppose I've gotten used to being the subject of scrutiny."

"And why is that?"

He laughed. "Really? You of all people are asking me that? Don't tell me the color of your skin or your religion has never caused the people you work with to question your loyalties."

Aadila nodded as if she were acknowledging his assessment. "Has this happened to you before?"

"It happens every day to some Muslim in the Western world. What happens to my brother, happens to me."

"You seem wise for your age."

He shrugged again. Aadila waited for a moment, but he didn't offer anything else, so she pressed on. "There are people here who think your friends were involved in the bombing."

"My friends?"

"Well, your cousin, Akbar Jafari, and Michael and Brian Barstow."

"Akbar is my cousin, that is true, but I don't know the others."

She flipped through a few pages on the notepad in front of her. "I'm sorry. You would probably know them better as Hasid and Abdul Kamal."

Sarah saw the slight shift in Naveed's eyes. He lied about not knowing them, but why? He had to know exactly where this was headed and he had to be aware they would've already connected him to the Barstow/Kamal brothers through the pending case in Dallas County.

"What did you call them? Barstow? I didn't recognize that name, but I know the Kamals."

"Excellent. I was hoping you did because we could use your help."

He looked surprised at Aadila's statement, relieved even, and it was only then that Sarah remembered how young, how immature he was. Not too young to help carry out a terrorist scheme, but he might be too immature to appreciate the enormity of what he'd done. Or he might just be evil. At this stage it was hard to tell.

She looked over at Trip, who was watching Naveed intently. "First impressions?"

"He's a cool customer, that one. But then again so are those kids who load up with weapons and march into schools to gun down everyone in their path. Just because he's young, doesn't mean he didn't mastermind the whole thing."

"Agreed." She looked back at the window. Aadila had opened a file folder and was thumbing through the contents, an act likely designed to give the impression she had hard evidence of the things they were about to discuss.

"What can you tell me about Akbar's father's charity, the Global Enterprise Alliance?"

Naveed looked confused, apparently surprised by the direction of the questioning. "I don't know much about it other than they do good work or at least that's what I've been told."

"Like your father's charity?"

"I think they might be more modern than my father. He embraces the past."

"And you are more modern?"

"I suppose you could say that."

"What can you tell me about your father's attorney, Ellery Durant?"

Sarah sucked in a breath at the mention of Ellery's name. "What the hell is she doing?" She felt a hand on her arm and looked over to see Trip standing beside her. He jerked his head toward the far corner of the room and she remembered they weren't alone although Agent Shirani still looked bored out of his mind. She nodded at Trip to signal she had her temper under control and resumed watching the interrogation.

"She was a good attorney," Naveed said. "She quit though, so she must not be too good at what she does. My father has a new attorney now."

Sarah almost laughed at the quick summation of Ellery's net worth. This kid didn't deserve someone like her on his side. He obviously didn't appreciate her or the lengths she was willing to go to protect him. Jackass.

"Why are you asking about Ms. Durant?" Naveed asked. "Did she do something wrong?"

Aadila didn't miss a beat. "I'm not sure. When we talked to her, she said she didn't, but I thought you might know differently."

He shrugged again, but Sarah noticed a hard glint in his eyes that belied the apathetic gesture. Before she could process what she was seeing, she heard Trip grunt. "What's with all the shrugging? Don't they teach kids to answer questions nowadays?"

Sarah laughed. "Shut up, you sound like an old man."

"I will be an old man before this interrogation is over."

She punched him in the shoulder and pointed at the glass where Naveed had started to talk again.

"I need to use the bathroom," he said.

Aadila hesitated for just a moment before she said okay. Sarah watched as she explained an agent would go with him, but only because of protocol. When Naveed left the room, she joined them in the observation room.

"Time to step it up," Trip said. "When he comes back, start hitting harder. He won't be expecting it since you've been so easy on him. It's got him off guard. He's smart enough to know he wasn't dragged down here just to help us out, but his ego wants to believe you're not smart enough to get to the truth. Start surprising him with some facts about the break-in."

Aadila started to answer, but the wall phone next to where Shirani was standing rang. He answered it and listened for a moment, and then covered the mouthpiece. "The kid wants to make a phone call. We took his cell when he came in. Told him they weren't allowed in the building."

Sarah looked at Trip and could tell he was thinking the same thing. "Let him," she said. "But get the number, dial it for him, and record the call. Maybe we'll get something decent out of it."

While Shirani gave the instructions to the agent with Naveed, Sarah excused herself to the restroom. What she really needed was a few minutes of quiet, away from anything to do with this case. She'd been fine until Aadila brought up Ellery's name. She understood why Aadila would want to touch on every point of reference in her conversation with Naveed, but the reminder that Ellery was wrapped up in the case was a distraction. Of course everything about Ellery was a distraction and it was taking every bit of self-control she possessed to keep the memory of coming in her arms from obliterating her focus. She stood in front of the mirror and stared at her reflection, at her furrowed brow, at the big black circles under her eyes. She looked unhappy, haunted even, and she knew it was the job. The job loaded with violence and evil. The job she'd moved across the country to escape. The job that for years had robbed her of a personal life and was robbing her still.

Because you let it.

As much as she tried to ignore it, Sarah knew her internal voice was spot on. On some level, she'd probably always known the truth, but she'd ignored the implications because if she admitted it wasn't the job that kept her from getting what she wanted, she would have to face the fact she was responsible for her loneliness. *Maybe I've always been afraid I wouldn't find the same charge from a relationship as I get from chasing bad guys.* With the revelation came the realization she'd been wrong. The question now was what was she going to do about it.

The restroom door opened and Aadila walked in. "We're about to start up again."

Sarah forced her focus back to the case. "You get anything from the phone call?"

"He called his girlfriend, the one who had the plans on her computer, but the conversation was short. He asked her to let his teacher know he wasn't going to be in school today. That's about it."

"Do you have someone watching her in case she gets wind of what's really going on and takes off?"

"Yes, but she's on campus. They'll pick her up again this afternoon after school."

"Okay. I'll be there in just a minute."

Sarah waited until Aadila left, and then turned on the water and splashed her face. As she patted away the water with a paper towel, she stared at her reflection again. The circles were still there, but her brow was less furrowed and the haunted look was fading. She would get through this day, but when it was done she was going to make some real changes. She was going to start by asking Ellery's forgiveness for her abrupt departure last night. In person. With kissing. A lot of kissing.

Ellery flipped the switch on the saw, raised her safety visor, and listened to the sound of her doorbell. She had it wired so it would ring in her studio in case she was working, but no one else knew that and she considered ignoring the intrusion. She wasn't in the mood for visitors and she was already deep into this project.

The ringing started up again and she glanced at the clock. It was just after noon and she realized the persistent caller might be

Meg. She set her visor on her workbench and made her way to the house where she found Meg standing on the front porch looking perturbed. She swung open the door and Meg walked in bursting with conversation.

"Damn, what a day. First Naveed no-shows and then I sat in court up in Collin County for an hour before the prosecutor finally showed up. Bitch scheduled two hearings at the same exact time. I love how they don't give a shit about our time, like I've got nothing else to do but sit around and wait until she's ready. Then she had the nerve to ask me if I could reschedule for next week. Well, I told her—"

"I get the point." Ellery had spent years listening to Meg's constant bitching about the adversarial nature of the business, and she'd written it off to a by-product of the job, but she no longer had to suffer through her rants. "I'm about to fix a sandwich. You want something?"

"I'm good. I've got a late lunch scheduled with Lena Hamilton. Need to do some damage control after last week. What did you need? Have you heard from Naveed?"

Of course Meg would want to get ahead of the bad publicity generated after the raid at her law firm. Ellery remembered her father urging her to use Lena's skilled PR services, but she didn't have the stomach to do the on camera interviews Lena would urge her to do in order to preserve her reputation. Meg would thrive on the attention. Not for the first time, she reflected on how much like her father Meg had turned out to be, which brought her back to the reason she'd asked Meg to stop by in the first place. "Let's make this quick. No, I haven't heard from Naveed, but I asked you to come by because I need to know why you didn't mention that you represent Sadeem Jafari."

Meg's eyes darted around the room while Ellery waited for her to settle on an explanation. "Take your time and make it good," she said.

"Maybe we should sit down," Meg said.

Ellery didn't budge. "Maybe you should just tell me the truth. Right now."

"Ellery, it's not that simple."

She offered one of her best imploring looks, but Ellery had given in to her too many times in the past to fall for her woe-is-me act now. "Meg, tell me the truth, or I'll go to the feds right now and tell them I think you're complicit in whatever Jafari is up to."

Meg's expression quickly morphed into defiance. "Fine, but there just isn't much to tell. I wanted to keep Amir's business. He came to me with his cousin. Jafari said he wanted to open a foundation to help his Muslim brothers and I figured asking a bunch of questions was not the way to keep on Amir's good side. I didn't do anything affirmatively wrong. I just filed the paperwork. If Jafari lied, it's on him."

"You can't really believe it's that simple."

"I'm not you. I don't spend all my time trying to parse all sides of an issue. A client hires me, I'm his advocate. End of story."

Ellery shook her head. Meg had always done well by her clients when it came to an all out battle because she would fight to the end. Her problem was she loved the fight so much she forgot to warn them away from danger in the first place. Here she'd committed a cardinal sin, letting a business decision override an ethical one, one that could cost her her license and maybe even her freedom if the feds thought she'd acted intentionally. "They're going to find the documents on your computer. How were you going to get around that?"

Meg's face turned red and she looked away. "I don't know. I guess I thought they might think your father drafted them since he prepared Amir's paperwork."

Anger welled up inside Ellery as she realized the truth. "Is it simply easier for you to lie than admit what you did? You know the documents weren't created until after my father left the firm. You figured the feds would assume I drafted them since they'd thought I helped Amir, isn't that right?"

"How do you know when they were created?" The minute the question fell from Meg's lips, her eyes went wide. "Wait a minute. You broke in to the firm, didn't you? Saturday. Kyle was certain someone had been there."

"Maybe you're not the only one who will go to extreme measures to help a client. And take it from me, when it's your own freedom on the line, nothing is sacred."

Meg's response was interrupted by the sound of the doorbell. Ellery glanced over at the door as she tried to decide if she was relieved at the interruption or reluctant to prolong her exchange with Meg. She pulled open the door and looked outside. A young blonde stepped in front of the entryway. She was dressed in what looked like a school uniform complete with a khaki skirt and a bulky blue blazer.

"Hello, Ms. Durant?"

The girl looked familiar, but Ellery couldn't quite place her. "I'm Ellery Durant."

She started to ask what she could do for her, but Meg appeared at her side and said, "Kayla, what are you doing here?"

Kayla. Ellery's memory flooded back. Akbar Jafari's girlfriend. She'd shown up at the courthouse with Amir and Naveed the morning she'd covered for Meg. She too wanted to know what Kayla was doing here, but before she could ask, Kayla waved to another young blonde standing off to the side and they both stepped into the foyer. Ellery registered both girls were wearing the same uniform, and she recognized the second girl as the one she'd seen at Naveed's house the day before. Jasmine. They were probably looking for Naveed, but she had no idea why they'd shown up here. She stood back and let Meg do the talking.

"Have you seen Naveed?" she asked. "He didn't show up for court this morning."

"No, we haven't seen him." Kayla turned abruptly to Jasmine. "There was only supposed to be one. Call and find out what to do."

Jasmine pulled out a cell phone and dialed while Ellery looked between them, attempting to decipher what in the hell was happening. As Jasmine whispered into the phone, she mentally calculated the facts. Two young, pretty girls stood in her entryway, presumably looking for one of their boyfriends. All outward signs seemed innocuous, but a chill ran up her spine and a sense of danger thickened the air. She wanted these girls out of her house now.

"Kayla, maybe you should go to Naveed's house and wait there, and Meg and I will make some phone calls to see if we can find him."

Kayla didn't respond, instead she said to Jasmine. "Well?"

"He said to take them both."

Kayla smiled a hard, humorless smile. "Ladies, I need you to come with us."

Ellery shot a look at Meg who merely looked confused, so she spoke for both of them. "I think it's time for you to leave."

"Oh, it's definitely time to leave, but you're leaving with us." Kayla unbuttoned her blazer and pulled it open.

Ellery heard Meg gasp, but she quelled her own stirring fear out of a deep-seated instinct of survival. Under her blazer, Kayla wore a black vest covered with straps holding what looked like black sticks of dynamite. Ellery had only seen something similar in the movies and on cable news, but she knew without a doubt she was looking at a suicide vest.

Was it real? Where was the detonator? She should care about the answers to those questions, but her mind was consumed with a single thought. In a moment she would walk out of her house with two terrorists and never see Sarah Flores again.

CHAPTER TWENTY-TWO

For the third time in the last fifteen minutes, Sarah looked at her watch and bemoaned the slow pace of the interrogation on the other side of the wall. After a couple of hours with Naveed and nothing to show for it, Aadila had started talking to Akbar Jafari. Akbar lacked Naveed's calm demeanor, but his willingness to admit an alliance with extremist views didn't extend to any sort of confession about the bombing. When it came to questions about the break-in at his old employer's building, he clammed up, no doubt well coached by the attorney his father had hired to represent him on that case. She looked across the room. Trip was reading the paper and Shirani, the HSI agent, had stepped out to take a call.

"Their attorneys were notified that they were being brought in, right?"

Trip looked up from the newspaper. "One of Aadila's people called them." He grinned. "It was kind of early though, so they may have had to leave a message."

"I thought you said this was being handled on the up and up."

"It is, for the most part. If you're worried about evidence we gather getting tossed, don't. As far as I'm concerned this is primarily an exercise. We've already got enough to charge them, and I don't expect we'll get much in the way of a confession out of any of these assholes. If they were really in it for public glory, they would've made sure everyone knew what they did right after the bombing. At this point, I'd be happy if they let us know where the Barstows are so we can scoop them up."

"If they even know," Sarah said.

"Oh, I bet Naveed knows. That little fucker is pure evil."

Sarah didn't disagree. She'd gotten Ted Bundy like vibes from Naveed the moment she'd seen him sitting in the interrogation room, and she sensed the more they sucked up to him, the more likely it was that he would start bragging about his involvement. "I think it's time for Aadila to start back up with Naveed."

Trip nodded. "I agree, but not until we've had lunch. It's after one and I'm about ready to eat this chair."

Sarah laughed. In all the years she'd worked with Trip she could always count on the fact that he'd never miss a meal, no matter how hard they worked. She pressed the buzzer on the wall and waited for Aadila to step back into the observation room so she could suggest the three of them reevaluate their strategy over lunch. When the door swung open she was surprised to see Liz instead of Aadila standing in the doorway. "Hey, Liz, what's up?"

"I'm not sure. There's a guy in reception who insists on seeing you. I told him you were busy today, but he refused to talk to anyone else and he won't leave. He said 'you'll have to force this damn old Marine out of here at gunpoint, but I'm not going on my own until I see Agent Flores,' which of course means we have him under guard. I plan to have him hauled off, but I figured it wouldn't hurt to check with you first."

Sarah's mind raced. The words damn old Marine brought a name to mind. "Is his name Leo?"

Liz looked surprised. "Yes. Do you know him?"

The minute Liz confirmed it was Ellery's neighbor who'd pushed his way into division headquarters, Sarah barreled out the door, certain something was very wrong. She rushed to the lobby of the building, but the only person there was the receptionist. "Where's the guy? The one who wanted to see me?" Sarah practically shouted the words, desperate for answers. The receptionist pointed to a door to the right and Sarah charged in. Leo was in a chair in the far corner of the room and two agents she didn't recognize stood on either side of him. Leo's face lit up when he saw her and he said, "See, there she is. I knew she'd want to talk to me." He pointed a finger at one of the agents guarding him. "If only you dumb lugs had just listened to me in the first place."

"Leo, what is it?" she asked, her anxiety mounting. "Why are you here?"

"Figures the day you call off your detail, something would happen. Ellery's gone. Took off in a car with her former law partner and two young girls. Left her front door unlocked and her wallet in the driveway, but I didn't need those clues to know something was up the minute those girls showed up at her house."

Sarah took a deep breath as she attempted to process the scattered bits of information. "Okay, I'm going to need you to start from the beginning. Slowly."

Leo grunted. "Fine. I'm sitting on my porch and this car drives up. I recognize the woman, she's Ellery's old law partner. Tall heels and lots of red hair, that one. Ellery comes to the door and lets her in. About a half hour later, a van shows up and parks in the street. Two young blond girls in school uniforms get out and go to the front door. One of them looks like a high school kid, the other one was a little long in the tooth to be wearing that outfit, but who am I to say?"

Sarah rolled her hand to get him to speed up.

"Okay, okay. So, the girls go in and about ten minutes later, all four of them come out and get in the van, but on the way there, Ellery trips and almost hits the ground. She recovers, they all pile into the van and drive off. Ellery was driving, and her partner, Meg, got into the backseat."

"And what about all this made you think something was wrong?"

He fixed her with a hard stare. "First off, why was Ellery driving a van that wasn't hers?" Sarah crunched her brow into a skeptical expression, but he kept talking. "There's more. After they drove off, I noticed Ellery's wallet, lying right there in her driveway. I figured she dropped it when she fell, so I walk over to get it, thinking I'll hang onto it until she gets home. When I go to pick it up, I see this sticking out of it."

He handed her a business card. It was hers. The one she'd given Ellery on Sunday when she'd seen her on the street outside of Breadwinners. She turned it over and saw her handwritten cell phone number.

"I called that number," he said. "But you didn't answer. I called the number on the front too, but they said you were busy. I figured if I came on down here, you would see me."

"You were right. Anything else you remember?"

"I tried her front door and it was unlocked. She'd never leave her place open like that. I looked around for the car you folks have had parked on the street since last week, but it was nowhere in sight."

Damn. Trip had told her they'd pulled the surveillance on Ellery that morning since they were bringing Naveed and his pals in. At the time, she'd been happy for Ellery, but now she realized the lack of police presence had placed her in jeopardy. "You did the right thing. I may need you to sit with a sketch artist and describe the girls."

"I can do you one better." Leo reached into his pocket and pulled out his phone. "Snapped a couple of pictures. Got the van and its license plate too."

Sarah could have kissed him, but instead she grabbed the phone and scrolled through the pictures. Her anxiety spiraled now that she knew exactly who had shown up at Ellery's door. She'd seen pictures of both girls in the files they'd reviewed just hours ago. "Wait here. I'll be right back."

She dashed out of the room and ran into Trip. The words poured out of her. "Ellery's been taken. It happened about an hour ago and she's in deep trouble."

"Slow down. What's going on?"

She shoved the phone at him. "Kayla and Jasmine showed up at Ellery's place and took Ellery and her former law partner Meg off in a van. Ellery's neighbor saw them leave."

Trip studied her for a moment and his expression, bordering on indulgence, drove her crazy. "What?" she asked.

"You're sure she was taken? That she didn't go willingly? Those girls could've gotten wind of what's going on down here with their boyfriends and decided to get some legal advice. Makes sense they'd go to the two attorneys who were already well acquainted with the case."

Leave it to Trip to stick to his usual mantra of the simplest explanation is usually the best. Normally, she would agree with him, but nothing about this case was simple, especially not when it came to Ellery. Sarah's gut told her something was terribly wrong, and Ellery, by leaving her card where someone could find it, relied on her for rescue. No way was she going to let her down. She squared her shoulders and faced Trip. She'd find Ellery no matter what it took, even if it meant she had to walk away from the job.

❖

Ellery gripped the steering wheel tightly as she listened to Kayla talk on the phone. She glanced in the rearview mirror at Meg who was seated in the back with Jasmine. Meg hadn't said a word since they left the house, but her face was pale and she looked like she wanted to throw up.

Ellery could relate. She'd managed to leave her wallet in the driveway, but it wasn't much of a clue. If anyone came looking for her, maybe they would get the hint and give Sarah a call, but she wasn't convinced that would do much good since Sarah wouldn't have any idea where she was. Frankly, she held out hope that it would be Sarah who came by her house. She'd left so abruptly last night. If she'd known she would never see Sarah again, she would have said something, done something to show her how she felt. To let her know the night had been about more than sex.

None of it mattered now unless she could figure a way out of this mess. She concentrated on figuring out Kayla and Jasmine's end game. They'd been in the car driving all over the city for the past forty-five minutes. In between snippets of conversation on the phone, Kayla had instructed her turn-by-turn, and Ellery was now certain they were headed back toward downtown. What she didn't know was what these girls had planned once they got there.

She tried to glean some idea of who might be on the other end of the phone, but Kayla's side of the conversation was too vague to give her any clues. Finally, after a few minutes, Kayla set the phone down and concentrated on the road ahead. "Turn right here."

They were on Ross Avenue now and Ellery could see the Dallas skyline just ahead. "So, we're headed downtown," she said.

"Don't pretend to act like you know anything about what's in store. All you need to know is that you're going to take part in something important whether you appreciate it or not."

"Important, like bomb another building important? Because if that's the case, you and I have very different ideas about what's important. It's not too late for us to turn around. Meg and I will help you get out of that vest and you can take off. It'll be like it never happened." She gave Jasmine a pointed look in the rearview mirror to make sure she understood she had a say in the matter, but Kayla cut her off. "Save it, counselor. We're ready to die for the cause. You should concentrate on getting ready to do the same when the time comes."

"You're crazy," Meg said, rising up from her seat. "Ellery, stop the damn car and let me out."

"Do it and you'll both be dead right now."

"Sounds like we're going to be dead soon anyway," Ellery said.

Kayla didn't argue the point. "I suggest you keep driving."

Ellery tried a different tack. "Jasmine, are you wearing a death trap too?"

"Ignore her," Kayla said. She looked over at Ellery. "What business is it of yours how we choose to exercise our faith?"

"When innocent people die, it's everyone's business." Ellery thought back to the night of the bombing and the memory of the broken bodies she'd helped pull from the rubble. The destruction had been devastating, and remembering the uselessness of it all made her angry enough to push for answers. "Besides, I have to wonder about this 'faith' of yours. Did you grow up in the Muslim faith or is it just something you do to impress boys?"

"It's not about them," Jasmine said.

Kayla made a zip it motion. "Seriously, Jasmine, shut up." She faced forward again and said, "And you too, shut up and drive. Turn left at the next light and then right on Main."

They were in the heart of downtown now. Ellery caught Meg's eye in the mirror and subtly shook her head. They would have to be very careful if they were going to get out of this alive. She had no doubt now Naveed and his friends were responsible for bombing the arena, and they now had a plan in place to bomb another location. Kayla was whispering into the phone again, and Ellery considered the possibility Naveed and Akbar were orchestrating this whole thing. What she didn't get was why they had involved her and why either of these girls would consent to suiting up with explosives. Were they truly convinced their actions were part of some glorious jihad?

While Kayla was occupied on the phone, she looked back at Jasmine. She kept crossing and uncrossing her legs and casting furtive looks out the window. Clearly, Kayla was the leader of this little expedition, and Jasmine was a reluctant follower. She needed to figure out a way to leverage that fact to help them out of this situation because right now things looked dire. Without a clue as to whether the explosives were real and how they were set to detonate, their options were severely limited. If they could get somewhere away from buildings and people, she could rush Kayla in order to give Meg a chance to get away, but if Jasmine was also wearing a vest, her action would be pointless. She didn't want to die today. Not today of all days, not after she'd spent the night in Sarah's arms and let her walk away. She should have done whatever it took to get her to stay, begging if necessary, but at the very least, she wanted to live long enough to have another chance to convince her what they'd shared was only the beginning.

Then again, what chance did she have? Sarah was a cop, through and through, and duty would always come first. Last night, the hours of pleasure they'd spent together, were an anomaly, a by-product of high emotions and physical attraction. When work called, Sarah made her choice, and Ellery could hardly blame her since her dedication was one of the qualities she found attractive about her.

Kayla's voice jarred her out of her reverie. "Here." She pointed to a parking garage entrance up ahead on the right. "Turn in there."

People were walking on both sides of the street, going about their regular routines while she was driving a van, presumably loaded with enough explosives to ruin the lives of everyone in sight. The idea of driving into an underground parking garage made her feel even more trapped and helpless than she had when Kayla had first ordered her into the van. She spotted a parking space on the street, said a silent prayer, and jerked the wheel until she was parallel to the sidewalk.

"What the hell do you think you're doing?" Kayla shouted.

If they were going to die anyway, she would decide the terms. "I'm not moving until you tell me what you're up to."

Kayla shot a look at Jasmine who turned her face to the window as if she was done participating in Kayla's little game. "We are taking revenge for the religious persecution of our loved ones. I would have thought you'd have more loyalty to the people you represent, but apparently, Naveed and his father were only dollar signs to you. I'm fully prepared to die for what I believe." She reached a hand inside her jacket and looked outside the van. "This isn't what we had planned, but if you're prepared to die with me right now, just say the word."

Ellery's eyes were locked on Kayla's hand. Was death really as close as the push of a button, the pull of a cord? The smart thing to do would be to keep Kayla talking, postpone any action until she and Meg could figure a way out or until they were rescued, but she doubted either option was likely. She glanced at Meg whose drawn expression signaled she was resigned to their fate. Fate. If this was fate, then everything that had happened over the past few weeks or even months had led her to this moment. Representing Amir and Naveed, leaving her practice, meeting Sarah—every action a cog in the wheel that propelled her life to this moment. But she wouldn't change a thing, especially if it meant taking back any portion of the time she'd spent with Sarah. Her only regret now was that she'd never see her again, never see the look on Sarah's face when she admitted she was falling in love with her.

Damn. The realization landed in her gut like a wrecking ball. Love was the reason it hurt so deeply when Sarah had walked out last night in favor of the job. Falling in love with Sarah would only bring pain because she'd always be the mistress, never the wife. Better that Sarah had left now, than later when she was more deeply invested in these feelings. Fate meant everything worked out the way it was supposed to, and if fate meant she would die today, then she was going to do so with dignity, which meant doing everything in her power to keep Kayla from killing innocent people.

She looked at Kayla's jacket. "I am prepared to die, but not your way." She pulled at the steering wheel, a hasty plan beginning to form. "I'll take you some place where you can blow the four of us to bits, but it's not going to be here." She started to pull out into the adjacent lane, but a DART bus had her blocked in. She began backing up when Jasmine suddenly yelled, "She docsn't have the detonator."

"What?"

"Hashid has it." Jasmine was crying now as she sputtered the words. "She can't do anything without him."

As Ellery tried to make sense of what she was saying, Kayla opened the passenger door and jumped out of the van. Ellery looked from Kayla to Jasmine and back again. Kayla was walking briskly toward the front doors of One Main Place, one of the largest buildings in downtown Dallas and a hub for the underground tunnel system that ran throughout the area. She asked Jasmine, "What was the plan?"

"I don't know for sure. We were supposed to get you here and he would tell us what to do then."

The cell phone conversation Kayla had kept going for the entire ride. Hashid was probably orchestrating their every move from the moment they'd shown up at her house. "Do you have one of those vests on?" She motioned to Meg. "Check her."

Jasmine shook her head and sobbed. Ellery looked out the window again. Kayla was almost at the door to the building where hundreds of people were sitting in their offices, wishing away the afternoon without a clue it might be their last. Fate may have brought her this far, but the rest was up to her. She slammed the van into park, tossed the keys back to Meg, jumped out of the van, and raced after Kayla.

CHAPTER TWENTY-THREE

Sarah edged her car around a woman with a jogging stroller and stepped on the gas.

"We're not going to get there any faster if you take out pedestrians along the way," Trip said. "The word's out. Someone's going to find them soon."

Someone wasn't good enough. She wouldn't rest until she saw Ellery with her own eyes. From the moment Sarah realized Ellery was in danger, her heart had been racing, propelling her to action. She'd started to rush out of headquarters, determined to find Ellery despite the fact she didn't have a clue where to look, but Trip had convinced her to wait at least long enough to formulate a rough strategy. She'd barely been able to contain her emotions as she watched Trip, Aadila, and Liz sketch out a plan. All she could think about was the end result.

Aadila stayed at headquarters to continue questioning Naveed and Akbar. Liz would monitor the search while the other agents fanned out to find clues, starting at Kayla's and Jasmine's houses. An all-points bulletin went out to local law enforcement with the license plate number and pictures of the girls and the van, and within an hour, a traffic camera picked up the van driving around the downtown area. Dallas Police were already in the area, combing the streets for another sighting. The minute they'd gotten news of the sighting, Sarah and Trip had hit the road. On the way, they'd gotten word the local police had eyes on the van.

Sarah sped up to pass a large produce truck. "They know not to approach, right?"

"They do," Trip said.

"They better." Sarah grimaced as she hit a patch of traffic and slowed to a crawl. She glanced around, but she was boxed in. She revved the engine, but the show of force did nothing to ease the fear of what she might find once they got to the van. Before they'd left headquarters, Trip had sketched out a plan of attack, but everything he'd said had been a blur against the picture of dread her thoughts had painted. She took a deep breath and willed calm to settle in. "Tell me again what you have planned."

"First thing, separate the girls. Then—" His phone rang and he looked at the screen. "Damn, hold on. It's Aadila." He set the phone in the cup holder. "You're on speaker with me and Sarah. Go ahead."

"I've got an address. The van's parked in front of One Main Place, at Main and Field."

"We're close," Sarah said. "Any signs of activity?"

"Nothing so far. DPD has a car just down the street keeping an eye on it, and I made it clear they aren't to move in until you get there, and then only under your direction."

The traffic ahead broke up and Sarah accelerated. "Five minutes, tops. Tell the locals what I'm driving and to keep an eye out. We may need their help, but they are backup only."

"Got it. And, Sarah?"

"Yes?"

"One Main Place is across the street from the federal building. I mean there's a small park in between, but that's still a little close for comfort. At some point we'll need to make a decision and it will have to be made quickly. I can't promise you'll have much time."

"Understood." A van with terrorist ties parked across the street from the federal building presented a precarious situation for everyone involved, especially since they didn't have a clue what was inside or what the girls had planned. Another bomb was highly likely. But why had they taken Ellery? It didn't make any sense. Unless Trip's earlier theory was correct, that the girls were spooked when Naveed and Akbar had been taken into custody and wanted legal advice. Except you didn't need to get into a van and drive around to get counseling on the law. Sarah was certain something more nefarious was happening. Something dangerous. "Any word from the agents who are searching the houses?"

"Not yet. Early word is the computers have been wiped. No one who lives with either of them professes to know anything. We'll be able to do data recovery, but it'll take time."

Time they didn't have. "Call us if you find anything." She focused her concentration back to the road and let Trip finish out the call on his own.

She honed in on the van the moment she turned on Main. It was parked in a space about fifty feet from the entrance of the building. "Get closer or park here and approach on foot?"

"Park here and figure out a plan before we blow into a situation we know nothing about."

"I have a plan and it involves getting to the bottom of what's going on as quickly as possible." She pulled into a loading dock and parked. With one hand on the door handle, she asked, "You with me?"

Trip shook his head as if he realized it was futile to argue with her. "I'm with you. Come on." He started to get out of the car, but his phone rang again. "It's Aadila, hang on." He put her on speaker again. "We're here. What's up?"

"The cops talked to a witness who saw two people leave the van a few minutes before they rolled up. One of them matches Kayla's description and the other appears to be Ellery Durant. They both entered the building through the front entrance."

"That's it. I'm out of here." Sarah walked as fast as she could without running and headed straight for the van. She could hear Trip's huffing breaths behind her, but she didn't slow her pace.

"Damn it, Flores, slow the fuck down."

She ignored him and walked straight up to the driver's side window and rapped on the glass. No one responded and she pressed closer only to see there was no one in the front seat. She wrenched open the door, stuck her head inside, and was greeted by the sound of crying. Sitting in the back seat was Jasmine next to a beautiful redhead. "What the hell?"

The redhead spoke first. "Who are you?"

"Special Agent Sarah Flores, FBI. Meg?"

She nodded and said, "You've got to do something. This girl and her friend are planning something terrible."

Sarah cared about that, but she cared about something else more. "Where's Ellery?"

"What?"

"Ellery Durant. I need to find her. Right now. Where did she go?"

"She's not involved with these people. When are you people going to stop chasing your tails and go after the real bad guys?" She pointed at Jasmine. "I'm telling you this girl is a terrorist and her friend just went into that building wearing a vest loaded with explosives and there's another guy on the loose with the detonator. Do something about that and leave Ellery alone."

Sarah struggled to process the information. "Kayla is wearing a suicide vest? And Ellery is with her?"

"Yes. Well, not like that. Ellery followed her, probably to try and stop her." Meg jabbed at Jasmine's arm. "Tell them."

Jasmine's words, offered between sobs were difficult to understand, but clear enough to convey the gist. Hashid Kamal was somewhere nearby with a detonator and Kayla, armed with explosives, was headed to a predesignated point in the tunnels beneath one of the most populated buildings in downtown Dallas. As if that weren't bad enough, Ellery was in the building with Kayla. "How is the detonator supposed to work?"

"Kayla is supposed to text him when she's in place and then he'll call her to set it off. When she answers the phone, the bomb goes off."

"You really think there's a good cell signal underneath the building?" Sarah asked.

"I know there is." Jasmine's voice was quiet, but sure.

The plan didn't sound airtight, but these little assholes had already had a successful run with explosives—it was probably best to assume they knew what they were doing and that this operation, in some form, had been planned in advance. Sarah ran through her options. She should stay here and question Jasmine to try to ascertain more details, but all she wanted to do was run into the building and find Ellery. Sarah felt a hand on her shoulder and looked back at Trip.

"Go, find her. Keep your phone close and check in. I'll stay out here and see if we can get a fix on Hashid. This feels like a pretty hasty move on his part, and I doubt he had much time to plan. He'll make a mistake. We'll get to him."

She didn't wait to hear more, and a few minutes later, she pushed through the doors of One Main Place and sized up the scene. Everything she saw said normal. People milling around the lobby, stepping in and out of elevators. She looked over at the security guard standing next to the information desk. His look of abject boredom said this was just like any other day on the job, uneventful and sleep-inducing. All of that was about to change. She walked over and surreptitiously displayed her credentials.

"Don't react," she said quietly. "I need to ask you a few questions and I need to know that none of the information I'm about to share with you will be passed on to anyone else without my express permission. Nod your head if you understand."

His eyes grew wide and he nodded.

"Okay, great." She pulled out her phone and scrolled through to find a picture of Kayla. "Have you seen this girl come into the building? It would've been in the last half hour."

He looked at the screen and scrunched his brow before nodding his head. "She took the elevator, but I'm not sure where."

"Thanks." She flipped to the next photo, the one Leo had taken that included a shot of Ellery. She pointed at the screen. "And this woman? How about her?"

"Yes. She came in shortly after. I remember because she seemed like she was late for something. She ran toward one of the elevators and got really frustrated when it closed as she got there. She went down the escalator over there. It goes into the tunnels. That's all I remember."

"That's good. Now, there is a potential terrorist threat to this building. I need to know the evacuation protocol and I need to know you're ready to call it in if I give the word."

He spent a minute taking her through the protocol and she tried to ignore the shake in his voice. Of course he was nervous. The entire city had been on edge immediately after the explosion at the arena, but the concern had faded into the reassuring conclusion that lightning wouldn't strike twice in the same place. But terrorism didn't behave like a natural disaster, and zealots could strike again at any time.

After she was sure he would be ready to call the alarm if necessary, she had a decision to make. Try and find Kayla or go after Ellery. Duty told her to find Kayla first and then make sure Ellery was okay, but instinct told her Ellery had gone after Kayla and finding Ellery would lead her to the bomb. "Will my cell phone work below this floor?" she asked.

"It should. Signal's actually pretty good down there." He reached into a drawer and pulled out a card. "This is my number if you need me."

Sarah typed the numbers into her phone and shoved the card into her pocket. She reached out a hand. "What's your name?"

"Phillips. Ed Phillips." He grasped her hand. "Do you want me to go with you?"

She shook her head. This guy hadn't signed up for the kind of danger she was headed toward. Besides, she needed someone in place who could initiate an evacuation if it came to that. "I appreciate the offer, but what I really need is for you to stay right here and be ready in case we need to evacuate the building. Okay?"

"Okay."

She shot him what she hoped was a look full of confidence, and then she jogged toward the escalator, determined to find Ellery, hoping they would both survive this day.

❖

The elevator door shut before she could reach it and Ellery cursed under her breath. She glanced around, finally locating the escalator that led to the tunnels. Every instinct told her Kayla was headed below ground and, as she took the stairs two at a time, she hoped she was right.

At the bottom of the escalator was a sparsely populated, wide corridor with a convenience store immediately to her right and a sign that said Field Street. Up ahead, the tunnel led to Renaissance Tower and to her left the path seemed to dead end. She didn't see Kayla in any direction. She reached for her cell phone before she remembered Jasmine had taken her phone once they'd gotten into the van.

Guess you should have thought of that before you went running after Kayla. She cursed her lack of foresight. She had two options. Go back upstairs, call the police, and let them handle finding Kayla or stay down here and keep looking for her. Right now, she was only steps behind Kayla, but in the time it would take to get help, she risked losing her entirely. After a few seconds consideration, she resolved to press on.

She walked a few steps to the right and glanced around. At the end of the hallway were glass doors that led out into an open, underground courtyard. If the explosion was planned to go off outside, there wouldn't have been any reason for Kayla to have entered the building in the first place. She looked back at the corridor directly in front of the escalator and decided it was her best bet. Feeling the pressure of ticking time, she abandoned all pretense of sneaking up on Kayla and broke into a run. Within seconds, she was standing in the middle of a food court and she pulled up short and turned in a circle, hoping to spot Kayla among the late lunch stragglers.

It didn't take long. She was seated in a popular sandwich chain, flipping through pages of a newspaper. To the casual observer, she looked like a student who'd just finished her lunch and was reading the paper to kill time.

Ellery looked around to assess how many other people were nearby. In addition to the two employees behind the counter, an older couple was seated at a table next to Kayla, eating their lunch and a middle-aged woman in a suit was sipping a coffee and reading a book a few tables away. While she was thinking about a subtle way to get these people away from here, Kayla looked up, directly at her.

Her eyes were vacant, but her lips formed a slow smile, taunting and malicious. Ellery remembered what Jasmine had said and silently repeated the words. *She can't do anything without Hashid.* She looked around again and didn't see anyone else in close proximity. If Hashid was running the show, he was doing it remotely. If she took any action at all, would she force his hand? Was it worth the risk? If she were one of the innocent people caught up in this cluster fuck, she'd want to know what was going on so she could make decisions about her own fate. She took a deep breath, pointed at Kayla, and yelled, "She has a bomb. Get out of here as fast as you can."

For a split second, the patrons and employees looked at her like she was a lunatic, annoyingly interrupting their lunch. She moved closer and lied to get her point across. "I'm with the FBI. She has a bomb. Leave now. All of you." She whirled in a circle to make sure everyone within the sound of her voice knew they were included in her warning. In what seemed like slow motion, one by one, the people in the food court dropped their lunches, grabbed their things, and started first walking, then running from the area. Ellery kept her eyes on Kayla the entire time, but she didn't move. She didn't even blink.

"Like that's going to do any good," she said.

"Why are you doing this?" Ellery asked.

"I told you," Kayla said. "I'm willing to die for what I believe."

"I know you aren't in charge. Hashid controls the explosives, not you. Did you ever ask yourself why he's not the one down here ready to blow himself up for what he believes?"

"Infidel. We all have our destiny. We don't choose our path, it is chosen for us. You don't understand and you never will."

Ellery realized it was pointless to argue with a zealot, and she considered her next move. She was about ten feet from Kayla, close enough to see her glance down at her cell phone every few seconds. She was certain the phone was the key. It had probably been Hashid on the other end of the cell during the entire drive from her house to this building. She imagined him huddled up somewhere nearby, safe from capture and ready to detonate Kayla's vest as soon as she was in place. Was he on the phone now listening, or was he waiting for a signal from her?

As if on cue, Kayla lifted the phone from the table. Ellery started to take a step toward her, but an authoritative voice stopped her in her tracks.

"FBI. Put the phone down and put your hands in the air. Now."

Sarah. The sound of her voice warmed the icy grip of fear that had Ellery in its grasp. She turned to see Sarah standing directly behind her, and her first instinct was to go to her and pull her close, but relief at Sarah's arrival quickly morphed to panic when she realized Sarah was alone and her threat wasn't accompanied by a show of force.

She might be panicked, but Sarah's appearance had done nothing to ruffle Kayla's easy composure. "I don't think so," she said. "If you're scared to die, you can leave."

Ellery looked between them. Did Sarah have a plan? If so, now was the time to let her in on it. She stepped back so they were close enough to touch and Sarah whispered in her ear. "You need to get out now."

"Not leaving without you."

"It wasn't a request."

Sarah's voice was a low growl, but her pleading eyes told her the command was born of caring. She injected as much warmth as she could into her words. "I'm not leaving you." She jerked her chin at Kayla and lowered her voice. "It's the phone. We need to get it from her."

Sarah grabbed her arm, squeezed her bicep, and then pushed her aside, saying in a loud voice. "Your clients have caused enough trouble. Get out now or I'll arrest you both." She turned so her back was to Ellery and started walking toward Kayla as she spoke. "Kayla, the building is already being evacuated. Your little plan is off the rails. Give me the phone and you might have a chance at something less than the death penalty."

Ellery watched as Sarah got closer to Kayla. Despite her terse words, Sarah's expression had been laced with concern, and she knew with every fiber of her being Sarah was trying to separate her from danger. Sarah may have more information than she did, but that didn't mean she'd make a better decision about what to do next. They should both get the hell out of here while they still could, but it was clear Sarah wasn't going anywhere, and Ellery decided she would rather face her fears than risk losing her. As long as Sarah was staying, she wasn't going anywhere.

Sarah was almost at the table now, and she stepped quickly to catch up. They would take Kayla together or not at all. She was practically on Sarah's heels when a loud ringing sound cut through the air.

Everything happened in slow motion. Kayla reached for her phone. Sarah launched through the air, her arm outstretched. Ellery lunged forward, but by the time she reached them, Sarah and Kayla were a tangled mass of arms and legs as they brawled for control of the phone. Ellery saw the phone in Kayla's hand and, saying a silent prayer that all the commotion wouldn't cause an explosion, she dove in, grabbing for Kayla's arm. She yanked Kayla's arm to the floor and slammed her wrist against the hard tile, willing her to let go. While she held Kayla's arm, Sarah got to her knees and tried to hold her still, but Kayla struggled against them like an angry cat, kicking with both legs.

Ellery heard a loud thud and glanced up to see Sarah grab her head. She started to reach out to her, but a quick look back at Kayla tore her attention in two. Kayla had taken advantage of Ellery's split second distraction and her thumb was inching toward the answer call button on the phone. Ellery growled and gripped Kayla's wrist until she felt the raw grind of bones breaking. Kayla screamed and the phone dropped from her grasp. Ellery scooped it up with her free hand and as she reached for Sarah, the phone stopped ringing and loud shouts filled the air.

CHAPTER TWENTY-FOUR

S arah struggled to sit up, but a strong arm kept her in place. "Don't move."

Whoever it was needn't have worried. Slowly and carefully, she opened her eyes. The paramedic kneeling next to her was wiping her forehead with a pad that reeked of pungent antiseptic. She tried to turn her head to look around, but spikes of pain sent a wave of nausea through her. At least she was alive.

The realization sparked her memory. Ellery struggling with Kayla for control of the phone, the incessantly ringing phone that held the power to send them all to a horrible death. The entire scene replayed in her head: the pain of Kayla's shoe connecting with her head, the sound of Kayla's screams as Ellery wrestled her for control of the phone, and then the mad chaos of federal agents swarming them just as Ellery won the battle. Everything after that was fuzzy. Had she passed out? She must have because she didn't have a clue what had happened next. She shifted in place and sharp darts burned behind her eyes. Obviously, she wasn't dead, but what about Ellery?

Suddenly, she didn't care about the nausea or the pain. She had to know what had happened. She braced a hand on the floor and pushed herself up. "Ellery. Where's Ellery?"

"Whoa there, hang on a minute."

The paramedic held her in place, but now that she was upright she could take in the entire scene. The food court was full of law enforcement personnel and buzzing with action. Her eyes were drawn to a group of agents huddled around a spot on the floor, and she spied Kayla's blond hair through one of the agent's legs. "The vest?"

"Intact. We got it off her and it's disarmed."

She smiled at the sound of Trip's voice and turned to see him standing behind her. The sudden movement sparked pain in her head. "Oh shit." The paramedic reached out a hand, but she brushed it away. "I'm okay. Got to remember to move slowly. Trip, help me up. Where's Ellery?"

He held her arm and she carefully pulled herself up. He looked around. "I haven't seen her. I just got down here. I was a little busy above ground locating Hashid. Looks like we got to him in the nick of time too. He had already dialed Kayla's number. If she'd answered, well…"

Sarah shuddered. She considered what might have happened had Kayla answered the call and her gut clenched. She'd been in danger before, but being shot at paled in comparison to the threat of being blown to bits. And Ellery. She'd tried to get her to leave, but Ellery had charged right in and joined the fight, never mind the fact she'd been falsely accused, and her name had been tarnished in the press. Would she have been as brave, as selfless if the tables were turned?

The answer flooded her mind with crystal clarity. She would do anything, everything, in her power to save Ellery's life, no matter what the consequences. Ellery had said last night that whatever was happening between them was important. What a colossal understatement. This thing between them was exactly what Sarah had been looking for when she left her career and moved across the country. Leave it to fate to give her what she wanted all wrapped in complications. Last night she'd walked away from love, but she'd be damned if she was going to do it again.

"Ellery stopped Kayla from answering the phone." Sarah shook Trip's arm. "She saved my life. I need to find her. Right now."

❖

Ellery strained to see over the agent's shoulder, but he was too tall. He was also becoming increasingly annoyed at her refusal to talk. Since he'd yanked her away from Kayla, handcuffed her, and started peppering her with questions, she had consistently repeated the same phrase over and over in response to every query. "I'll only talk to Agent Flores." The words became her mantra.

Finally, he threw his hands in the air and snapped, "Your right to remain silent is going to put you on death row." He pushed his chair back and ordered one of the other agents to keep an eye on her before he stalked off. With his large frame no longer blocking the view, Ellery could see a large contingent of officers blocking off the area where she and Sarah had wrestled with Kayla. She could make out what looked like a paramedic bent over someone, but the angle kept her from telling who. *If it's Sarah, please let her be okay.*

She had no idea what had happened to Sarah while she was wrestling with Kayla. She'd wanted to go to her, but she knew she had to keep fighting Kayla if they were going to have a chance to make it out alive. The rest of the scuffle had been a blur ending with agents pulling her off Kayla, ripping the phone out of her hand, and hustling her away from the scene.

She glanced around the room, praying she would spot Sarah, but she was nowhere in sight. When she looked back at the paramedic, he had moved, and now she could tell the person he'd been tending to was blond. She flexed her fist which was still sore from gripping Kayla's wrist. She hoped she'd broken it into pieces.

"Ellery?"

The voice behind her was soft and tentative, but after last night its lush tone would forever be engraved in her memory. She sighed with relief. Sarah, accompanied by a man she didn't recognize, stood in front of her with a large bandage on her forehead, her clothes disheveled. Ellery stood and, ignoring the glare of the agent who'd been left to guard her, she raised her hands to touch Sarah's cheek. "You're okay?"

Sarah put her hands on her still cuffed wrists. "Yes. You?"

"I'm fine." She motioned to her guard. "Except I think I might be under arrest."

Sarah looked at the man beside her. "Trip, can you take care of this?"

"On it."

The man motioned to the guard and instructed him to unlock the handcuffs. Once her hands were free, Ellery rubbed her wrists. "Thanks."

"Ellery Durant, meet Trip Sandler. He's a friend."

Ellery nodded. She noted the way Trip held Sarah's arm, protective and caring. He was clearly a good friend, and under other circumstances, she would have been happy to meet someone Sarah cared about and who so obviously cared about her, but right now all she wanted was to be above-ground and alone with Sarah. Last night's intimacy seemed so long ago, but after today's danger, the tangled feelings Sarah had left behind came roaring back. She was in love with her, but did Sarah feel the same way? After staring down death just moments ago, she didn't want to wait to find out.

"Come on."

Sarah's soft words were a welcome command, and she followed her out of the building, past the agents, past Kayla still prone on the floor, toward a future she hoped they would share.

Sarah pulled her car into Ellery's driveway and shut off the engine. She looked over at the passenger seat. Ellery was staring at the front door, but she couldn't read her expression. Should she stay or go? They hadn't talked much on the ride over, both of them seemingly sucked out of adrenaline. She leaned back in the seat and waited for Ellery to make the first move. A few seconds later, her phone rang and she rushed to silence it, the sound a painful reminder of the ordeal they'd just endured.

"Do you need to get that?" Ellery asked.

Sarah looked at Danny's name on the display. By now she'd probably heard what happened and was worried, but Sarah didn't want anything to interrupt whatever was about to happen between her and Ellery. When the message icon appeared on her screen, she typed a quick text to let Danny know she was okay, switched off the ringer, and stowed the phone in the console. "Sorry about that."

"Don't be. I understand you have a job to do."

Sarah started to say she wasn't here because of the job, but Ellery spoke first. "Walk me in?"

"Absolutely."

They were halfway up the walk when she heard Leo's gruff voice call out. "You found her."

Sarah raised a hand to wave at him and he leaned over the railing of his front porch as they approached. "I said I would."

"You look like you got a little beat up in the process," he said.

"You should see the other guy."

Leo grunted his approval and gave her a quick salute before returning to his chair.

As Ellery pushed open the front door, she said, "Something going on between you two I should know about?"

"We seem to have formed a bond." Sarah followed her into the kitchen. "Actually, there's probably a lot of detail we're both missing about what went down today. Are you up for talking about it?"

"Maybe."

"Maybe?"

"There are a bunch of things I'd like to talk about. If you want to start with what happened today, we can do that."

Sarah glanced down the hallway. The door to Ellery's bedroom was shut, but every inch of the interior was emblazoned on her mind and she sensed it always would be, no matter what happened next. She'd brought Ellery home because it had seemed like the right thing to do, but now that they were here, every detail about the night before came rushing back, and she wasn't sure if her motives were fueled by arousal or something more permanent. Back in the tunnel, she'd been ready to call what she felt for Ellery love, but was that a by-product of danger or a real feeling?

Ellery's voice cut through her thoughts. "Kayla and Jasmine showed up here around noon. They said they were looking for Naveed. Apparently, he missed his court appearance this morning. Meg was already here when they arrived. She'd called earlier to ask about Naveed and I asked her to come by to talk about something that was on my mind."

Sarah looked into Ellery's eyes as she relayed the simple facts. She saw pain and something else. Longing? Whatever it was, Ellery had apparently decided not to push for some big discussion about feelings, instead choosing to sort through the events that had brought them to this point. It couldn't hurt to meet her halfway.

"HSI took Naveed into custody this morning," she said. "When we took a break, he made a phone call to Jasmine. It sounded innocuous at the time, but we think he must have given her some kind of code to signal her to initiate this plan."

"Is Meg okay?"

"For now. After you and Kayla left the van, Jasmine became a big soppy mess. I don't think she was ever really committed to any of this. She just wanted to be close to Naveed. As for Meg, she has a lot of questions to answer. You should know HSI has connected her to Jafari and they've only begun to scratch the surface of the evidence they gathered from her office."

Ellery sighed. "Whatever she's done, she didn't deserve what could have happened today. I'm fairly certain those girls intended to take us out with them."

Sarah shook her head to clear a mental image of the downtown building exploding with Ellery underneath it. "Thank God for Leo. After he saw Kayla and Jasmine drive off with you and Meg, he showed up at headquarters demanding to see me. Clever trick with the card in your wallet."

"I figured it was a long shot, but I'm glad it worked. I think we'll let Leo stay on as head of the neighborhood watch," Ellery said as she reached into the fridge, pulled out a beer, and tilted it in her direction. Sarah started to shake her head no. Any minute now, she could get called back in to deal with the aftermath of the scene she'd just left. HSI had both of the Barstow brothers in custody now and they'd want to try to question them. Aadila's crew would be spread thin, and she imagined she and Trip would be asked to help out. The process would be long and tiring, and it would consume her while it lasted.

She stared at the beer in Ellery's hand and closed her mind against all the distractions. She reached for the bottle and, as she grasped it, her fingers closed around Ellery's, and she braced against the onslaught of opposite sensations. The heat of Ellery's touch and the chill of the bottle—the contrast pretty much summed up everything about their relationship. Relationship. Outside of the bonds she'd formed on the job, the entire concept of a relationship was foreign. Was she ready to accept this most personal challenge and have a life defined by more than her work?

She looked into Ellery's eyes and she knew. She didn't want the push and pull of working this investigation. She'd come to Dallas to find something new and exciting, someone she could love who would love her back. Standing here in front of Ellery, she was absolutely certain she'd found exactly what she was looking for, and she wasn't going to let anything get in the way.

She set the bottle on the table and pulled Ellery into her arms. "I want to talk about something else."

Ellery pulled back and met her eyes, her expression hopeful. "Okay, what do you want to talk about?"

"I'm falling in love with you."

Ellery grinned. "You really know how to change the subject."

Sarah play shoved her. "Is that all you have to say?"

Ellery caught her hands and pulled them to her lips. She kissed the tips of her fingers one by one, as she withheld her answer with delicious delay. Sarah groaned in response to her soft, teasing touch. "You have incredible skills, but are you going to answer my question?"

"I'm saying plenty here." Ellery kissed another fingertip. "I'm pretty sure I fell in love with you when you showed up at the design show in that blazing hot red dress. Or maybe it was when you met me for coffee and then dashed off in your shiny blue Corvette. You're bold and smart and full of life." She leaned in for a kiss and murmured against her lips. "How could I not fall in love with you? All this time, I guess I've been waiting for you to catch up."

Sarah melted into the kiss, into the heat of Ellery's embrace, and let her uncertainty about her job and her role in the investigation recede. Her body hummed with anticipation and, for once, the suspense wasn't about a mystery she was trying to solve, but about the path her life was about to take. She was in love, and all that mattered was she was here with Ellery, and Ellery loved her back. She had no doubt everything else would fall into place.

THE END

About the Author

Carsen Taite's goal as an author is to spin tales with plot lines as interesting as the cases she encountered in her career as a criminal defense lawyer. She is the author of a dozen previously released novels, *truelesbianlove.com*, *It Should be a Crime* (a Lambda Literary Award finalist), *Do Not Disturb*, *Nothing But the Truth*, *The Best Defense*, *Slingshot*, *Beyond Innocence*, *Battle Axe, Rush*, *Switchblade, Courtship*, and *Lay Down the Law*. She is currently working on her fourteenth novel, *Above the Law*, the second book in the Lone Star Law series. Learn more at www.carsentaite.com.

Books Available from Bold Strokes Books

Deadly Medicine by Jaime Maddox. Dr. Ward Thrasher's life is in turmoil. Her partner Jess has left her, and her job puts her in the path of a murderous physician who has Jess in his sights. (978-1-62639-4-247)

New Beginnings by KC Richardson. Can the connection and attraction between Jordan Roberts and Kirsten Murphy be enough for Jordan to trust Kirsten with her heart? (978-1-62639-4-506)

Officer Down by Erin Dutton. Can two women who've made careers out of being there for others in crisis find the strength to need each other? (978-1-62639-4-230)

Reasonable Doubt by Carsen Taite. Just when Sarah and Ellery think they've left dangerous careers behind, a new case sets them—and their hearts—on a collision course. (978-1-62639-4-421)

Tarnished Gold by Ann Aptaker. Cantor Gold must outsmart the Law, outrun New York's dockside gangsters, outplay a shady art dealer, his lover, and a beautiful curator, and stay out of a killer's gun sights. (978-1-62639-4-261)

The Renegade by Amy Dunne. Post-apocalyptic survivors Alex and Evelyn secretly find love while held captive by a deranged cult, but when their relationship is discovered, they must fight for their freedom—or die trying. (978-1-62639-4-278)

Thrall by Barbara Ann Wright. Four women in a warrior society must work together to lift an insidious curse while caught between their own desires, the will of their peoples, and an ancient evil. (978-1-62639-4-377)

White Horse in Winter by Franci McMahon. Love between two women collides with the inner poison of a closeted horse trainer in the green hills of Vermont. (978-1-62639-4-292)

The Chameleon by Andrea Bramhall. Two old friends must work through a web of lies and deceit to find themselves again, but in the search they discover far more than they ever went looking for. (978-1-62639-363-9)

Side Effects by VK Powell. Detective Jordan Bishop and Dr. Neela Sahjani must decide if it's easier to trust someone with your heart or your life as they face threatening protestors, corrupt politicians, and their increasing attraction. (978-1-62639-364-6)

Autumn Spring by Shelley Thrasher. Can Bree and Linda, two women in the autumn of their lives, put their hearts first and find the love they've never dared seize? (978-1-62639-365-3)

Warm November by Kathleen Knowles. What do you do if the one woman you want is the only one you can't have? (978-1-62639-366-0)

In Every Cloud by Tina Michele. When she finally leaves her shattered life behind, is Bree strong enough to salvage the remaining pieces of her heart and find the place where it truly fits? (978-1-62639-413-1)

Rise of the Gorgon by Tanai Walker. When independent Internet journalist Elle Pharell goes to Kuwait to investigate a veteran's mysterious suicide, she hires Cassandra Hunt, an interpreter with a covert agenda. (978-1-62639-367-7)

Crossed by Meredith Doench. Agent Luce Hansen returns home to catch a killer and risks everything to revisit the unsolved murder of her first girlfriend and confront the demons of her youth. (978-1-62639-361-5)

Making a Comeback by Julie Blair. Music and love take center stage when jazz pianist Liz Randall tries to make a comeback with the help of her reclusive, blind neighbor, Jac Winters. (978-1-62639-357-8)

Soul Unique by Gun Brooke. Self-proclaimed cynic Greer Landon falls for Hayden Rowe's paintings and the young woman shortly after, but will Hayden, who lives with Asperger syndrome, trust her and reciprocate her feelings? (978-1-62639-358-5)

The Price of Honor by Radclyffe. Honor and duty are not always black and white—and when self-styled patriots take up arms against the government, the price of honor may be a life. (978-1-62639-359-2)

Mounting Evidence by Karis Walsh. Lieutenant Abigail Hargrove and her mounted police unit need to solve a murder and protect wetland biologist Kira Lovell during the Washington State Fair. (978-1-62639-343-1)

Threads of the Heart by Jeannie Levig. Maggie and Addison Rae-McInnis share a love and a life, but are the threads that bind them together strong enough to withstand Addison's restlessness and the seductive Victoria Fontaine? (978-1-62639-410-0)

Sheltered Love by MJ Williamz. Boone Fairway and Grey Dawson—two women touched by abuse—overcome their pasts to find happiness in each other. (978-1-62639-362-2)

Asher's Out by Elizabeth Wheeler. Asher Price's candid photographs capture the truth, but when his success requires exposing an enemy, Asher discovers his only shot at happiness involves revealing secrets of his own. (978-1-62639-411-7)

The Ground Beneath by Missouri Vaun. An improbable barter deal involving a hope chest and dinners for a month places lovely Jessica

Walker distractingly in the way of Sam Casey's bachelor lifestyle. (978-1-62639-606-7)

Hardwired by C.P. Rowlands. Award-winning teacher Clary Stone, and Leefe Ellis, manager of the homeless shelter for small children, stand together in a part of Clary's hometown that she never knew existed. (978-1-62639-351-6)

No Good Reason by Cari Hunter. A violent kidnapping in a Peak District village pushes Detective Sanne Jensen and lifelong friend Dr. Meg Fielding closer, just as it threatens to tear everything apart. (978-1-62639-352-3)

Romance by the Book by Jo Victor. If Cam didn't keep disrupting her life, maybe Alex could uncover the secret of a century-old love story, and solve the greatest mystery of all—her own heart. (978-1-62639-353-0)

Death's Doorway by Crin Claxton. Helping the dead can be deadly: Tony may be listening to the dead, but she needs to learn to listen to the living. (978-1-62639-354-7)

Searching for Celia by Elizabeth Ridley. As American spy novelist Dayle Salvesen investigates the mysterious disappearance of her ex-lover, Celia, in London, she begins questioning how well she knew Celia—and how well she knows herself. (978-1-62639-356-1)

The 45th Parallel by Lisa Girolami. Burying her mother isn't the worst thing that can happen to Val Montague when she returns to the woodsy but peculiar town of Hemlock, Oregon. (978-1-62639-342-4)

A Royal Romance by Jenny Frame. In a country where class still divides, can love topple the last social taboo and allow Queen Georgina and Beatrice Elliot, a working class girl, their happy ever after? (978-1-62639-360-8)

Bouncing by Jaime Maddox. Basketball Coach Alex Dalton has been bouncing from woman to woman, because no one ever held her interest, until she meets her new assistant, Britain Dodge. (978-1-62639-344-8)

Same Time Next Week by Emily Smith. A chance encounter between Alex Harris and the beautiful Michelle Masters leads to a whirlwind friendship, and causes Alex to question everything she's ever known—including her own marriage. (978-1-62639-345-5)

All Things Rise by Missouri Vaun. Cole rescues a striking pilot who crash-lands near her family's farm, setting in motion a chain of events that will forever alter the course of her life. (978-1-62639-346-2)

Riding Passion by D. Jackson Leigh. Mount up for the ride through a sizzling anthology of chance encounters, buried desires, romantic surprises, and blazing passion. (978-1-62639-349-3)

Love's Bounty by Yolanda Wallace. Lobster boat captain Jake Myers stopped living the day she cheated death, but meeting greenhorn Shy Silva stirs her back to life. (978-1-62639-334-9)

Just Three Words by Melissa Brayden. Sometimes the one you want is the one you least suspect. Accountant Samantha Ennis has her ordered life disrupted when heartbreaker Hunter Blair moves into her trendy Soho loft. (978-1-62639-335-6)

Lay Down the Law by Carsen Taite. Attorney Peyton Davis returns to her Texas roots to take on big oil and the Mexican Mafia, but will her investigation thwart her chance at true love? (978-1-62639-336-3)

Playing in Shadow by Lesley Davis. Survivor's guilt threatens to keep Bryce trapped in her nightmare world unless Scarlet's love can pull her out of the darkness back into the light. (978-1-62639-337-0)

Soul Selecta by Gill McKnight. Soul mates are hell to work with. (978-1-62639-338-7)

The Revelation of Beatrice Darby by Jean Copeland. Adolescence is complicated, but Beatrice Darby is about to discover how impossible it can seem to a lesbian coming of age in conservative 1950s New England. (978-1-62639-339-4)

Twice Lucky by Mardi Alexander. For firefighter Mackenzie James and Dr. Sarah Macarthur, there's suddenly a whole lot more in life to understand, to consider, to risk…someone will need to fight for her life. (978-1-62639-325-7)

Shadow Hunt by L.L. Raand. With young to raise and her Pack under attack, Sylvan, Alpha of the wolf Weres, takes on her greatest challenge when she determines to uncover the faceless enemies known as the Shadow Lords. A Midnight Hunters novel. (978-1-62639-326-4)

Heart of the Game by Rachel Spangler. A baseball writer falls for a single mom, but can she ever love anything as much as she loves the game? (978-1-62639-327-1)

Getting Lost by Michelle Grubb. Twenty-eight days, thirteen European countries, a tour manager fighting attraction, and an accused murderer: Stella and Phoebe's journey of a lifetime begins here. (978-1-62639-328-8)

Prayer of the Handmaiden by Merry Shannon. Celibate priestess Kadrian must defend the kingdom of Ithyria from a dangerous enemy and ultimately choose between her duty to the Goddess and the love of her childhood sweetheart, Erinda. (978-1-62639-329-5)

The Witch of Stalingrad by Justine Saracen. A Soviet "night witch" pilot and American journalist meet on the Eastern Front in WW II and struggle through carnage, conflicting politics, and the deadly Russian winter. (978-1-62639-330-1)

Pedal to the Metal by Jesse J. Thoma. When unreformed thief Dubs Williams is released from prison to help Max Winters bust a car theft ring, Max learns that to catch a thief, get in bed with one. (978-1-62639-239-7)

Dragon Horse War by D. Jackson Leigh. A priestess of peace and a fiery warrior must defeat a vicious uprising that entwines their destinies and ultimately their hearts. (978-1-62639-240-3)

For the Love of Cake by Erin Dutton. When everything is on the line, and one taste can break a heart, will pastry chefs Maya and Shannon take a chance on reality? (978-1-62639-241-0)

Betting on Love by Alyssa Linn Palmer. A quiet country-girl-at-heart and a live-life-to-the-fullest biker take a risk at offering each other their hearts. (978-1-62639-242-7)

The Deadening by Yvonne Heidt. The lines between good and evil, right and wrong, have always been blurry for Shade. When Raven's actions force her to choose, which side will she come out on? (978-1-62639-243-4)